BY THE SAME AUTHOR

The Eagle of the Ninth

Outcast

The Silver Branch

Warrior Scarlet

The Lantern Bearers

Tristan and Iseult

Blue Remembered Hills: A Recollection

Flame-Colored Taffeta

The Shining Company

Sword Song

ROSEMARY SUTCLIFF

Sword Song

Farrar, Straus and Giroux
New York

Text copyright © 1997 by Anthony Lawton
Map by Jill Taylor, copyright © 1997 by The Bodley Head
All rights reserved
Printed in the United States of America
First published in Great Britain by The Bodley Head, 1997
First American edition, 1998

Library of Congress Cataloging-in-Publication Data
Sutcliff, Rosemary.
    Sword song / Rosemary Sutcliff. — 1st American ed.
        p.   cm.
    Summary: At sixteen, Bjarni is cast out of the Norse settlement in the Angles'
Land for an act of oath-breaking and spends five years sailing the west coast of
Scotland and witnessing the feuds of the clan chiefs living there.
    ISBN 0-374-37363-9
    1. Vikings—Juvenile fiction. [1. Vikings—Fiction.   2. Great Britain—History
—To 1066—Fiction.   3. Seafaring life—Fiction.]   I. Title.
PZ7.S966Sw   1998
[Fic]—dc21   98–16827

CONTENTS

A NOTE ABOUT THIS BOOK

Throughout her working life my godmother and cousin, Rosemary Sutcliff, wrote each of her books in three consecutive drafts. *The Sword Song of Bjarni Sigurdson* (later re-titled *Sword Song*) was two-thirds through its second draft when she died suddenly in July 1992. Since then, as her executor and chairman of the company which looks after her books, I have transcribed her manuscript, with the encouragement of her agent for some years, Murray Pollinger. Her long-time editor and friend Jill Black has edited the result. Many thanks are due to them.

In this, her final book, Rosemary returns to the Norse world she had so memorably portrayed many years earlier in *The Shield Ring*.

Anthony Lawton
October 1996

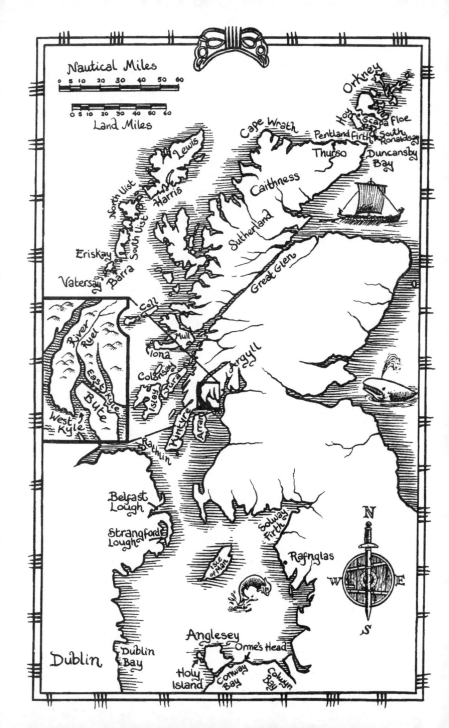

Sword Song

1

Dublin on the Morning Tide

Halfway up the Hearth Hall the man and the boy faced each other.

The man sat leaning forward a little, hands spread-fingered on the carved foreposts of the High Seat. The boy stood before him, stubbornly returning his accusing blue gaze with eyes that were just as blue under a thatch of barley-pale hair.

Bjarni Sigurdson was not much over sixteen; a tall raw-boned stripling whose voice, when he spoke, still sounded faintly rough at the edges, betraying the fact that it had broken not so many years ago.

'He kicked my dog,' said Bjarni Sigurdson.

'Your dog having just attacked him.'

'Her pups are no' but three days old, her temper a bit shaken.'

'And so you killed him.'

'I was not meaning to – only the horse-pond was near-hand, and he cannot have had much hold on life to have drowned in the little time I held him under.'

There was a long silence. At the lower end of the Hall women were about their ready-making for the evening meal, with anxious glances towards the High

Seat. From outside came the sound of metal on wood and men's voices as they worked; all the sounds of the young settlement; and beyond that the crying of the gulls. Beside the turf fire one of the hunting dogs was snuffling after fleas in his flank. Bjarni heard them all with great clearness; and yet he had the feeling of silence that went on – and on.

He had hoped, when he was summoned to stand before Rafn the Chief here in his Hall, instead of being held to appear before the Thing – the Law Gathering – on a charge of man-slaying, that nothing so very bad was going to happen after all. He had not meant to kill the old man in the long brown kirtle who had come to the settlement to tell them about his god, as though they had no gods of their own. Anybody could make a mistake. But looking into the unforgiving face of Rafn Cedricson he felt less hopeful as the moments passed.

'How long since you came west-over-seas to join the settlement?' the Chief asked at last.

'Half a year,' Bjarni said sullenly.

Half a year. It seemed longer than that, somehow, as though he had already begun to put down roots. Half a year since the Grandfather, too old to pull up his own roots, but wanting to get the young ones out of Norway (which King Harald Finehair was making too hot for those who valued their freedom to live as they chose) had sent him to join Gram his elder brother in the settlement of Rafnglas, which their own chief's brother had made here on the north-west coast of the Angles' Land.

'Time enough to learn that in this land-take the men of the White Christ walk safe.'

'I did not think – I had forgotten – '

'Then listen,' said the Chief, 'and I will tell the thing over to you again. When I was a bairn, I was fostered,

2

according to common custom, on a friend of my father's. His son and I grew together, closer than brothers-in-blood, as is often the way with foster-kin. In young manhood he came – no matter how – under the influence of folk who worship the White Christ. He left his own gods behind, and turned to theirs, and in time took the cowl and the shaven forehead, and became one of their holymen. So I lost my brother from the hearth fire and the shield ring. But for his sake I swore on the Hammer of our god Thor that within my land-take and among men of my own following, the men of his kind should be safe.'

The silence came back. Bjarni said nothing. There seemed nothing to say.

'Therefore you have made of me an oath-breaker, and that is a thing I do not lightly forgive,' said the Chief at last. 'But it is a thing between you and me, and not a matter for hearing out there at the Thing.'

And Bjarni knew that he was waiting for sentence just as surely as though he stood before the Law Gathering of the settlement, after all.

Rafn's hands tightened on the foreposts, the carved heads of Odin and Frigga that made the High Seat the sacred place in any hall. 'Kraka will give you a sword from the weapon kist. Take it and get out of my sight, out of the settlement until you have learned the meaning of an oath. Heriolf the Merchant sails on the morning tide.'

Bjarni stood while the words sank in. 'Just – go?' he said at last, his mouth feeling oddly dry.

'Just go! A man with a sword need never lack the means of life – or death. If after five years you still live and you shall be free to return and take your place in the settlement again, it may be that I shall be able to stand the sight of you.'

'If I still live when the five years are up, it may be

3

that I shall not wish to return to this boat-strand,'
Bjarni said.

The Chief let out a kind of moan. 'Then – the seas
are wide, and you may sail them until you fall off the
far end, if you choose.'

Kraka, foremost of the Chief's hearth companions,
who rowed first oar in his galley when she put out to
sea for the summer's raiding and trading, gave him a
sword from one of the great weapon kists against the
gable wall. A good serviceable weapon with a grip of
age-darkened walrus ivory. Not such a sword as he
would have chosen for himself, but well enough. He
had had no sword of his own until now, but his prac-
tice sessions with the other boys had taught him to
recognise the balance of a blade. And a little later,
knotting the sword-thongs to his belt as he went, he
was heading back through the settlement for his
brother's house-place. And Gram, who must have
been waiting in the foreporch, was suddenly beside
him.

'If he asks me now, out in the open with half the
settlement looking on,' Bjarni thought, 'I'll kill him.'

But all Gram said, glancing down at his new sword,
was, 'Tha's got that on the wrong side.'

'Not for a left-handed swordsman,' Bjarni said
between his teeth. And heard the other's surprised
silence. It was wonderful how folk that weren't left-
handed themselves never thought of things like that.

They walked on without another word, up through
the settlement, crossing the log bridge over the burn
and following the stream upwards for half a mile until
they came to the side glen, to the steading that was
the nearest thing Bjarni had now to a home. The smell
of cooking came out through the house-place
doorway, but that must wait. As though the thing had

4

been decided between them, they turned aside and ducked in through the low doorway of the store-shed. Inside were kists and bundles, farm tools, the dry smell of corn dust from last year's harvest. Nothing moved but a mouse. Then the hound bitch in the corner looked up and thumped her tail but could not come without upsetting the blind and rat-like pups feeding all along her flank.

Gram seized him by the shoulder and swung him round. 'Now – what passed between you and the Chief?'

'He gave me a sword and bade me be out of the settlement. Heriolf the Merchant is sailing on the morning tide.'

'For all time?'

'Until I have learned the meaning of an oath; five years he said.'

Gram cursed softly. 'It could have been longer. But the gods alone know what the Grandfather will say.'

'The Grandfather in Norway will never know,' Bjarni said, and felt, even as he spoke the words, how far he had come already from the place where he had been born and bred.

Gram had begun to chew his lower lip as he did when he was trying to clear his mind. 'I should come with you – '

'Why?' Bjarni demanded.

'You're too young to set sail on your own.'

'I'm sixteen and more. There's some that's sailed on their first Viking raid when they'd seen but twelve summers. I'll do well enough.'

Gram was still chewing his lower lip. 'Tha'll have to,' he said at last. 'I cannot leave the steading and Ingibjorg, not for five years, not now she's in whelp.'

'Who's asking you to?' Bjarni demanded, and then, seeing the trouble still in his brother's face, 'Bide here and keep the place for all of us. In five years' time I may be Emperor of Byzantium – I may just be dead – but if I'm neither, I'll like enough want to come home to it.'

He still felt stunned by what had happened in this day that had wakened like any other, and torn his familiar world to shreds before evening. But if he was to launch out into strange seas, and win his own way and his own fortune, he certainly did not want an older brother along with him to spoil it.

The hound bitch, as though sensing trouble in the air, heaved to her feet and, shaking off the fringe of pups, came padding across the floor, moving stiffly from the holy man's kick, and thrust her shaggy head against Bjarni's thigh; but even as he stooped to rub her muzzle, she turned and made her way back to the protesting pups.

'I can't take her with me, with the pups not yet weaned,' Bjarni said, watching her flop into the midst of her young and gather them once more against her flank. 'You'll keep her? The whelps are mostly spoken for.' There was an ache in his throat. Astrid had come with him west-over-seas. He was not good at loving, but he was unpleasantly surprised to find that he loved the rough-coated bitch. She was not young. Even if he came back after five years, likely she wouldn't be there . . .

'I'll keep her when I'm here.' Gram was a great one for having things cut and dried. 'In the summer she'll do well enough with the rest of the pack that gets left behind during the summer sea-faring.'

Bjarni nodded. 'Then I'll be gathering my gear, and away.'

'You'll come in and sup first. Ingibjorg'll have cooked for the three of us.'

Bjarni did not like his brother's new wife. She had

6

a little pink greedy face, but she was a good cook. His stomach was crying out to him that he must eat somewhere, and he certainly was not going to eat among the Chief's house-carles in the Hearth Hall.

He followed Gram into the house-place, and sat down in his usual seat beside the fire.

Ingibjorg looked up as they came in. 'Well?' she demanded, spooning eel stew into three mazer-wood bowls. So the thing had to be told again.

She said all the proper things: that he should have a care of that temper of his, that five years would pass, that they would keep his place warm for him. But he saw in her face that she was glad of his going.

When the meal was over – a silent meal with spurts of uneasy talk that died like flames in wet wood – Bjarni went up to the loft where he had slept above the cowstall, and collected his worldly goods: a spare pair of brogues and his feast-day sark, a small dolphin made of sea-blue glass that he had picked up one day among the ruins of the Redcrests' fort above the settlement. He bundled them into his weather-stained wadmal cloak, retied the belt-thongs of his new sword and checked that his sheath knife was tucked safely into the same broad leather strap.

When he scrambled down again into the living place, Gram was working at the battered silver arm-ring he wore above his left elbow, dragging it off, while Ingibjorg watched him with her lower lip caught angrily between her teeth.

'Take this with you,' Gram said. 'You'll be needing journey silver.'

Ingibjorg broke in, clearly continuing an argument that had been going on while he was in the loft. 'It was your grandfather's! You have told me so often enough, you must keep it for our son!' She patted her belly, which was just beginning to swell like the sail of a ship in a light breeze.

Gram took no notice. He held the bracelet toward Bjarni.

Bjarni wanted to refuse it, but his common sense told him that he might indeed need journey silver for one purpose or another. He took the bracelet with a mutter of thanks, partly for the pleasure of annoying Ingibjorg, who had begun to cry, and pushed it above his own elbow.

'Fair sailing to you – I have work outside to do before dark,' Gram said, already halfway through the doorway.

That would be true. In another year or so there might be a few captured thralls if the summer raiding went well, to help with the crops and the few lean cattle; but till then the men of the settlement must work each for himself. There was also, of course, the matter of getting away from Ingibjorg's tears. Well, he, Bjarni Sigurdson, was going to escape all that.

He hitched up his bundle and set out, across the steading garth and down the burnside, leaving his old life behind him and whistling like a blackbird as he went, to show all men, himself included, how little he cared. But halfway down the burn, on his way to the bridge and the houses of the main settlement, his steps began to slow. Then he paused and, hardly knowing why he did so, he turned into a little valley that led off the main path and sloped back towards the surrounding hills. No one had yet built a steading there, though the land seemed to Bjarni good, and there was a little stream that ran through it, down to the main burn. Finding a soft, flat piece of ground halfway up the glen, he scratched a hole with his knife and buried the blue glass dolphin there. Perhaps the valley would still be empty in five years' time and perhaps his dolphin would still be waiting for him. Was it a kind of promise to himself? he wondered, as he walked back to rejoin the main track down to the settlement.

The settlement was so new that some of the house-places were still roofed with sails and ships' awnings, though others had their proper roofs of heather thatch; and the God-House, raw with newness, stood among staked ash saplings, where in years to come the sacred grove would be.

Here and there, folk with their evening meals inside them were out again, about work that needed doing while there was still light to see by; and faces turned to him as he passed, friendly enough, nobody holding it against him that he had broken the Chief's oath, yet with something, an uneasiness, behind their eyes. Nobody holds it against the oak tree that it draws the lightning flash, but men stand clear of an oak tree in a thunderstorm, all the same. An oath-breaker was unlucky, and he knew that they were glad to see him go.

Down on the ship-strand was the smell of fish and salt water, rope and timber and pitch, the fisher-boats lying heeled to one side like sleeping seals. The Chief's longship was drawn out from the ship-shed onto the slipway and men were still busy along her flanks where they had been all day, pitching her seams and making her ready for the seaways of summer. Bjarni went past them all, heading for the broader-beamed merchantman lying in the shallows, her crew wading to and fro between her and the shore with the last bales and bundles of her cargo.

In the bows of his ship, *Sea Cow*, Heriolf the Merchant stood muffled in an old sea-cloak watching his goods come aboard.

Bjarni swung his own bundle onto his shoulder and

waded out towards her. With the silver ring on his arm, he had the price of his passage to – wherever she was bound; but he saw no point in paying when there might be another way. Thigh deep in the swinging shallows, he paused and stood looking up at Heriolf across the dark ship-shoulder as a man on foot looks up at a man on horseback.

'Where away?' he said.

'Dublin, on the morning tide.'

Dublin. That would do well enough. 'I am for Dublin, too,' Bjarni said.

'Have you the price?' the merchant said. He must have known, the whole settlement knew by now, about the holy man and the horse-pond, but he said nothing as to that.

'Not in goods or gold,' Bjarni said. 'I pay in service.'

'And what service would that be?' Heriolf leaned over the bulwark, grinning. 'I think you are no seaman, as yet.'

'Not as yet.' Bjarni returned the grin. 'Though I can handle an oar none so ill. Meanwhile, I am a better hand with this – ' And he hitched at his sword belt.

'So-o! A bodyguard? I, a peaceful trader? Have the Viking kind forsworn overnight the custom by which they raid the land-folk and their own kind at sea, but leave the traders to go about their trade?'

'There will always be some who forget a custom that was not of their own making,' Bjarni said, hopefully.

'Just as there are some who forget an oath that was not of their swearing.' The shipmaster shrugged. 'Nay then, we can all make mistakes. Tell me, what do you plan to do when you come to Dublin?'

Bjarni had not had time to think of that. He knew only that Dublin was a fine rich town with the world from Iceland to Byzantium flowing through its streets.

Plenty of chances there. 'Join the war-band of Halfdan the King,' he said on the spur of the moment. He did not think that Heriolf was listening to him, for he had turned aside to watch the stowing of some particularly precious bale; but he turned back, saying, 'The man who sells his sword-service should have a care who he sells it to. Halfdan is not such a king as was Olaf the White. Wolf that he is, he sits uneasy in the King Seat, and has been toppled out of it once already.'

'That might make for an interesting life for the men who follow him,' Bjarni said.

'Or a short one.'

Thigh deep in sea water, Bjarni was growing uncomfortably cold. 'Dublin first, any road. After that, wherever wind and tide may take me. Do I come aboard?'

The merchant laughed. 'Throw up your bundle.'

Bjarni threw up his bundle and the man caught it, and reached down a hand. He grabbed it, and sprang like a salmon out of the shallows; and next instant was scrambling over the side to land on the rising and dipping foredeck of the merchant vessel.

When the tide turned seaward on the dark edge of day-spring with the shore birds crying, the *Sea Cow* went with it, her crew swinging to the oars in time to the chant of 'Lift her! Lift her!' from Heriolf at the steering oar. And Bjarni squatted at the feet of the merchant shipmaster, with his naked sword laid across his knees.

2

The Streets of Dublin

Bjarni had never imagined that there could be a town like Dublin in all the wide world. Even Miklagard, that some men called Byzantium and others Constantinople, whose streets, as he had heard, were paved with gold, could hardly surpass it; though the narrow winding streets of Dublin seemed to be paved for the most part with split logs half sunk in springtime mud, where they were paved with anything at all. But the size of the place, and the close-huddled buildings and the shifting crowd . . .

It had taken him the best part of the day, hanging around the High King's Hall, among the fighting men and merchants, craftsmen and harpers and sea-captains already crowding the royal garth, to get word with the captain of Halfdan's bodyguard. And when he did, the captain had stood with his hands on his hips and laughed at him. 'What makes you think that Halfdan Ragnarson needs green striplings among his house-carles? Go you and sprout yourself a beard, and come back in two years' time.'

'I will go and sprout myself a beard. But I shall

have better things to do than come back here in two years' time!' Bjarni had told him furiously.

And someone among the onlookers had laughed. 'Hark to the cockerel crowing!'

So here he was, loose and lonely like a hound that has slipped his leash, in the winding ways of Dublin. The day was on the edge of dusk, that turned the passers-by shadowy about him, and no idea of what he should do next, and rage still twisted with the hunger in his belly. Well, he could do something about the hunger, at all events. Heriolf had changed the silver arm-ring for him for its weight in coins and precious metal shards and several links of a broken silver chain, so that he had usable buying-money to jingle in a greasy leather pouch tied to his belt. And wine shops and ale-houses seemed to be as thick on the ground as leaves in autumn.

From one open doorway a particularly rich smell of stew spilled out with the glow of torchlight into the narrow wynd, and he went in.

Inside there was peat-reek and the smoky light of a couple of torches, and a snotty-nosed boy tending to the needs of a knot of men at one end of a rough trestle table. Bjarni hitched out a stool and sat down at the other end of the table, the end nearest the door. He hadn't bothered to remember most of the advice Heriolf had given him that morning – he was not a bairn to need such warnings – but he did remember that this was the best place to be in a strange ale-house. He called for ale and something to eat. The boy brought him ale in a leather jack, and a bowl of stew swimming in fat and a hunk of hard brown bread. And the men at the far end glanced round at him and then returned to the game of dice that they were playing among the platters and ale-pots of their own supper.

Bjarni reckoned that they were Irishmen by their checkered cloaks and the meaningless tongue that they spoke, and then lost interest in them altogether.

He had matters of his own to think about, such as what he was going to do next. There was an old ale stain on the table that looked like a grotesque face looking up at him, seeming to ask jeeringly, 'Well? What now, Bjarni Sigurdson? Go back to Heriolf, squealing that they wouldn't take you? Asking to be taken on to the next port of call?'

He could do that, he knew. Heriolf was heading up the coast with dressed furs and amber and a fine foreign saddle for Evynd the Easterner, who held the North Irish coast-lands clear of raiders from his base on Belfast Lough. Maybe Evynd would take him on, even without a beard. At the worst he could work among the ship-sheds for a year or so whilst it grew. But how they would laugh at him, *Sea Cow*'s crew! His belly curdled at the thought of their laughter. He took a gulp of the sour ale and slammed the pot down in the middle of the leering face on the table, so that a few drops flew out to add to the stains on the boards.

A stray dog which had just wandered in out of the dusk flinched aside at the sudden clatter. The dark flash of movement caught Bjarni's eye, and he looked round and met the half-fearful, half-hopeful gaze of a pair of amber eyes. A half-grown black cur, lean as a wolf at the end of a famine winter, looked back at him, crouching and ready to spring away at the first sign of danger, but with a faint hopeful flickering at the end of its disreputable tail. Bjarni threw it a gobbet of bread, and it snapped it up and came nearer; he tossed it a bit of gristle from his stew bowl; and presently it was within arm's length, sniffing at the fist he held out to it. It was the first thing that had seemed friendly in all Dublin, and half unwittingly Bjarni turned his hand over and began to rub behind its lop ears in the warm hollows where Astrid had liked to be rubbed. The dog leaned against his hand, eyes half closed in bliss.

In the end, it had a reasonable share of his supper, and when there was no more to eat, sighed and lay down under the trestle. And busy with his own problems, Bjarni forgot about it.

Presently he got up, paid for his supper after some haggling with two links from the broken silver chain, and heaving his bundle onto his shoulder drifted out into the dark wynd.

The next thing was to find somewhere to spend the night. Maybe somewhere down toward the harbour, among the wharves and ship-sheds – though he would not be going anywhere near *Sea Cow*. So he turned downhill into the faint mist creeping up from the river. He did not notice that the black dog, sleeping with one ear and one eye open, had gathered itself together and come padding after him. Nor did he notice that one of the men playing dice at the other end of the table had risen and with a silent gesture to his fellows had also followed him out.

Dublin was quietening from the crowding bustle of its daytime self. From every ale-house doorway cheerful uproar spilled into the street and stray knots of men from the ships or the garrison went roistering by from one to another; but between them the streets seemed filled with a quieter coming and going as of shadows. In one such patch of stealthy quiet between ale-house and ale-house, Bjarni caught a faint pattering behind him and, looking round, saw by the light of the May moon coming toward the full that the black dog was coming after him. He cursed it, and it gave back a little, but when he walked on again the sound of four feet was still behind him. A knot of shadows jostled past him, but when they were gone, the padding was still there. Fiends take the dog! As though he had not enough problems of his own to handle! He stopped and grubbed up a loose billet of wood from the walk-way, and threw it at the animal, just to let it know that it was not wanted. It dodged, and came on. Maybe if he kept on walking for a while before he tried for somewhere to sleep, and simply took no more notice of it, it would give up in the end . . .

He strode on, resolutely not checking or looking back. The streets seemed more crowded down here toward the harbour, and in a while he lost the sound of padding paws in the general surf-sound of voices and feet, lapping water and creaking timbers all around him. He never heard at all the light prowling feet of the dice-player behind him.

But he felt the light tug at his belt, and swung round to find a dark figure almost pressed against him. He was aware of an up-reared arm that sent something free and arching across the face of the moon, into the midst of a ragged knot of revellers that had just emerged singing from a side alley, where a hand was up-flung to receive it. In the same splinter of time he caught the white blink of moonlight on a knife blade, and the next instant his own knife was in his hand. He felt the ringing jar of blade on blade, and then a slash of pain bright across his knuckles.

No one among the shifting street-crowd took any notice of the small vicious knife-fight that had flared up in their midst. Nothing unusual in a knife-fight, and if it was not one's own, better to keep well clear of it. A fist fight would have been another matter –

For Bjarni, the seeming lack of all reason for the attack made it like something leaping at him out of a nightmare. His hand was growing slippery with his own blood, or his attacker's, and trampling to and fro he knew one moment of cold fear; the fear that he was going to die here in the dark street of a strange town and no one of his own would ever know what had happened to him.

And then a snarling blackness with the speed and force of Thor's thunderbolt hurled itself upon the other man. The fight, which had been almost silent before, flared into a yowling and worrying and shouted curses. And then, as quickly as it had begun, it was over, and the man was running, with the black dog baying in pursuit.

Bjarni snatched a gasping breath and was after them, not caring about the man, but remembering all too clearly the glint of the moon on the knife blade. He tried to whistle but his mouth was dry; he tried to call the fool-dog off his hunting, but he had no name to call him by . . . Then the baying became a string of yelps drawing nearer, and as he ran, a black shape come streaking back to meet him out of the crowding shadows ahead, and the next instant the dog was panting and quivering against his legs. He stooped to fondle and reassure the creature, and his hand came away sticky. He hauled it over into the light of a nearby ale-house doorway, and saw a long shallow gash in its shoulder; a blow that had gone astray and done little damage, but was bleeding all the same.

'Why me?' he thought, cupping the creature's muzzle consolingly in his free hand. He could not be the first who had ever thrown the brute a scrap of bread. Maybe he was the first who had ever rubbed it behind the ears. Clearly it was as masterless as he was, it had taken a knife-gash for his sake, and he could not abandon it to fend for itself in this howling wilderness of the streets of Dublin. Well, he had enough silver to feed them both for a while. He slid his knife back into its sheath, his hand expecting the feel of his pouch beside it. It was not there. And glancing down he saw the pouch strings neatly cut through, and remembered the faint tug at his belt, the dark thing arching across the moon on its way to be caught by someone else in the crowd. The knife had not been meant for him, only to separate him from his pouch. The fight had grown from that only because he had felt the tug and turned before the thief had a chance to get clear.

What now? It was not only his silver that had gone, but the time it would have bought him. Time to work out what to do next, find someone to sell his sword-service to. Everything in him shied away from the thought of going back to Heriolf and *Sea Cow*, telling him how he had fared in the King's garth. 'The captain told me to go and grow myself a beard.' Now he would have to add, 'And some cursed bog-brother has stolen my pouch.' He did not think that he could do it.

The dog looked up at him hopefully, wagging its tail.

'I haven't anything more,' Bjarni said. Already he seemed to hear the jeering, the rough, good-humoured laughter. Well, that would be the price to be paid; there was generally a price to be paid for things.

'Come,' he said with a small slap to his thigh; and the dog gave a little bounce and came, willing and eager. Bjarni would have slipped a strap round its neck if he had had one to spare, but all he had was his belt, without which both his sword and his breeks would fall down. But when, twisting his bleeding knuckles in one corner of his cloak, he turned and walked on, the creature paced at his knee with the proud submission of a good hound.

There was a gaggle of ale-houses strung out along the keel-strand; and Heriolf and several of the *Sea Cow*'s crew were taking their ease in the third he looked into.

The merchant master looked round from the bench on which he was sprawling, and saw them in the doorway, and waved a greeting with the ale-pot in his hand.

And Bjarni jostled his way into the crowded peat-reek of the place, the black dog still at his knee.

'And what brings you down this way from the High King's Hall?' Heriolf demanded.

'I was thinking you'll be needing a bodyguard up north to Evynd's keel-strand,' Bjarni said.

'Will I so? And what of the King's house-carles?'

'I changed my mind! I have no wish for the King's house-carles, nor for his town.' Bjarni grinned, standing with his feet apart.

'Which, it seems, has lightened you of your silver.' Heriolf's brows were up and his small dark eyes flickering with amusement along Bjarni's belt where his pouch had been knotted.

'I exchanged it for the dog,' Bjarni told him, and all the weather-burned grinning faces along the table. It was true in a way.

There was a splurge of laughter, good-natured enough, and every eye was on the gangling black creature standing pressed against his leg.

'What?' said Heriolf. 'For that half-grown, half-starved gutter-cur?'

Their laughter twisted in Bjarni's gut. But he answered steadily, 'He'll be a fine hound by and by, fed up a bit, and when he's grown to match his legs.'

'And you so eager to get him that you paid the pouch along with the silver, cutting the purse strings rather than waiting to untie them?' Heriolf jerked a thumb at the end of knotted thong still fastened to Bjarni's belt.

'Yes,' Bjarni said, and looked him eye into eye, knowing that the man did not believe a word of the story, but sticking to it all the same.

'And your bundle too? Was that part of the bargain?'

Until that moment, Bjarni had forgotten all about his bundle, abandoned, presumably, when he needed both hands for other matters. Still, what was an old cloak and a spare sark? 'Yes,' he said again.

'And having just bought him at such a princely price, I am thinking you will not be minded to leave him behind in Dublin.'

Bjarni shook his head, his mouth suddenly dry.

'Ach well – ' Heriolf took a long reflective pull at the ale-jack, then held it out to him. 'Have a swallow, you look as though you could do with one . . . It is not the first time that I have carried hounds among the *Sea Cow*'s cargo. You had best go down to her now. I have kept a guard on board. Tell him I sent you, and get your head down; we'll be loading a fresh cargo in the morning.'

3

Sword for Sale

The great sea-lough ran for half a day's rowing into
the heart of the land; and on its north shore, far
enough from the open sea to gain shelter from the
mountains behind it, near enough to have its longships quickly out into the open water in time of need,
the fleet base of Evynd the Easterner lay clear in late
sunlight under a great over-arching bank of cloud.

'Weather brewing,' said Heriolf, sniffing the wind
like a hound, one eye on the threatening cloud bank
as the sail came rattling down and the oars were run
out; and *Sea Cow* came about in answer to his hand
on the steering oar, and headed for the long keel-
strand. 'Well, we shall be snug enough out of storm's
reach tonight.'

Bjarni, squatting at the master's feet with his sword
across his knees, his free hand twisted in the bit of
old rope round Hugin's neck – the black hound had
a name by now, taken from that of one of the god
Odin's ravens – looked along the straining backs of
the rowers and out past *Sea Cow*'s up-reared prow
as the distance narrowed between ship and shore.

He saw long turf-thatched buildings, high-gabled

ship-sheds, the long dark shapes, like basking seals, of galleys lying on the slipways or on the open beach. And mingled with the land scents of sun-warmed grass and heather, the sea-reek of pitch and rope and timber came to his questing nose.

Along the strand, men were making all secure for foul weather; and some among the nearest came wading out to add their strength to that of *Sea Cow*'s crew as they sprang overboard into the shallows; and so they ran her ashore and well up the beach above the tide-line, where they set to work to rig the storm covers and drive in the chocks that kept her on an even keel.

Scarce a couple of oars' lengths further along the strand two slim war-galleys were being made ready for the waiting timber rollers to take them up to a nearby ship-shed. Bjarni, who had splashed ashore with a hand still twisted in Hugin's makeshift collar, looked up from the rope's end which somebody had tossed to him with orders to hang on to it, to see the tall dragon-prow of the nearest up-reared against the gathering storm clouds and the wheeling gulls.

Coming as he did of a sea-going people, he had seen a good few carved wooden dragon-prows before now; but none the like of this one for beauty or for a kind of shining wickedry that lifted the hair a little on the back of his neck. Like many of its kind, it was not all dragon, but held within it traces of some other beast, and looking up at it, letting his eyes follow the long wave-break curves of carving that almost broke into leaves and blossom but never quite, Bjarni realised that this one was part vixen, long-necked, slender and savage, the same curve from throat to chin, the same laid-back ears, the same snarling mask . . .

'That's *Sea Witch*. She's a beauty, isn't she?' said

Heriolf's voice behind him. 'They do say she barks like a vixen when her lord comes near.'

'Her lord?'

'Onund Treefoot. Best have a care to that rope.'

And Bjarni turned back to the work he had forgotten. But when *Sea Cow* had been made secure, and her master had seen the main part of the crew bestowed in one of the seamen's longhouses that mingled with the ship-sheds along the keel-strand, and with his remaining men was making his way up the sandy track that looped inland through the furze, Bjarni, following with the rest, returned to the subject. 'Why Treefoot?'

'Why Treefoot?' somebody said, clearly surprised at his ignorance.

'Seems an odd name.'

'Lost a leg in battle, to Harald Finehair,' Heriolf said. 'Six – seven years since, that would be.'

'And he still goes sea-faring?' It seemed an unlikely way of life for a one-legged man.

'Well enough, with a leg of good stout oak-wood under him.'

'It must be chancy on a pitching deck?' Bjarni half questioned.

And Heriolf laughed. 'There's always somebody's shoulder to grab.'

The track lifted over a low furze-grown ridge, and there ahead of them rose the Hall of Evynd the Easterner, its high, antlered gable-end catching the last of the stormy sunlight against the murk of the mountains northward, though already the lower buildings clustered about it were swallowed up in the coming night.

Later, with the evening meal inside him, his eyes full of torchlight and his ears full of harp-song, Bjarni sat with Heriolf and his men on the guest bench at the foot of the great Hearth Hall, and felt that life was good. Soon, maybe in the morning, he would take his sword to Evynd the Easterner. There must be room for another sword, always room for another sword, among the seamen and fighting men who kept the coastwise lands of Northern Ireland against the raids and river-farings of the Viking kind.

He looked at the big dark-haired man with a noble paunch on him who sat in the High Seat, midway up the Hall, and wondered what sort of lord he would be to follow. A giver of gold? Surely a giver of gold by the look of him, and by the glint of the yellow metal on fine weapons and arm-rings that showed among the men around him. The two who sat nearest to him, also, were men worth looking at; the one, younger and less paunchy than Evynd, but clearly of the same blood, was Thrond his brother, ship chief of the second galley on the keel-strand. The other was built altogether on lighter and swifter lines, with hair like a fox's pelt growing low onto his forehead, thick, upward-quirking brows, and a mouth which Bjarni judged could look kind or cruel as the mood took him. 'Loki might look like that,' he thought; Loki the God of Fire, who could warm your hearth or burn the roof over your head, also as the mood took him. The man's legs were lost among the smoky shadows under the trestle table, but even if he had not been told, Bjarni would have known him at once by the kinship between him and the dragon-head of his galley.

'Always they hunt in couples, those two, Thrond and Onund,' Erik of the *Sea Cow*'s crew had said earlier as they bent their heads together over a shared bowl of pigmeat. 'You wouldn't think that the first time the foxy one beached on this strand, ten year past that'd be, that Evynd was all for pitching him back into the sea.'

'Why was that, then?'

'Evynd's woman is daughter to an Irish king. Barra in the Outer Isles was part of his territory until Onund and his friends drove him out of it and took the island for their own living place. Therefore Evynd had small love for Onund, until Thrond, they do say, made some sort of peace between his brother and his foxy friend.'

'Gossip, gossip, gossip like an old fisherwife,' Heriolf had said, overhearing. 'That is threadbare history; and I'm thinking Evynd Easterner would be feeling the lack, these days, if he couldna' call on yon pirate and his war-keels from Barra when he had the need of them.'

Now the food was done, and Evynd's flame-haired woman who was daughter to an Irish king had risen and swept the other women after her from the cross-benches at the end of the Hall, away to their own quarters. The trestle boards had been taken down, and many of the younger men were sprawling at their ease among the hounds beside the long hearths. Game-boards had been brought out, and games of fox and geese were going forward, and here and there a man was patching his own breeks or renewing the binding of a spear, while the Hall harp went round, passing from hand to hand, as man after man woke the strings with more or less of skill and offered up riddle or song or story; a bright web of sound to keep out the menace of the rising storm that had come beating up the lough to hurl itself against the settlement out of the dark. There were wonderful stories that came from the Northman's world, of water-horses and baresarkers' ghosts and troll-women who rode the roof-ridges of halls on winter nights.

Bjarni, listening spellbound, woke suddenly to the

fact that the troll-women story had been told maybe
too often. There began to be a restlessness among the
listeners, a snort of laughter in the wrong place from
the lower benches. Then heads got together, and a
knot of young warriors who had been drinking
together in a corner got up, grinning, and were
somehow gone through the foreporch doorway into
the stormy darkness, scarce noticed in the constant
coming and going of the great Hall.

A squall of rain came spattering into the fire; and
once Bjarni thought he heard a snatch of laughter
outside in the wild weather. Then suddenly in a
trough of quiet between gust and gust, there came
a flurry of sound high overhead on the highest crown
of the roof near the smoke-hole; a trampling of feet
and a thick shouting, and something small and dark
fell through the hole into the fire beneath. There was
a smell of singed fur, and a moment's high squealing
as the rat streaked free of the hot embers. Then the
dogs lying around the hearth were up and onto it,
and the squealing stopped. Men scrambled up also to
cheer on the dogs, and the harper flung his harp aside
between note and note.

And in the general uproar a young tawny-haired
giant rose to his feet, swaying a little and holding an
ale-jar high in one hand. 'No call for troll-wife tales,
for seemingly the real thing is come upon us by the
sound of it.' His voice rose to a joyful bellow. 'And
that is a thing Sven Gunnarson will not be having on
any roof he drinks under!'

And slamming the jar on a friend's head in passing,
he set a somewhat wavering course for the foreporch
door. A good few of the young men scrambled
whooping after him, and with them most of the dogs
in hopes of a rat hunt. Bjarni and Erik went with
them, Bjarni still with a hand on Hugin's makeshift

collar, for he had no mind to let the dog run loose among his own kind with the gash only half healed on his shoulder.

Outside the wind buffeted by, and the light came and went as the racing clouds let the moon swim free, then caught and swallowed it again in their dark stampede as another squall of rain came trailing up the lough. There were dark figures on the roof-ridge, found and lost in the swiftly changing light. And below in the garth figures more fiercely lit by the wind-teased flames of the pine-knot torch someone had carried out from the Hall. In the russet flame of it, Bjarni saw Sven Gunnarson already climbing by way of a friend's back onto the roof, which on that side came down to within not much over a man's height from the ground. Next instant he had swung himself onto the heather thatch, and with a handhold on one of the weighted ropes that held it down against the winter storms, was heading for the roof-ridge.

High against the racing moonshot sky, one of the dark shapes rose and stood to meet him, crouching a little with arms outspread.

Afterwards Bjarni never knew whether there was so much ale in Sven Gunnarson that he really thought it was a troll-wife there on the ridge, or whether he knew well enough that it was a bunch of his own kind who had caught a rat in the grain store and dropped it down the smoke-hole to enliven the evening. Clearly he was the kind to find one reason as good as another for starting a fight when the drink was in him. Yelling defiance, he scrambled up the steep slope towards the waiting figure, and made a kind of flying upward dive at its legs, striving to bring it down. The figure kicked out, shouting defiance in its turn; Bjarni thought he heard laughter, snatched away on the wind. The kicking foot was captured and the two figures became one sprawling darkness of arms and legs, then shook itself apart into two once more, half-sitting, half-kneeling astride the roof-ridge, heads down and arms locked. From further along the roof and from the torchlit garth below, their friends and sword-fellows cheered them on. Darkness swept across the moon with the next flurry of rain, and when it cleared again they were on their feet, each struggling for a wrestler's throw, looking scarcely human but more like two bears struggling up there, swaying together and trampling to and fro. Once Sven was on his knees, but managed to twist clear and come up again on the twist, once the other man was half over the far side of the ridge before he could check himself and come swarming back.

It was a good fight while it lasted, but it did not last long and the end came unexpectedly with a sudden eddying change in the wind that sent a great belch of smoke and a trail of sparks from the smoke-hole side swooping along the roof to engulf the two battling figures. Even the watchers in the garth were coughing and spluttering; and Sven, caught off balance and blinded by the choking cloud, missed his footing on the heather thatch made slippery by the rain and came rolling and clawing down the steep slope.

From the eaves to the ground was not a long drop on that side, but flying off with a yell, all arms and legs, he landed awkwardly, pitching down on the point of an elbow. Bjarni, who was among those nearest, heard the sharp unreal crack of breaking bone.

There was a sudden silence, and in the midst of it, in the midst also of the flaming light of the pine-knot torch, Sven Gunnarson lay with his right arm under him, bent at an unlikely angle between elbow and shoulder. But even as they closed in around him, he sat up, and got slowly to his knees and then to his

feet, cradling his right arm with his left. His foe of the
roof-ridge had come sliding down to join them, still
coughing and spluttering from the smoke. Somebody
went to put a steadying arm around Sven, but he
backed away – he seemed for the moment quite steady
on his feet and stone-cold sober. 'If anybody touches
me,' he said, speaking quietly but through his teeth,
'I'll kill him.' And he turned towards the pool of light
that spilled from the foreporch doorway.

He went back into the Hall under his own sail and
walked up it, the rest of them following close but
keeping their hands to themselves, until he came to
his own place on one of the side-benches, and sat
down in it rather suddenly, as though his legs had
given way beneath him.

Somebody came through the crowd, walking with
a sideways lurch of the shoulders; and Bjarni got the
feeling that they were all being swept back to make
room, though no word was spoken about it. 'What
fools' game hast been a-playing here?' demanded a
voice, swift and light as the speaker himself; and
Onund Treefoot was standing in the midst of the small
space that had fallen clear about him, his fox-yellow
gaze taking in the rigid figure on the bench.

'No game but a fight with the troll kind. Their hair
is in my eyes even yet,' said Sven.

'Fell off the roof and broke his arm,' other voices
struck in.

'So I see,' said Onund Treefoot. 'His sword arm,
too. The goddess Ram, the Mother of Foul Weather,
would see to it that it is his sword arm . . . Well, we
must be doing what we can . . .'

Evynd the Easterner, seeing that it was no man of
his own, had returned to a game of draughts with his
brother Thrond. A general shout went up for Hogni
Bone-grinder, and a man who might have been a troll

himself for his hairy ugliness and the length of his arms appeared as from nowhere, followed by a boy carrying flat billets of wood and strips of binding rag.

Onund sat down on the bench beside his man, his wooden leg stuck out in front of him, and braced himself behind the other's shoulders, holding his upper arm in a grip that looked easy to Bjarni, watching, until he saw how the muscles stood out like cords on the ship chief's own arm, as the bone-setter got to work. Hogni was pulling the damaged arm out straight, twisting and drawing it, frowning a little over what he did. Sven turned not so much white as a kind of dirty yellow, his mouth shut and his breath whistling a little through flared nostrils. Bjarni heard the two ends of bone creaking together with some curiosity. He had never been so near to a broken bone being set before, and he was interested accordingly. The thing seemed to take a long time to do; all the while it was as though Hogni Bone-grinder was feeling and listening and looking through his hands at what he did. At last, with one slow powerful heave, it seemed that it was done, the sweat springing on the faces of all three men shone in the torchlight, and the arm was more or less straight once more. Still holding it, the troll-man took the bits of wood from his boy and began to splint it, binding them on tightly with the strips of rag. A little blood pricked through, but not much: the bone had barely pierced the skin. And when it was done, and Onund had taken his hands away, the bone-setter fashioned a sling to take the weight and knotted it around Sven's thick neck.

Onund got up, and stood looking at his tawny giant without sympathy. 'You mazelin!' he said. 'Now we shall be lacking a man from the rowing benches and the sword-band all this summer!' But the tone was not as harsh as the words. To the others of *Sea Witch*'s crew he said, 'Get him drunker than he is already, and bed him down in the byre.' And to Evynd, sitting with a draught piece in his hand, 'He'll be good for neither man nor beast until the bone is knit. Will you give him hearth-space until I come again at summer's end?'

And Sven Gunnarson's friends got to work on him with a fresh jack of ale, before carrying him away. To be borne into the Hall like a swooning maiden would have shamed him, but there was of course no shame in being too drunk to leave it on one's own feet. And the rest of the company returned to whatever they had been doing before.

Bjarni stood where he was, thinking hard and quickly. 'Lacking a man from the rowing benches and the sword-band all this summer,' Onund had said. 'Lacking a man' – Oh! But where was the sense in hiring one's sword to a one-legged ship chief who must in the nature of things be less worth following than a captain with two good legs under him . . .

He started up the crowded Hall, Hugin following as usual at his knee, towards the High Seat where Evynd the Easterner sat over his game of draughts.

But not knowing that he was going to do so, he stopped short, where Onund Treefoot sat with his wooden leg stuck out in front of him, leaning his shoulders against the weapon-hung wall and watching the sparrows who had built in the thatch.

'Onund Treefoot,' said Bjarni, bright-eyed and formal, 'I have no lord to follow. I can handle an oar, and my sword is for hire. I am your man.'

4

Harvest on Barra

Bjarni lay on his stomach in the short mountain grass, his chin propped on his forearm, and gazed away over the windy emptiness. From up here on the shoulder of Greian Head you could look out over the score or more of islands that went to make up Barra and on northward past Eriskay and Uist away and away along the great wild-goose skein of the Outer Isles.

He had been across to one of the native fisher-villages on the south shore, after a new pair of sealskin brogues. There was a little black-eyed hump-backed man over there who claimed to have been taught the art of making them by the Lordly People and charged accordingly. A whole silver coin with a king's head and three ears of corn embossed on it, these had cost, but Bjarni knew that they would be worth it; they were his second pair.

Now he was on his way back to the settlement with them tucked into his belt. But there was no hurry. It was good up here. Beside him Hugin thumped his tail, head alertly up into the wind. It was over a year since he had followed Bjarni out of Dublin, and he had grown and fleshed out into a big powerful hound, black as midnight save for some white hairs under his chin, and still those surprisingly light amber-coloured eyes.

Bjarni, his hand rubbing behind the pricked black ears, let his mind drift back over the time, to the Hearth Hall of Evynd the Easterner. 'I have no lord to follow,' he had said to Onund Treefoot. 'I can handle an oar, and my sword is for hire; I am your man.'

And Onund Treefoot had looked him up and down as a man looks over a horse he is minded to buy, and agreed, 'You are my man.'

It had meant leaving Hugin behind along with Sven Gunnarson for the three months' summer sea-faring. But when at summer's end they had returned for Sven, whose arm had mended somewhat out of shape but as strong as ever it had been, they had picked up Hugin too, out of the dog pack. Bjarni had earned that, and had the hands to prove it; hands that had blistered on the oarloom and grown red-raw when the blisters burst and healed over into thickened and calloused skin that marked him for a seasoned rower.

Another sea-faring summer since then. Merchant runs – not the long open-sea runs down as far as Spain for slaves and spices from the Saracen traders, but coastwise and island-hopping with salt and hides; once north as far as Orkney with farm-slaves for Jarl Sigurd. He remembered lying off the Great Head waiting for the right stage of the tide that they might slip through from the Pentland Firth without falling foul of the roaring, down-sucking turmoil of the whirl-pool there, the Eater of Ships, the Widow-maker. He remembered the tide races between a score of islands, the storms and the occasional calms. He remem-bered the land journey with Evynd against a flare-up of three native Irish kings and the Danish war-bands they had brought in to help them. A southward raid on their own account upon the Danish settlements on the Welsh coast.

Onund and Thrond, Aflaeg and Thormod Shaff, sometimes hunting in couples, more often running their longships together as a fleet. Three who had come west-over-seas together, to be done with King Harald Finehair: one, Aflaeg, who was on Barra already, a friend from earlier raiding days, older than the rest and of mixed breeding so that the Isles were already in his blood. Maybe that was why in land matters he took the lead; why it was he who sat in the High Seat in Hall when the others gathered from their steadings in the settlements round about, and had the last word as to the time for barley sowing or the start of the seal hunt, while in all matters to do with sea-faring, it was Onund Treefoot, without argument, who was the Sea-King, the ship chief over them all.

Away between the islands the sea was changing colour with the turn of the tide, and his belly told him that it was time to be getting back for the evening meal. Bjarni rolled over and sat up, and remained a few moments with narrowed eyes gazing across the shining water toward the west. No more islands that way, only emptiness until one fell off the edge of the world – unless one came upon those other islands that Aflaeg's harper sang of sometimes, the islands beyond the sunset, the lands of the ever young ...

Meanwhile, the surf was going down, the pale feather of a new moon was in the sky, and he was hungry. He drew his legs under him and scrambled to his feet, Hugin leaping up beside him. Together they started back towards the settlement. Down from the high bare rock and grassland of the mountain shoulder into the lower country of hills and heather

moors that sank at last to the *machair*, the fine grazing-
land behind the white sands that ringed all the
western length of Barra. Just where moorland fell
away to *machair* a stream came down from the higher
ground, pushing its way through a narrow glen suddenly and unexpectedly choked with trees a-tangle,
birch and rowan and willow and thorn. Checking a
moment with an odd cold fascination to look down,
Bjarni saw the corner of a turf roof half lost in thicker
woodland, a dense clump of ash trees, old and wind-
twisted, and felt, as he always did, the darkness and
the chill that seemed to lie over the place. He shook
his shoulders, jibing at himself for a fool. It was no
more than the God-House, just such another as the
God-House at Rafnglas. But at Rafnglas they seldom
offered more than a tassel of hair cut from a horse's
tail, a blood sacrifice only seldom and in time of need.
Here they kept to the old ways. Here there were bones
in the sacred grove, things that had once been alive
hanging from the trees. Downwind, you could smell
this place from a long way off . . .

He turned away and went on down, following the
spur of moorland, making for the place where the glen
opened out and the burn ran clear of the shadow,
before crossing over, whistling as he went. But just
above his chosen crossing place, in a thicket of bram-
bles spilling down the bank, he came upon a girl.

She was sitting there, forlorn as a fledgling fallen
from the nest, the skirts of her grey homespun kirtle
bunched to her knees, nursing one foot, and at her
side, an over-set creel, trickling a few blackberries
into the grass. Bjarni knew her well enough for the
daughter of the settlement's Odin Priest. He stopped,
looking down at her. 'Thara? What's amiss then?'

'I slipped among the stones crossing over, and
twisted my foot.'

He squatted down for a closer look. She had been going barefoot and he could see that her instep was already swollen and turning red.

'It hurts,' said Thara in a small whimpering voice.

'I can see it does. Can you walk on it?'

'No – it hurts.'

'So you said before.' He looked at her consideringly. She was a plump little thing, but small-boned. Probably not heavy. 'I'd best carry you,' he said somewhat grudgingly and got up, thrusting Hugin's exploring nose aside. 'Leave that,' he said as she reached for the over-set creel. 'Someone else can fetch it by and by – the bramble fruit is not full ripe yet, anyway.'

She abandoned the creel and held out her arms to him, and as he picked her up he got the distinct feeling that despite the pain of her foot she was beginning to enjoy herself. 'Put your arms around my neck,' he ordered. 'There, that's the way of it.'

It was none so easy fording the burn, for the stones rolled underfoot and, feeling him lurch, the girl giggled excitedly and craned round to see how near the water might be. 'Don't wriggle, or I'll like enough drop you,' Bjarni told her, and she was quiet again.

He gained the opposite bank safely, Hugin leaping out after him and showering them both with burn water as he shook himself. Bjarni whistled him to heel and set out once more for the settlement.

'But you're so strong,' Thara said, continuing where they had left off in midstream. 'You feel so strong. You would never drop me.' And somehow she made it sound as though his strength was something that she was proud of, something that belonged to her.

He glanced down, and found speedwell-blue eyes surrounded by feathery silver-gilt lashes gazing up at him, and noticed for the first time how bonny she was in a kitten-witted kind of way. He had never carried a girl before, and the feel of her in his arms was warm and soft and pleasant. But she was heavier than she looked, and there was still quite a way to go, and he had to stop once or twice to heave her further up when she started to slip.

'I have seen you when you come under Onund's armpit, for him to use you as a crutch. So strong you are . . .'

And that was true. At most times Onund Treefoot was as swift and able on his wooden leg as though it were a part of him, but there were times, just now and then, when the stump grew hot and red and even wept a little, so that it would not bear his weight. He had a crutch for such times, but most often he used who came nearest. And Bjarni was just the right height. Also he was left-handed . . . 'Together, we make a fine two-bladed swordsman,' Onund had said, and they had practised the thing, half in jest, half in deadly earnest, with the rest of the crew baying them on. It did not in fact take all that much strength. But Bjarni would have braced himself to it gladly, if his chief had been built like a bull walrus.

But it was not a thing he wanted to talk about, especially to a girl. He grunted, making a great thing of how heavy she was becoming, until soon after on the edge of the settlement, he came to the fine long house-place of Asmund the Odin Priest – after the chieftain, the priest, with his barns stacked with tribute, was generally the richest man in any settlement. And there he let her down on the threshold and left her to the scolding care of the woman thrall who came in answer to his shout, and went on, stretching the strain out of his shoulders as he went, up through the in-take fields toward the Hall.

In one of the harvest fields the barley was already cut and stacked; in the others it still stood, whitening under the footsteps of the wind, waiting for the sickle. On Barra the main work of the fields and cattle-garths was done by thralls, but at harvest time, with the longships back from their summer sea-faring, everybody lent a hand. Tomorrow, Bjarni thought, with a seaman's content at being back on land, he would take his turn with the sickle among the dry hushing masses of the grain.

Thara Priestsdaughter was already out of his mind.

There were strangers in the Hall that night, the crew of a small trading vessel out from Kintyre. But in the constant coming and going among the islands there was nothing unusual in that. Bjarni saw them on the guest benches, but took no particular notice of them, as he set to work on the great trenchers of oatcake and salt fish, laverbread and ewe-milk cheese on the trestle boards before him. Outside the wind had begun to rise, blowing up into one of the great westerlies that sent the steep seas pounding onto the beaches from the world's end. The wicker shutters had been pegged across the small high windows, to add their strength to the panes of stretched membrane which were prone to burst like an eardrum under too much pressure when the gale blew from that quarter. But the wind came in through every chink and cranny, the skin rugs and the painted sail-cloth hangings on the walls billowed out, and in the draught-teased flamelight of the torches and the long central hearth the painted dragon-knots on the sail-cloth seemed to stir on the edge of life.

Something, a piece of torn-off thatch from one of the outhouses maybe, came floundering across the roof, and for the second time that day, Bjarni's mind went back to Evynd's Hall, over a year ago. 'Another troll-woman riding the roof-ridge,' he thought.

Almost, he said it to Sven Gunnarson sitting beside him, Sven Gunnarson with an arm that was as good as new, but who still had a bony lump just above the elbow to show for that night's work. Almost, but not quite. Sven's neighbour on the other side said it instead, and got a handful of boiled fish and laver-bread ground into his face to teach him that the joke was stale.

A moment more, and it would have come to fighting; one of those small snarling scraps that broke out sometimes in Hall among the men on the benches as among the dogs under the tables, and Bjarni was just making ready to join in. But in that moment a girl's voice between laughter and exasperation said, 'Salt fish needs good ale to wash it down,' and a thin yellow stream descended on the heads of first Sven and then his neighbour. They fell apart like dogs separated by a pail of cold water, shaking their heads and spluttering. And glancing up, Bjarni saw that the girl standing over them with an ale-jar poised in her hand was Aesa, the daughter of Aflaeg the Hall Chieftain.

As always a certain resentment rose in him at sight of her, not against anything in the girl herself, but because she was betrothed to Onund Treefoot, with the bride-ale set for that autumn as soon as the harvesting was over. And surely nothing would ever be quite the same between Onund and his ship-carles once he had a wife to come home to – and one almost young enough to be his daughter at that – though of course all men knew that the chief purpose of the mating was the bonding together of the Barra fleet. But seeing her standing there, her face laughing but determined, he had to admit to himself that not many of the girls sitting on the cross-bench or carrying round the ale-jars would have headed straight into the centre of a threatening dogfight on the warrior-benches and broken up the trouble before it could start.

Aesa turned and went her way. Sven's neighbour was wiping dark green laverbread out of his eye amid a general burst of laughter, and supper went on.

It was not until the eating was over, and the strangers on the guest benches had been properly filled, that Aflaeg in the High Seat raised his great silver-bound horn to drink to them, demanding of their captain, 'What news from the seaways and the landing-beaches?' the customary question asked of all strangers, though it was only a few days since the Barra longships had returned from their own summer sea-faring.

The captain raised his own cup in reply, and answered across the Hall, 'You have na' heard, then?'

'What is there to hear?'

'That Vigibjord and Vestnor are in these waters.'

There was a sudden silence in which everybody seemed to crane a little closer, and the booming of the sea grew very loud.

'So-o-o,' said Aflaeg softly into his greying beard, as he set down his ale-horn, 'this is sure? No mere wind-blown tale?'

'As to that . . .' growled the merchant captain with feeling, 'Findhorn has been raided, and the God-House gold; and the people gathered to some festival of their god carried off for the slave market. And the word is already along the coast up from the south that 'tis them and their fleet. We barely escaped them off Colonsay. Only got clear, I reckon, because they were heavy with loot and weeping captives.'

Onund, who had been silently gazing into the depth of his drink horn, looked up and asked quietly in a voice which Bjarni had never heard from him before, a voice with fur on it, but none the less terrible for that, 'Vigibjord and Vestnor?'

'The word is for both brothers,' said the merchant.

'How many ships?'

'The word is for eight, when they come all together.'

'Quite like old times,' said Onund, with a kind of laughter like the cold flicker of sea-fire at the long corners of his mouth. He drained his drink horn and held it up.

'More ale! My throat is as dry as the salted cod.'

The girl Aesa brought the ale-jar and poured for him. And a great roar of voices broke out; men baying for the hunt, shouting for an autumn sea-faring, men calling that the ships could not be ready for sea again in less than half a moon, one old blind warrior who lived in the warmest corner of the Hall lifting up a quavering voice to demand why it must be for the Barra fleet again, why could not Red Thorstein of Mull or one of the other sea lords put an autumn fleet to sea. But it was only Fredi White, and all men knew that age had made him foolish, so no one even troubled to answer him.

Under cover of their voices Bjarni turned to Orlig Anderson, the oldest and most full of knowledge of Onund's ship-carles, who sat beside him, his face at the moment hidden in the ale-jack they were sharing between them, and asked, 'Who are they?'

Orlig took his face out of the ale-jack. 'Who are who?'

'Vigibjord and Vestnor?'

'Old enemies. They used to come raiding along the Irish coast before Evynd Easterner took on the defences.'

'That would be a good while back?'

'A good while – when Onund had two sound legs under him, in our own sea-raiding days.' He wiped the back of his hand across his mouth, and held the jack out to Bjarni. 'These waters weren't big enough for the three of them then, and I doubt they're big enough for the three of them now.'

Bjarni drank thoughtfully and returned the ale-jack to the hand that came out for it. 'It sounded – Onund sounded – as though it was something more. Like a kind of holm-ganging, a duel to the death.'

'You're not so witless as you look,' Orlig told him kindly. 'Aye well, they never had much care, those two beauties, for the custom that protects merchantmen at sea. They captured a small trader, one time; they had heard there was gold on board, and when they found none, only salt and hides, they sank her and left the crew to drown . . . One of them was Onund's young brother – younger than you, he'd be.'

'What did he do? Onund?'

'Oh, he went after them, of course, when he heard. Thought he'd settled the debt; seems he hadn't.' Orlig held the ale-jack high. 'More drink here!'

In a short while first Thrond and then Thormod, summoned from their own steadings and each with a knot of his own men, came striding into the Hall, throwing off storm-wet cloaks to steam before the fire, and the four sea lords, joined by the merchant captain and young Raud, who captained the fifth longship of the Barra fleet, drew together into a huddle between the High Seat and the fire.

It was not a long council, for clearly all of them were of one mind; and Onund got up, and stood with his drink horn held high, looking round him at the crowded benches and from the benches the crews of the Barra longships, *Sea Witch* and *Wave Rider*, *Reindeer* and *Red Wolf* and *Star Bear*, looked back at him, knowing that this was a sea-faring and sea-fighting matter, and therefore the leadership was to him.

'With captives aboard they'll likely enough be making for the Dublin slave market,' someone said.

The storm, which had quietened somewhat, came swooping back, filling all the dark world beyond the torchlight with a turmoil of black wings, and Onund lifted his voice against it, reaching to the far end of the Hall. 'This harvest time it must be for the women and the bairns with the thralls to cut and carry home the sheaves – whatever the harvest is worth that the wind and rain have left to us. For the longships of Barra there is fine hunting down the Dublin sea, maybe a kill waiting to be made.'

And tipping back his head he drank long and deep from the silver-circled horn, as men drink to an oath that has been made. A roar went up from the warrior-benches, a hammering of ale-mugs on table-boards, and men caught down their weapons from the walls behind them as though they would be launching on the next wave. Blades were half out of the sheath, men thumping each other on the shoulders, the four sea lords with the rest.

'Did I not say there was not seaway enough for them and us in these waters?' grumbled Orlig joyfully into his beard.

'Why Dublin?' Bjarni asked.

'Did even you know a raider keep living captives aboard a day longer than need be? They'll be south along the sea-road to Dublin slave market.'

5

Sea Fight

For three days the gale lasted, pounding the steep western seas onto the coasts of Barra. But the time was not wasted, for the longships that had been drawn up onto the slipways ready for their winter refit had to be hurriedly made ready for sea again. There was torn canvas to be renewed, water-kegs to be filled and stowed, while on every hearth the women were baking the flat oaten sea-bannocks that never grew stale. The gear and rigging was brought down again from the ship-sheds and hastily overhauled before being stowed once more aboard, stores and spare weapons stowed in the narrow spaces below the deck planking; the dragon-heads, still rimed with salt, shipped at each prow.

Even so, on the third day, with all things ready and ship-shape and the gale sunk to no more than a stiff breeze, Arnulf Grimson, who was steersman of *Sea Witch*, found an unsuspected weakness – the start of a crack, maybe the work of sea-worm – in the vital steerboard side of the stern post, and would have had the sea-launch put back a day while repairs were made.

Sea Fight

Onund, with the smell of his old enemy already in the wind, would have none of that. 'We have lost ten years as it is, another day may like enough lose us the quarry. It has held up through the summer, it will hold up a few more days.'

Arnulf shrugged. 'Or fail tomorrow. Very pretty you'll look, drowning.'

'You've always been one to croak like an old woman. We'll take a log of wood for repairs if need be.'

And so they ran the five longships down into the shallows, with a serviceable baulk of timber stowed beneath the deck planking, and sailed on the turning tide.

Bjarni, settling to his oar, cast a parting look out past the high curve of the stern to the boat-strand they were leaving, and saw the crowd that had gathered to see them away; old men – not many of those – women and bairns and dogs, Hugin's lean black shape among them. The first summer Hugin had tried to swim after *Sea Witch* and Bjarni had had to go overboard himself and drag him back to land and beat him to make him understand, but now he had settled into the life-pattern of his kind, who followed at their master's heels while the longships were in their winter quarters and ran as a pack or hung around the women and bairns during the summer sea-faring. So now he barked furiously but made no attempt to follow. There was another pair of eyes to watch Bjarni go. Thara Priestsdaughter had hobbled down on her still-sore foot to see the galleys away; but he never noticed her.

'Lift her! Lift her!' came the call of Onund at the steering oar. At sea Arnulf his second-in-command was *Sea Witch*'s steersman. But always Onund Treefoot himself took her to sea and brought her in to harbour.

'Lift her! Lift her!' as *Sea Witch* led the Barra fleet out into open water.

In the fore-dawn darkness half a moon later, Bjarni was squatted among the thin scrub of hazel and dwarf willow at the southernmost head of the Dark Islet, Eilean Dubh in the tongue of the Old People, and gazing southward, his sword naked across his knees because somehow that made him feel more ready for action and less like to fall asleep at his watch-post than if he had left it in its old wolfskin sheath at his side. Behind him Loch Ruel ran away up into the mainland mountains; ahead, dark and furry as a crouching beast, the mass of Bute lay nose-on-paws on the paleness of water, where the water divided to become the tideway of Eastern and Western Kyles flowing past on either side of the island to the sea. The moon was still up; and in the light coming and going with the drifting cloud-roof, he had been able to glimpse from time to time scatters of low-lying islets and the ruffled bars of shoal water that spread their danger across the head of the Eastern Kyle, even between the muzzle of the crouching beast and the thrust like an elbow where the Western Kyle changed direction and was lost to sight, the half-fallen remains of one of those strange towers that some people said had been built by the Old People for defence against the Viking kind, but not even the Old People knew for sure.

Onund had been right about the slave market. They had picked up the wake of the raiders as they headed north again out of Dublin, lightened of their load of captives. But in open water five against eight was odds that not even Onund was crazy enough to take on needlessly. Better this way, this kind of shadow-hunting among the islands. In all likelihood Vigibjord and Vestnor must have guessed before long that the shadow ships, now glimpsed, now lost again like a wolf pack on their flanks biding its time, were fewer than themselves, but even so they would know that they must get rid of them, whoever, whatever they were, before they could run freely on their own hunting trail. And so Onund had drawn them northward back and back into this chosen spot that could even all odds.

The Barra fleet had slipped into the Western Kyle at dusk, when the last of the fighting light was gone; up to the place where they lay now quietly waiting behind the Dark Islet. With any luck the scouting galley that they had glimpsed the previous evening would have carried back word to Vigibjord that the fleet was only five keels strong. If any among the raiding fleet knew these waters well, they would know the Kyles for open tideways, coming together at the mouth of Loch Ruel, but even if they did, even if they came in up the Eastern Kyle, chancing the shoal water and tided eddies among the islets there, hoping to take them in the rear, the Barra scouts that Onund had sent up last night onto the highest point of Bute would bring the word in plenty of time for the Barra ships to fall back into Loch Ruel ahead of their coming. Loch Ruel, like the Kyles, was only wide enough for five keels to come in line abreast, with fighting space, at a time.

However, Vigibjord and Vestnor, it seemed, were not well-knowing of those waters, and to a stranger's eye the Western Kyle had the look of being a sea-loch because of the way the land seemed to close in where it rounded the beast's elbow and changed direction. They might think that the shadow fleet taking shelter there for the night had run themselves into a trap. That would be best of all, for there they – the raiders

– could be brought to battle under the walls of the ancient tower, the tower where Onund had set ashore a band of stone throwers last night with orders to gather up fallen stones and prise others from the walls, and carry them up to the highest point . . .

Late into last night – a long time ago it seemed – one of the scouts had got back to them with word that the raiders had indeed come in after them up the Western Kyle, and reaching the elbow of Bute and finding that open water went on beyond, had pulled up for the night on the good landing-beach there, kindled a couple of shore-fires and set scouts of their own around their flanks. There had been those among the sea lords who had been all for attacking them then and there, but to do that, Onund had pointed out, would be to lose all the advantage that they had gained and hurl themselves against a war-band nearly twice as large as themselves. So they held to the original plan.

That was when Bjarni had been ordered off to keep his solitary watch on the southern lip of Eilean Dubh, to watch out for anything that might be happening on Bute. There was a small hard knot of pride in him at having been sent there with maybe – who knew? – the safety of the Barra fleet in his hands. But he knew in reality that it was only because, like the rest of the scouts, he could swim. Most of his kind could not, holding by the old belief of seamen since seas began, that if the ship went down you would drown anyway, and drowning was quicker and less trouble if you could not swim.

He found himself thumbing the edge of his sword blade, for the familiar feel of it as much as anything else, hanging on to that pride. He hated this quietness and aloneness before battle. It wasn't natural, it was strange somehow. In the normal way of things he

48

could have been with the rest, and there would have been noise and to spare; battle-singing and the thunder of weapons on shield rims and the flare of fire and torches to set the blood racing and bring the blood-smell into the back of one's nose before ever the fighting joined. And the silence wasn't the only thing that was strange; or rather it was only the beginning of the strangeness. Bjarni had been with the Barra men long enough to know that Treefoot had odd ideas about sea warfare, and this would not be the customary Viking battle, which had almost the formality of a duel, in which ships were lashed together into a fighting platform on which enemies fought it out like land armies on a dwarf battlefield. Onund had ideas about manoeuvring his fleet so that the ships themselves took on fighting power and became weapons in their own right. It was a frightening way of battle because there was no known pattern to follow: only the shifting pattern in the mind of the leader, which might change at any moment as need or chance arose.

The moon was down now, but an ashy paleness as yet without warmth or colour was spreading behind the mountains eastward; and the sea birds were beginning to call again along the rocky ledges. The tide, which had been running strongly southward, stood at slack water, was on the turn. Slowly, slowly the first promise of colour was stealing back into the world, feathering the edges of the drifting cloud-roof with dim foxglove colour, though the hills and shoreline were still bloomed with darkness. The waters of the Kyle, faintly reflecting the promise of a squally sunrise, ran seemingly empty of all life save for the wings of the wheeling gulls, as Bjarni strained his eyes for any sign of movement on the shoreline of Bute. Then something dark – a man's head – appeared on the brightening surface, and as Bjarni knelt up, his hand instinctively tightening on his sword-hilt, Leif Johanson pulled out onto the rocks like an otter, close beside him, shaking back his wet hair.

'What word?' Bjarni demanded.

'They're dousing the fires,' Leif said, 'running the keels down into the water.'

And he was gone, crashing away through the willow-scrub toward the far end of the islet and the fleet lying there.

Bjarni waited a few moments wondering whether he should keep his watch any longer, but with the word gone through that the raiders were on the move there could be no further need for a lookout on Eilean Dubh and it was for him to be getting back to *Sea Witch*. Also there was the chance of something still to be had of the morning issue of bannock; for now that the solitary waiting time was over and the ready-making for the fighting had begun, the coldness had gone from his belly and he was wolf-hungry.

He got up and headed in the direction Leif had taken. But though Eilean Dubh was little more than a bowshot in length it was home to a pair of sea-otters and the sundry other beasts that he had heard going about their own lives in the dark. And as he went, suddenly the ground went from under him, as he put a foot into the hole that was the mouth of some creature's lair, and pitched headlong. There was a sharp crack somewhere, and a small starburst of col-oured sparks inside his right temple, and for a few moments sky and earth and water spun around him. Then, as the world cleared and steadied, he found himself lying with his head on what seemed to be an outcrop of rock. He went on lying there for a short while, wondering, though at a distance, where he was and how he came to be there, until the thought came to him that it might be a good idea to get up. He rolled over and sat up, feeling a little sick and still a little dizzy, and the light, which had grown, though not much, while he lay there, showed him his naked sword still clenched in his left hand, and at the sight, thought and memory shook themselves into place in his head. *Sea Witch*. He must get back to *Sea Witch* . . .

He got to his feet. The world dipped and swam a little, then he steadied and lurched off in Leif's wake towards the northern point of Eilean Dubh. But still somewhat deaf and confused from the bang on his head, he forgot to allow for the fact that Leif must have got back to *Sea Witch* some time ahead of him and she and the fleet would likely have up-anchored and be under way by now, and he did not hear, or at least did not properly take in, the sounds of voices and creaking timbers and the dip and thrust of oars passing between him and the mainland. And when at last he did hear, and altering course blundered out through the willow-scrub onto the shore, *Sea Witch* was already clearing the southern point of the islet, and *Wave Rider* was already past him with Thrond at the steering oar.

It would have been more sensible to head for *Star Bear*, following after, but the only thought in Bjarni's still slightly addled head was to get as near to Onund and *Sea Witch* as he could. He drove his sword into its sheath and plunged into the water and struck out after *Wave Rider*, shouting, 'I come – wait for me!'

Luckily they had not worked up any speed yet, but the oar-thresh was in his eyes and ears and he came near to getting another crack on the head from a swinging oar. Then willing hands hauled him in over the stern, and he stood shaking himself like a dog on the stern planking.

'It's Bjarni Sigurdson,' somebody said and somebody else asked, 'What have you done to your head?'

Bjarni put up a hand to his forehead and when he took it away the half-light showed him the darkness of blood on his fingers. 'I had a fight with a rock – it tried to bar my path,' he said with dignity. He was not going to have *Wave Rider*'s crew laughing at him for falling over and banging his head like some three-year-old bairn.

They laughed, all the same, Thrond with them. Still laughing, the ship chief said, 'Well, now that you are aboard, you may as well get forward and join the fighting men.'

Bjarni said steadily, 'I will go forward and join your fighting men for this while, but do not count on my sword, for the first chance that comes I will be over the side to join *Sea Witch*, for I am Onund's man.'

'I will blame that piece of insolence on your split head,' Thrond said, his gaze on the waterway ahead, 'and therefore it may be that I shall not demand your head from Onund in payment, when the fighting is over. Nevertheless your fighting today will be with *Wave Rider*. Fighting time is no time to be dog-paddling from ship to ship, unless you would be having what few brains you possess knocked out by the blade of an oar. Now get forward.'

And as Bjarni made his way toward the bows he heard the ship chief raise the rowing chant behind him.

'Lift her! Lift her!'

The last of the Barra ships cleared the southern point of Eilean Dubh, and the fleet spread out sideways wing-wise with *Sea Witch* in the centre and in the lead, headed down the Kyle, straightening from wild-goose formation to line-abreast as they went. And as they went, suddenly, rounding the elbow of Bute, appeared the longships of the enemy fleet.

Sea Fight

It seemed to Bjarni that *Wave Rider* checked for an instant then surged forward, with the rest of the fleet, like so many hounds slipped from the leash. A great shout went up, the rowers swinging to the increased rowing-beat, 'Lift her! Lift her! Lift her!'

Tide and wind were both against them, and behind the enemy keels; they must use all the speed that was in them to come up with Vigibjord and Vestnor before they drew level with the old shore fortress, to make full use of the plan laid by the slight man at the steering oar of *Sea Witch*. Once the fight was joined, wind and tide, which now seemed friend to the raiders, would be their enemy, making it hard to pull back when they had need to.

Bjarni, standing among the fighting men, sent up a spear-thought of gratitude to all the gods of war and sea-faring, that even though he was in the wrong ship, he was not among the rowers, pulling backwards into battle, missing the fine fierce sight of the two fleets drawing towards each other, the ruffled waters of the Kyle narrowing between. He could sense that the dragon-prow of every ship rose higher, like the heads of great sea beasts lifted for a better sight of their foe, a better judgement of each other's fighting-power, eager for blood.

The light was broadening on the oar-thresh, glinting on shield rim and war-cap. The gulls were crying round the ruined tower on the shore as the Barra fleet surged past.

'Lift her! Lift her, my heroes.' The rowing chant came almost as a caress.

The tower with its crowd of crying gulls fell astern. Ahead, the raiders were almost within hailing distance. The timing was perfect.

For a few heartbeats of time as they drew together it seemed that the fight was going to follow the old formal pattern after all, the two fleets meeting prow to prow all across that narrow Kyle, where there was space for only five galleys under oars to come abreast while the three remaining raiders must hold back in the rear. But there was no lashing of prows together, so the fight would remain loose and free to manoeuvre. For a long breath of time the two fleets confronted each other, little more than a spear's length apart, and something like the very old formal salute before battle, each using their oars just enough to hold station. The silence was filled with no more than the lapping of the water and the sky-wide diving of the gulls.

Then the man high in the prow of the centremost enemy vessel flung up his arms, the first sunlight jinking on the boss of his painted shield; and his bellow came clear across the water. 'Who are you that comes playing wolf pack in our hunting runs?'

From the stern of *Sea Witch*, where he still stood at the steering oar, Onund's voice, that light clear voice of his that carried like a hunting horn, made answer, 'Do you not know me, Vigibjord? I am Onund Tree-foot, whom you have good cause to remember. And with me Thrond, brother of Evynd Easterner, who long ago made these waters unsafe for your kind. Also Thormod and Aflaeg, all of us the sea lords of Barra.'

Vigibjord laughed, and his laughter rang and re-echoed to and fro between the rocky shores. 'I never yet saw a man go into battle who could not get there on his own two feet!'

Then Onund laughed also, flinging his own challenge into the wind, 'Did you not? Aye well, there must be a first time for all things – a first time – and a last! Best be turning tail and heading for the skyline now, lest this be the last fight you see at all – you and your pack of curs.'

There was a sudden roar of fury from the enemy longships. And the rowers who had been lightly, sullenly, backing water against the tide, bent to their oars and sent their vessels plunging forward on the full thrust of the oars.

'Hold water,' came the order from the man in *Sea Witch*'s stern, echoed from *Wave Rider, Red Wolf, Reindeer* and *Star Bear*. 'Lift her,' and again, 'Hold water.'

The two fleets came together with a shock, a grinding kiss of prow against prow, quarter against quarter, like herd animals trying to shoulder each other off; and instantly the champions on the fighting deck thrust forward against each other. Bjarni, tensed among *Wave Rider*'s lesser fry, his drawn sword waiting in his left hand, glimpsed through the reeling press men bounding forward, one foot on the bulwark, the blink of morning light on the up-swung blade of sword and war-axe. The shouts and the weapons rang. But chiefly he was aware of what he could not see, for it was almost behind him: Onund braced on his wooden leg at the *Sea Witch*'s steering oar, watching the fight with narrow eyes, watching for the exact moment to pull back his fleet, as the swordsmith watches a cooling blade, waiting for the exact change of colour that marks the instant for plunging it into the tempering trough. Would he be able to whistle the Barra ships off in time . . . long enough for the enemy to get their blood up, not long enough for the Barra men to forget that this was only the skirmish to draw them into the trap, not yet the full Ravens' Gathering after the trap was sprung . . . The moment was not long, not long enough for the thing to pass from skirmish into full fight. How it happened, Bjarni did not know; in the uproar he did not hear the orders to the rowers, he only knew that before he had even had a chance to blood his sword, the fighting-line was falling apart, the rowers backing water, raggedly. One by one the Barra ships shuddered and fell away; seemingly a fighting fleet that found itself outmatched, falling back shamefully from more than it could handle.

For one incredulous moment clear water showed churning between the bows of the two fleets. Then with a yell of triumph Vigibjord's rowers sent their vessel surging forward in pursuit, the rest of the reiving pack with them.

Back and back in disorder, unable as it seemed even to turn away, and huddling closer and closer to the Bute shore; at any moment Bjarni thought to feel the check and shock and lift, the grinding crash as *Wave Rider* ripped her bottom out on the rocks. Then they were close upon the ruined tower. Two – three more oarstrokes, and they were clear of the crumbling walls and the raiders yelling in pursuit were close beneath them. And in that same instant the jagged crest of the tower sprang to life with heads and shoulders against the drifting sky and a flight of jagged stones came whistling down upon the close-packed reivers beneath.

They were not, for the most part, big stones, though one boulder went straight through the bottom of a smaller vessel so that she began instantly to fill and settle in the water, but coming from that height and with the throwers' power behind them, they spread chaos on the rowing benches, crashing down on the oarlooms and the heads of the rowers, while on the narrow fighting decks men dropped to clog the feet of their sword-brothers. While the Barra men rested on their oars, looking on.

Unable to pull clear for the force of the tide and their

own reserves behind them, unable to thrust forward through the Barra fleet across their way, the pirate ships were caught like beasts in a hunter's net. And still the stones came whistling down and from the trapped reivers the turmoil of furious shouting and desperate cries and screamed-out curses burst up and echoed to and fro between Bute and the mainland shore.

Then the hail of stones thinned and stopped. 'Out oars,' came the order up and down the Barra fleet, and then, 'Lift her! Lift her!' In the stern of *Sea Witch*, there was a shifting and change of pattern and Arnulf the Steersman thrusting up beside Onund to take his place at the steering oar. And from his place among the *Wave Rider*'s fighting men, Bjarni, snatching a sideways glance between the forward-thrust of bodies and shield rims, saw the slight unmistakable figure of Onund Treefoot lurching sword in hand up the crowded, pitching length of *Sea Witch* to take his leader's place among the champions on the forward fighting deck.

To Bjarni, Thrond's orders went for nothing. All he knew was that his place was with his lord as the two-sworded beast was going into battle. He slammed his sword into its sheath, having enough sense even in that moment, with the blood-smell rising in the back of his nose, to know that to swim with it in his teeth in clogged and flailing waters would be to go begging for death. He ducked out and back along the rowing benches toward the stern. Shouts and curses followed him but he never even heard them as he went over the side. He dived down into the rolling churn of water under the slow-beating oars, and struck out for *Sea Witch*. The two keels were scarce their own oars' lengths apart, but he came within hailing distance of death twice all the same, once from being knocked on the head and drowned among the oar-thresh, once at the hands of the men in the stern of *Sea Witch* who mistook him, the first moment of his surfacing beside them, for one of the enemy. But a friendly voice from the rowing bench shouted above the tumult, 'It's that fool Bjarni Sigurdson!' and the hands, turned friendly, hauled him in and dumped him all a-sprawl at the steersman's feet.

Almost in the same instant he felt the shuddering jar beneath him and heard the rising battle shouts above the general turmoil as the two fleets came together again. He lurched to his feet, shaking himself like a dog, and lurched off between the rowing benches, where the oars were being swung in, war-axes and swords drawn, weapons caught up as alternate rowers turned warrior, drawing his own sword as he went, thrusting his way through the press heedless of who he trampled on or heaved off balance and half overboard. But it seemed slow going, and he was still amidships when the shout went up from the heart of the press ahead of him: 'Onund's down!'

Sick shock lurched in his belly. 'He could have waited for me! He should have waited for me!'

How he hurled his way through the last distance and arrived in the midst of the champions on the fighting deck he never knew. He only knew that as he arrived there, of all unlikely things, the sudden check and following roar of vengeful fury began to be shot through with a gale of laughter.

On either side the rest of the Barra keels were locked in battle.

'Wrong leg!' somebody shouted, and he knew that it was Onund.

The ship chief was already coming up again from his sprawl among the feet of his champions, his arm across someone's shoulder, his war-cap gone and his fox-pelt hair flying free, and on his face that white-lightning laughter covering a certain greyness beneath. Several of his carles had locked shields to cover him from the enemy. And Bjarni, looking down to see what was the damage, saw what the laughter was about; saw that Onund's wooden leg was gone, splintered and cut through a little below the knee, and the light throwing-axe that had done it lying close by on the rocking and tilting deck. He kicked it aside as he charged in, thrusting the other men aside to come up into Onund's armpit in his place.

'Bring me my milking-stool!' the ship chief was shouting.

The baulk of timber with its carved dragon-knots was fetched up and thrust under Onund's bent knee. 'Hands off, you dripping seal-man,' said Onund and Bjarni felt the other's weight and balance go from him and took his arm away. Onund was his own man again, his sword, Skull-Splitter, ready in his hand. The whole incident could have taken only a few racing heartbeats of time.

The covering shields parted as the fighting deck of *Sea Witch*, which for that blink of time had been held back like hounds in check within the shield-wall, defending, roared into battle.

It was not Bjarni's first experience of a sea fight, but he had never known anything quite like it before. The splintered wounds of the ships themselves as they joined and juddered together; men slumped broken or dead on the enemy rowing benches; and fighting men who had found death without even reaching an enemy to strike at before it came whistling out of the sky. He was not aware of the rest of the fleet at all, only *Sea Witch* and her nearest enemy, and the fight that was now swinging to and fro across the bulwarks, as Vigibjord's men with despairing courage strove to board and, yelling with the rest, Bjarni hurled himself against them. He saw snarling, wild-eyed faces like the faces in a savage dream, and the wolf-glint of weapons in the morning light. He drove left-handed under someone's shield, and felt the blade bite deep, and dragged it out, reddened halfway to the hilt, as the shield's owner went over backwards with a surprised-sounding grunt to be lost across the side of his own ship. To and fro swung the fighting, war cries beating against war cries in a surge of sound under the screaming of the gulls. And in the midst of the weapon-storm Onund Treefoot stood like a rock swept by pounding seas, wielding his sword in great sweeping blows that kept open space before him.

Bjarni, fighting grimly, well up among the champions, found the lurching deck growing slippery underfoot. A fresh wave of Vigibjord's reivers came crashing in against them, swarming in over the sides, their dead and wounded made good by men pouring in from their reserves astern. At their forefront a huge man rose suddenly in their midst, war-cap wide-horned against the sky, the light glinting on the blade of his up-swung battle axe as he made for the place where Onund Treefoot stood to meet him – as though it were a meeting long arranged.

The battle axe came swooping down. No sword could have turned the blow, but somehow, no one, not even Onund, knowing afterwards how it was done, the one-legged sea lord wrenched sideways without losing his balance on his one remaining leg, and the axe came whistling down to bed itself deep in the log of wood beside his knee.

In the instant that the man was unarmed and struggling to drag the blade free, Onund brought Skull-Splitter crashing down in a great blow that took him between neck and shoulder, hacking his arm all but free of his body so that it hung only by splintered bone and a strip of flesh above a great hollow pumping red. Vigibjord crumpled on to his face, making a horrible sound, oddly thin and pitiful to come from that great bull throat, but rising above the fighting-roar like the scream of a hare in a trap.

Onund stood, leaning on his sword, looking down with cool satisfaction at the man twitching convulsively against his foot. 'So you never saw a man come to battle that could not come there on his own two feet,' he said in that hard, high, carrying voice of his. 'Yet having come there he might do well enough.' And he laughed, spurning the great body with his sword. 'At least one leg makes a better showing in the killing time than one arm does, I'm thinking.'

But the twitching and the high whistling cry had ceased.

Their leader down, the men who followed him began to give back across decks grown slippery with blood, and the men of *Sea Witch* were pouring after them, yelling as they went. It was the same to right and left as the tide-turn spread along the lines of the opposing fleets; but Bjarni had no awareness to spare for them, the bows of *Sea Witch* and the enemy bumping and grinding against her was his whole world just then. Onund's hand had come down on his shoulder and Onund's voice was in his ear, 'Now, my hero, time for the two-sworded beast!' And he had come up, his shoulder into his lord's armpit, his lord's arm round his neck, and they went forward with the wave of men, the two-sworded beast. One leg might be well enough in battle, but not so good for pursuing a desperate and fleeing foe across planks covered with blood and battle filth. But, three legs and two swords biting deep, they did none so ill. The enemy turned in the stern and put up a desperate fight against them, and with the yelling wave of Barra men around and behind them, the two of them swept the pirate longship from stem to stern, their battle yells changed to singing; the splendid and terrible singing of the Viking kind in the moment of victory.

When evening came, the five longships of the Barra fleet lay above high-tide mark on the beach below the elbow of Bute where last night Vigibjord's pirate keels had lain, and with them three captured ships, all sluiced down with sea water to be freed of the worst of the battle-fouling. Two of the pirate fleet had been sunk in the fighting, and one they had sunk themselves, with its cargo of dead men lying tangled among its oar-shafts and broken spars, as being too sorely damaged to be any further use. Two enemy ships, both of the reserve, had escaped in the final stages of the fighting, bearing away Vestnor, his own ship sunk by Thrond and the men of *Wave Rider*, and as many of the enemy reivers as could reach them and scramble aboard.

The Barra men had made no attempt to give chase or hunt them down. 'Vestnor has lost brother for brother and most of his fleet, and the feud-price is paid. Let him away to lick his wounds,' Onund had said peaceably, sitting on his milking-stool with his sword across his knees and looking much as though he had just come out from a slaughterhouse.

They had taken a few captives, not many, for the Dublin slave market, and they lay at a little distance, roped like cattle. A few survivors had reached the shore and disappeared into the high country of Bute or the mainland. The pirate wounded they had dealt with according to the usual custom, and tipped them overboard. There would be dead men all along the coast on the next few tides.

They had dead of their own, and these they had tipped over likewise, though more gently and with much of their heavy war gear still on them to keep them down. Their own wounded they had seen to as best they could, and the sorest scathed of them lay now beside the ships with sails rigged over them for shelter from the fine chill rain-mist that had set in with the dusk. All along the beach among the rocks the Barra men had kindled drift-wood fires and, gathered about them, they had supped well on captured stores and half-singed, half-raw meat – there were red deer for the hunting among the high moors of Bute. And sitting beside one of them on his gashed milking-stool which his men had brought ashore for him, Onund Treefoot was making himself a new wooden leg; replacing the splintered end of the old one with an oarloom from one of the captured galleys. Bjarni had cut it to the right length for him with a blow from somebody's war-axe, and was squatting beside him steadying one end of it while his lord jammed the other into the boiled-leather cup with its dangling straps, and bound it in place with a length of fine sealskin cord.

'That should hold until we come again to Barra and they can make a neater job of it in the ship-sheds,' he said when he was satisfied, and began to buckle it on as another man might buckle on a piece of his war gear. He jerked the buckle tight on the last strap, the one that encircled his waist beneath his sword belt, and stood up to a cheer from the men about the fire.

'Timbertoes is himself again.'

He looked round at Bjarni, who had risen also with an odd feeling that he was being left behind, and his mouth quirked into its rare, fierce and fleeting smile. 'Not but what I'm minded to keep it as it is to mind me of a day well spent and in good company.'

6

Bride-Ale in Barra

They spent three days lying close under the elbow of
Bute, patching up their own ships and the captured
reiving vessels, before they swung out the oars again
for Barra. They met squally weather in the open
waters beyond Arran, but on the third morning the
southernmost islets of Barra rose like faint cloud
shapes out of the sea; and before evening they were
nosing in past Vatersay toward the main island
harbour.

The sails had come rattling down and the crews
had taken to the oars and Bjarni, pulling with the rest,
saw only the tall graceful up-thrust of the stern post,
and beyond, *Wave Rider* and *Red Wolf, Reindeer* and
Star Bear and the three captives, with prize crews
aboard them, following each in another's wake, and
beyond again the empty seaway that they had crossed.
Onund was standing braced on his renewed wooden
leg at the steering oar, bringing *Sea Witch* into harbour,
leading home the fleet.

All along the rowing benches men were beginning
to snatch glances over their shoulders as the coasts
slid by. And Bjarni, glancing back also as he swung

to his oar, saw the high-pitched gables of the ship-sheds above the gull-grey shingle of the landing-beach that had been stranger-strand when first he came that way, but grown familiar as the months went by until the sight of it brought with it a sense of homecoming.

The next glance snatched over his shoulder showed him the whole landing-beach and the rough grass slopes beyond freckled with people. Clearly they had been seen from afar – a look-out on Vatersay maybe – and the whole of the mainland settlement had come crowding down to see them return in triumph. Eight war keels returning, where they had seen five away.

Onund's voice quickened in the rowing chant, 'Lift her! Lift her!' and *Sea Witch* leapt forward like a mare that scents her own stable and is eager to be home. Onund put over the steering oar and she came round in a sea-swallow curve, the others following in the white oar-thresh of her wake. The water was green now in the steep shallows, and they were heading straight in through the broken water where the weed-grown jetty thrust out to give shelter from the storms and the swinging tides.

'Now! In oars! Out rollers! Run her in, my heroes!'

They unshipped the oars and swung them on board and caught up their rollers from their places under the thwarts. They were out over the sides, belly-deep into the icy water, running her up through the shallows, the rest following after. The people at the settlement came plunging out to meet them, set their shoulders to the ship's sides and helped with the rollers as they ran her up the sloping shingle, shouting and cheering as they went.

The whole settlement seemed to be there, old men and boys, women and bairns and the usual flurry of dogs. Bjarni was still shin-deep when the black and joyful shape of Hugin was thrashing about his legs,

trying to leap up on him, adding his frenzied showers
of barks to the general tumult. Bjarni thrust him off
with one foot; but only a few gasping moments
later, with *Sea Witch* safely stranded, he was squatting
on his heels to receive the loving onslaughts of the
great black dog. All around him men were greeting
their women, tossing up their bairns, joyful reunions
all along the ship-strand, save where a woman here
or there stood looking for her husband or son who
had not come back with the rest. Here and there were
girls who had kilted up their kirtle skirts and came
running down to meet the returned ships; and among
them, Thara Priestsdaughter. She passed close by
Bjarni, slanting her eyes at him and holding her
shoulders back to make the most of her little round
apple breasts. But he never saw her, because his face
was buried in Hugin's neck and his hands were up,
working into the warm hollows behind the great
hound's ears.

Later, when the longships had been run up the
beach and tended like hard-worked horses brought
back to their stables, when the reunions were over
and the evening meal had been eaten, the captured
booty was brought up to the broad garth before the
Hearth Hall and the crews gathered to the share-out,
with most of the rest of the settlement looking on. The
harvest, by now gathered in by the thralls and the
womenfolk, had been a poor one, thin in the ear and
storm-battered, but this other kind of harvest would
help to see them through the long lean winter. Daylight was fading, and torches had been brought out
and here and there the flamelight through the smoky
dust struck out blinks of coloured light from the
growing piles of booty as the wicker sea-kists and
the sail-cloth bundles were opened and their contents
flung out on the beaten earth.

Bjarni, squatting among the rest of *Sea Witch*'s crew, watched the coming to light of the fruits of a whole summer's raiding; fine weapons and rapiers of narwhal ivory that would be sold in the south as unicorn's horn. Furs and enamels and good stout copper cooking pots. He saw a thick russet woollen cloak that might be a prosperous farmer's best, and sea-spoiled striped silks from foreign parts; a hacked silver cross, and a painted picture of a woman with a golden straw hat on the back of her head and a babe in the crook of her arm, also damaged by sea water, which he knew by now probably came from a God-House of the White Christ. There were hangings worked with writhing dragon-knots that must have been torn down from a chieftain's hall; horse harness and five hide ropes; bags that spewed gold and silver and copper coins and small broken-up bits of metal, whose value, like that of the coins, would be by weight. There was even a carved wooden manikin dressed in a wisp of soaked cloth and a string of blue beads, that must have been a bairn's toy before it took the fancy of some freebooter with maybe a bairn of his own to take it home to.

The share-out was done in several stages and took a long time, so that long before the end the autumn night had closed round them, blotting out the world beyond the smoking wind-teased torches. First the tribute-share of Evynd the Easterner was set aside for him. Most of the church treasure was in that pile, seeing that though he was not exactly a follower of the White Christ himself, his queen and many of the household were. Then the ship chiefs made their choice. Onund took only one thing for his share, a splendid and beautiful ice-bear skin, yellow as old ivory, and flung it down before Aesa, who had come out with the other girls to look at the sea-harvest that the men had brought home: 'Here's a bonnie thing for our marriage bed, that shall keep you warm when *Sea Witch* puts to sea.' And there was a cheerful roar of laughter, while the girl, flushing in the torchlight, bent to gather the heavy folds against her.

The rest of the booty was divided into five; five steep piles stacked each on a spread cloak before one of the ship chiefs; and each from his own pile the ship chiefs began the gift-making among their own crews.

Most of the things would be used simply to trade – for what use is a silver-mounted drinking cup to a man who needs seed corn for his plot or a new pair of sea boots? That was understood. But there were things that would be kept and treasured as the gift to a carle from his chief; an enamelled arm-ring, a fine pattern-forged sword blade, a chain of silver and turquoise for a woman's neck.

Bjarni, a mercenary who had sold his sword-service to the one-legged sea lord for one sea-faring summer and then one more and received steady pay for it as a mercenary should, had not had anything from the share-out before, and he did not expect it. But at the very end he heard his own name called, and when he scrambled to his feet and answered the call, Onund grinned up at him, saying, much as he had said once before, 'For a good fight in good company,' and tossed him something shapeless and bright. Bjarni caught it and, feeling it unexpectedly light and warm as loops of it tumbled through his fingers, saw that he was holding a string of massive amber beads that caught the torchlight like gobbets of clouded honey.

'A good fight in good company,' he agreed, and returned the grin. And turning away he met the eager gaze of Thara Priestsdaughter standing among a chattering cluster of girls nearby. He looked away quickly, pretending not to have seen, pretending not to know that she wanted him to give her the string of amber. Quite a few of the longships' crews were making gifts out of their share to the girls of their choice. He saw Sven Gunnarson on the fringe of the torchlight, with great care and concentration hanging a heavy coral and silver drop in his woman's ear and following it up with a smacking kiss before they both disappeared into the darkness. He grinned again and put the fragile beauty round his own neck, squinting down at it and not heeding the angry whisk of a girl's blue skirts as she swung away to become deeply interested in somebody else.

In the next days the interrupted ready-making for Onund's wedding got under way again. There was a great baking and brewing; best clothes taken from storage kists, shaken out to air and mended if need be; a black ram and a milk-white ewe were chosen out of the bridegroom's flock and set aside for sacrifice to Odin, the lord of all the gods, and to Frigga, his wife, the lady of all things to do with marriage and in the home. Traders began coming in, too, for word of what was in the wind had spread out beyond Barra to the Island Seas and the coasts of Alba and Erin, and a chief's bride-ale was always good for trade.

On the day that Aesa, in the midst of much advice from the older women of the settlement, was baking her great bride-cake, the broad-beamed serviceable shape of *Sea Cow* appeared, beating into harbour out of an autumn squall; and towards evening Bjarni, heading down to the boat-strand on some errand, met Heriolf Merchantman on the track up to the settlement. They greeted each other with much cheerful thumping on the shoulders, and turned aside into the lee of a peat-stack out of the wind for a few words before going their separate ways.

'A fine beard you have grown yourself,' Heriolf said.

And Bjarni laughed, but flushing to the roots of his hair; for his beard was not much more than chicken-down as yet, and he was well aware of it. He had not thought that Heriolf knew about that; but the little merchant had a way of knowing more than one expected. 'They do say that the Hero Cuchulain must needs paint his down with bramble juice.'

'Na, na, no need for that,' the other said consolingly. 'And you've a man's shoulders on you.'

'Two summers at the oar,' Bjarni said.

'Two summers? It seems not so long since you sold your sword-service to my Lord Timbertoes . . . Good summers they've been, have they?'

'Aye, good enough.' Hugin, who had been off about his own affairs, came up smelling strongly of fish guts, and nosed lovingly into his hand.

'Not feeling the wind in your sails then?'

Bjarni shook his head. 'Not as yet – tho' there's three years and more my far-faring still before me and maybe I'll get the itch for strange seas before they are all spent.'

And an eddy of the wind dipped round the shoulder of the peat-stack and blew a cold spatter of raindrops into his face.

Two days later came the appointed day for Onund Treefoot to take Aesa from her father's hearth. Almost before daylight the whole settlement had begun gathering in the broad garth before the Hearth Hall. It was a day of thick yellow sunshine and sudden glooms under a sky of high-piled hurrying storm cloud threatening wild weather to come; but the harvest was in and the fleet home from the sea.

With the rest of *Sea Witch*'s crew, Bjarni had spent

the night in Onund's house, and in the early morning, all clad in their best, they went up with him – Onund walking with his familiar sideways lurch and swagger on the fine new wooden leg which the shipwrights had made him from the one he had rough-cobbled from a captured oarloom on the shore of Bute – to demand the bride.

The women brought her out to him, clad in a kirtle of poppy-red merchant's stuff, and with her hair bound back under the heavy silver-gilt bridal crown taken in some long-past raid. And Aflaeg set her hand in Onund's over the fire, binding and unbinding them together three times with a supple sealskin thong. Then they drank together from the same cup in the sight of the whole settlement. 'I take the woman from her father's house to mine,' Onund said. 'Henceforth I am her man.'

And Aesa lifted her head stiffly under the weight and balance of her crown, and smiled at him. 'I go with the man from my father's house,' she said. 'Henceforth I am his woman.'

And so the thing was done.

After, bride and groom and closest kin, having drunk the sacred juice that made the gods' fire come into the priest's head in time of sacrifice, went out to the God-House in its dark sacred wood, where Asmund the Priest waited with the black ram and the white ewe; and when they returned, walking behind Asmund, whose own robes were spattered, both Onund and Aesa had a streak of blood on their foreheads. But that was to do with seeking the favour of the gods on the marriage that was already made.

After that it was the time for feasting. The kegs of bride-ale were brought out and the huge bride-cake was broken up and given to all comers. And the rest of the day went by in feasting and harping, while bride and groom and priest and chieftains sat beside the chieftain's fire in the Hall and the young men of the settlement wrestled and raced against each other, between fresh attacks on the little dark carcasses of hill mutton, the seal meat and cod and great dishes of bannock and ewes'-milk curds and honey.

Evening came at last, with the tawny light of the feast fires beginning to draw men's faces out of the gathering dark, and the sound of the sea growing louder as it always seemed to do at dusk. Bjarni, pleasantly weary after a day spent enjoying himself, full with much feasting and in a pleasant haze of bride-ale, had cast himself down beside Heriolf on the comfortable fringe of things, their backs propped against the pigsty wall.

'Thunder coming,' said the merchant, sniffing the air like a hound. 'Aye well, 'twill come in the night and be cleared by morning.' He had a personal interest in the weather for, having done good trading through the past few days, he was for the seaways again next morning.

'And what sea-road this time? Or are you reckoning to be making for a haven and laying *Sea Cow* up for the winter?'

Heriolf shrugged. 'The Misty Isle, maybe, or further south to Mull. Thorstein the Red is generally worth a visit before the winter closes in.'

'Any bride-ales there?' Bjarni asked idly.

'Three daughters the man has, all too young for their bride-ales as yet. But I've an enamelled cup set with river pearls might please his mother – the Lady Aud has an eye for beautiful things and money of her own to pay for them.'

'That would be her they call Aud the Deep-Minded?' Bjarni said after a moment.

The merchant laughed. 'Aye, that would be her. But she has the wisdom not to let it show too much . . .'

Out in the clear centre of the garth someone was playing a pipe, and some of the men and older women had begun to sway and stamp and clap their hands for dancing. The hunter's moon was up, broad as a buckler and yellow as corn sheaves, among the tumble of cloud and clear, its quiet light mingling with the fierce flare of fires and torches; and thrusting through the crowd in answer to the piping, Bjarni saw that in the clear space in the midst of it all, the girls had formed themselves into a ring-dance facing outward, laughing, arms linked and feet moving in little neatly braided steps under them. The young men had gathered also and stood idly looking on, pretending not to be much interested, passing the ale-jack from hand to hand. The clapping women had taken up the pipe tune and begun to make the quick lilting mouth-music that has no words but set the feet jigging and the blood to dance, and the young men drew closer and forgot the ale-jacks.

Bjarni, watching the girls circling by, saw Thara's pretty, stupid little face go by with bursts of coloured silk twisted into the pale bright braids of her hair. Three times he saw her go by. Then, circling still, the girls slipped their arms free of each other and the steps became wider and looser, the circle swifter and more ragged as each girl darted out from it to catch whichever of the young men caught her fancy and swung him back with her into the dance. Bjarni found Thara's face close to him, flushed and foolish, and next moment she had flung herself upon his chest, her arms round him, laughing, trying to kiss him wetly, trying to drag him into the jigging, bounding circle behind her.

If he had been stone-cold sober he would not have

done it. He would have had too much sense, or maybe too much kindness. But the bride-ale was strong and he had drunk a good deal of it, and he did not want to find himself caught up with Thara Priestsdaughter, who seemed to be forever hanging round him. He pulled her arms away and thrust her cheerfully into the arms of the man next beside him, and himself grabbed the next girl to spin by and swung her off her feet as he pranced out with her into the ring of dancers. He scarcely knew the girl, but she came willingly, squealing with laughter, and they danced together in the ragged spinning circle. The whole night was spinning, swimming and circling under the yellow moon to the lilt of the pipes and the fog of ale and the nearing scent of thunder in the air.

Once he caught sight of Thara in the swirl of the dance, her head turned over her shoulder to watch him, her face without its prettiness, her big blue eyes seeming turned to splinters of ice as they met his and with a look in them that reached him through the torchlight and the ale, and for the moment almost sobered him. Then the pattern of the dance closed over between them and he almost forgot about it – almost, but not quite.

The thunder-clouds were coming up against the wind in the unchancy way of thunder, banking thick behind the hills, soon to swallow up the moon. And at the same time the men of *Sea Witch*, Onund's ship-carles and hearth companions, were beginning to gather also, knowing that their lord would be wanting to get his bride back beneath his own roof before the storm broke. It was then that Bjarni found Hugin missing. He whistled, the shrill two-note call that at most times brought the great hound leaping back from wherever he might be. But this time no black shape answered the call. Always, when *Sea Witch* was in harbour, Hugin slept at his feet, and there was just enough of the old uneasiness left in the back of his neck – maybe it was the low mutter of the nearing thunder and nothing more – made him unwilling to leave the dog here and go back to Onund's house without him tonight. He knew Hugin's ways and the good friends that he had among the kitchen thralls, and headed for the cookhouse, fairly sure of finding him.

In the lea of the kitchen peat-stack he sensed rather than saw two figures, one of them clinging to the other. There would be many such couples among the outbuildings of Aflaeg's Hall tonight. He took no notice of them and, among all of the comings and goings, Bjarni's feet in his lightest brogues for dancing made scarcely any sound, so they remained unaware of him. Then the man spoke. 'It was for this that you brought me out here?'

And the girl answered, 'Oh my father, I could not have speech with you in Aflaeg's Hall.'

And Bjarni knew the voices, Asmund the Priest and his daughter. And something, some unreasoning sense of danger, made him check and freeze.

'Surely this is a woman's matter, and you should be making your plaint to the goddess who protects women, the Lady Frigga herself,' Asmund said. 'She should listen kindly, having had her own sacrifice this feast day.'

Thara was almost sobbing. 'Nay, but you do not understand – it is not kindness that I seek – '

'And that's true enough. For I'm minded that it's revenge, my daughter.'

'And should I not? – Shaming me before the whole settlement – ' Thara was almost whimpering. 'He has used me so ill – I could show you the bruises on my arms – '

Well, she couldn't be talking about him anyway. He hadn't used enough force on her to raise a bruise the size of a finger-tip.

The thunder muttered again, nearer this time, and the girl seemed to seize upon it with a kind of triumph. 'Do you not hear? It's Thor! It is the Lord of Thunder, who grows angry for lack of a sacrifice on his altar. Tell that to the chieftains and the people and they will not dare gainsay you – '

The thunder rolled closer, swallowing the last of her words, and when it had muttered away into the stillness, the two shadows had moved on.

Bjarni stood where he was for a few moments. What he had overheard made very little sense to him; except that Thara wanted revenge on somebody who had used her roughly – a revenge that her father as the Priest could work for her. And likely, in one way or another, she would get her own way. He was glad that whoever the man was, it wasn't him.

After a moment he moved on, kicking a stone out of his way and cursing, to make sure that anyone could hear him coming, and whistling for Hugin as he went.

Almost at once there was a scuttering of paws from the direction of the kitchen midden, and the great hound's muzzle was thrust into his hand.

'Come, greedy one,' Bjarni said, twisting a hand in his collar as they turned back towards the Hall.

The thunder muttered again and there was a distant flicker of lighting over Ben Harr; the storm was circling to the north and seemingly no nearer than before, as they rejoined the others who were gathering in a cheerful and jostling crowd before the Hall. Onund had come out to them and in the broad fore-porch doorway Aesa stood with all her bridal finery muffled in the folds of a thick hooded cloak, and her mother and all the women of the household fussing about her.

'Let you bide until the storm be passed,' said the chieftains, but Onund said, 'Nay, the way it's travelling 'twill be half the night before it breaks this side of the ben,' and he laughed, reaching out to slip Aesa against his side. 'And I'm minded to have the lass under my roof before then.'

Aesa said nothing at all.

And so they set off, with torches to light their way, singing and a little unsteady in the way of wedding parties, to bring home the bride. But it is not easy in coast and mountain country to judge the speed and pattern of thunder coming up against the wind; and Onund, though agile as a goat on his wooden leg, was less swift than he had been in his younger and two-legged days; and always forgot to allow for that.

The thing became a race and they had only just reached the edge of his own in-take land, when the storm broke over them with great booming crashes of thunder that rolled and re-echoed from the hills to the sea, and flash on flash of lightning that set the whole sky a-flicker. Then, driven before the wind that came upon them with the speed of a galloping horse, came the streaking rain.

It drove hissing against their faces and quenched the torches. Onund flung his cloak over Aesa, and Bjarni heard her laughter skirling like a curlew as he dragged her close. And ahead of them the light of the steading fires glimmered ragged through the swathing rain, swelling on the sight as they pelted towards it.

They plunged in through the house door at last, laughing and cursing, gasping, half-drowned. Warmth and light met them. The house thralls had kindled the wall-torches and the drift-wood fire down the centre of the hall burned high. The last bride-cup was brought, and Onund and Aesa drank together, their hands meeting on the sides of the gilded cup, and then disappeared together through the heavy painted curtain of the bridal chamber, *Sea Witch*'s crew cheering them on their way with wishes for many sons.

And when they were gone, Bjarni and the rest flung off drenched cloaks and settled down among the dogs in the rushes along the fire, with a keg of ale to keep the night from going flat, while the storm hurled itself across the roof and the lightning sent flash on blue-white flash through the chinks in the wicker shutters.

Bjarni was half-asleep, sprawling with his feet to the fire and Hugin's black flank pressed companionably against his thigh, when the storm-curtain over the foreporch was wrenched back. The storm seemed to leap into the hall, and three figures appeared in the doorway with the flickering lightning behind them. The hounds sprang up snarling, and in upon the startled men around the fire strode Asmund the Priest, and his two huge God-House thralls behind him, naked save for their blood-stained leather aprons.

The men round the fire were scrambling to their feet, Bjarni with the rest, his hand twisted in Hugin's collar. There seemed to be a quietness all around him, a core of quietness in the midst of the raving storm. He saw the tall drenched figure in the firelight, Asmund, Thara's father, swallowed up in Asmund the Priest of the High Gods. He saw the widened pupils of his eyes and the flecks of spittle in his beard and knew that he had drunk again of the sacred juice that brought the gods' fire into his head in times of sacrifice. As he looked into those widened eyes, the understanding leapt in him with the speed of the lightning flash, and made sense of the talk that he heard behind the peat-stack. He knew that it had been him they spoke of, after all, and Thara was quite capable of making the needful bruises herself. Fool that he had been not to think of that . . .

'Seize the black dog,' Asmund commanded. 'Thor demands the black dog!' and the thralls dived forward to do his bidding.

In the same instant Bjarni took his hand from Hugin's collar and dealt him a stinging blow on the rump, shouting, 'Off with you! Go!'

The door was unguarded to the storm, and if the dog was fast enough he might get clear. But Hugin was bewildered, knowing only that his lord was in trouble, and crouched for a moment unsure what he was to do, and in that moment the God-House thralls were up, snaring with their ropes. He was struggling like a wild thing for his freedom, his black face become a snarling wolf-fanged mask. 'Let him go! Let my dog free!' and in the same instant Bjarni hurled himself against them, his dirk in his hand. Everything had the confusion of an evil dream.

Hands were on him, friendly hands of men who had rowed and fought with him through two sea-faring summers, but dragging him back, twisting the dirk from his grasp. Voices shouting in his ears not to be a fool, not to call down upon himself the wrath of the Lord of Thunder.

Hugin had all but broken free, leaving one of the thralls with a fang-slashed forearm running red, before he was seized again, and in the same instant Bjarni had torn himself free and, unarmed as he was now, hurled himself into battle. The smell of blood had come into the back of his nose and the leaping flame-light made a red mist before his eyes. And he was not aware of the baying crowd around him, of the hands again on his arms, of anything but the faces of the men who were dragging Hugin away . . .

The curtain over the inner doorway was wrenched back and Onund stood there, stripped to sark and breeks, his sword naked in his hand. Then Onund's voice cut through the uproar, demanding in a tone that cut like a whiplash, 'What means this fighting at my wedding feast?'

And the whole ugly scene checked into stillness under the fading rolls of thunder. Bjarni stood panting in the grip of Sven Gunnarson and another of *Sea Witch's* crew, while Hugin still struggled and snarled against the ropes that were half strangling him, though the men had checked for an instant in dragging him towards the door.

'They are taking my dog,' Bjarni said, snatching at his breath. 'They are taking him for the sacred trees.'

But the voice of Asmund the Priest closed over the words before they were spoken. 'Thor the Thunderer is angry that there is no sacrifice on his altar at this feast. He demands the life of the black dog!'

'It is not the custom for Thor to receive sacrifice at a wedding feast,' Onund said.

Spittle was trickling into the Priest's beard and again the thunder sounded, though less loudly than before. 'Hark to his Hammer in the clouds! Who are you – who am I – to question the demands of the Lord of Thunder?'

'If it is his demand, and not rather the demand of the Priest,' Onund said at his most silken. The two faced each other, their wills crackling in the air between.

Then the thunder rolled again, fading westward over the open sea.

And Asmund, as though feeling the power slipping from him, let out a baffled howl. 'The Priest speaking with the voice of the god, the thing must be done, and done swiftly to quench his wrath – ' And suddenly his right hand, which had been hidden in the folds of his mantle, appeared, and in his hand the sacred blade. He gestured with it to the flat bake-stone beside the fire.

Bjarni, his arms twisted behind him, was shouting desperately, 'The sacrifice must be willing! He's not willing – look at him – and no more am I! I'll fight you for him. I'll fight anybody for him – '

'Will you fight Thor himself?' shrieked Asmund.

'It's not Thor, it's only you with too much of the sacred juice in you, and you know why – '

He half expected the wrath of the Lord of Thunder to strike him into nothingness in that instant, and yet the other half of him knew that it was true, that it was only Asmund with spittle in his beard and Thara's malice working in him that he had to fight.

Then Onund's voice came between them again. 'There is one quick way to put an end to this matter,' and he walked with that stiff swinging strut of his, down the hall to where Hugin, half strangled with the ropes about his neck, still struggled in the hands of his captors. Bjarni saw the firelight catch the naked blade in his hand, and unbelieving horror rose like vomit within him. Someone was bellowing, 'No! No!' and it was him – unless it was him making that terrible howling noise. Then in the confused horror of the moment he heard Onund ordering, 'All's over! Let him go – let them both go!'

The thing was over between one heartbeat and the next, and next instant Bjarni and Hugin were crouched together, the hound suddenly silent, thrusting against him and the blood pumping from the place where his left forepaw now lacked the ends of its two long central toes.

'You have lamed my dog!' Bjarni shouted, glaring up at the ship chief where he stood wiping his blade with a handful of rushes, with Hugin whimpering against his breast and scattering bright droplets everywhere.

'You have robbed the Thunderer of his sacrifice!' the Priest was almost shrieking. 'For how may I offer a maimed beast on his altar?'

'How indeed?' said Onund simply, and in Bjarni there began to be a glimmer of understanding.

Chieftain and Priest stood confronting each other. The wind was dropping away moment by moment, the bruised darkness beyond the door growing lighter, the crown of the storm over. 'A fine thing it must seem to both of us that the Lord of Thunder seems not so angry as you had feared,' Onund said into the sudden after-storm stillness. 'You will have a moon to light your homeward path.' Asmund seemed to be trying to say something, but in the end he turned away with it still unsaid, and strode from the hall, his two thralls following like hounds behind him.

When they were gone and when Bjarni, his hand twisted in Hugin's collar, had got to his feet, Onund spoke again. 'There is a time for battle and a time for peace and *Sea Witch* has no place among her crew for a man who cannot tell the one from the other.'

'They would have taken my dog for sacrifice,' Bjarni said, thinking desperately that he could not have understood.

But Onund Treefoot had understood. 'You would not have been the first man to lose a dog in such a way. So now, take him and be gone from Barra.'

Bjarni could not believe it. It could not be simply because he had got into a fight at the wrong moment. No ship chief was so set against a scrap among his crew. It could not be because he had raised hand against the Priest in defence of Hugin – it was Onund himself who had made Hugin unfit for sacrifice . . .

He was just starting to urge these things, but what he saw in Onund's face stopped him. Instead, he said only, 'Loyal sword-service you have had of me these two summers past, Onund Treefoot.'

'So now do I give you back your sword-service with honour,' Onund said, 'that you may take it elsewhere.'

7

Thorstein the Red

There was a heavy swell running and *Sea Cow* wallowed through it, not so much like her namesake as like a farrowing sow. Bjarni had forgotten how different the motion of the broad-bellied merchantman was from that of the slim Barra longships he had grown used to in the past two years, but it was last night's ale partly, and with it the cold shock of all that had blown up like storm out of a clear sky, that had given him today's queasy belly and splitting head, though it was only the ale that he blamed. He crouched against the bulwark, Hugin stretched beside him, his left forepaw lashed up like a small blood-stained pudding in dirty rags. Sometimes Hugin tried to bite the pudding and Bjarni would put out his own foot to thrust the dog's muzzle aside.

He was going over last night in his mind, not remembering very clearly through a haze of ale and firelight and the dark and levin-flash of storm. Faces crowded in on him, Onund's face, Thara's and the drugged face of the Priest her father; faces of the men striving to drag Hugin away, the faces of his fellow ship-carles turned into the faces of troubled strangers.

And again, Onund's face as he wiped his sword blade. A chill spatter of spindrift in his face brought him back to the present, and the sickness in his belly twisted itself into a sudden hard knot pressing up behind his breast bone. He dragged himself up, leaned over the side, and threw up like the veriest landlubber on his first sea-faring.

Putting up his hand to wipe the back of it across his mouth when the heaving was over, he found the string of amber swinging forward through the neck of his leather jerkin, and wished that he had flung it at Onund's feet – foot – last night, even as he gathered it up to thrust it back inside. But whether the thought made him harshly clumsy, or the thing happened by chance, the cord snapped and suddenly the honey globules were purling down through his fingers into the long green trough of the swell. Gone like the Barra years, the years that he had been Onund's man. He opened his hand and found that a single bead was left, lodged between two of his fingers. For an instant he thought to keep it, thought maybe he was meant to keep it. Then he parted his fingers and let it go after the rest.

Someone had come lurching up, and was beside him. For a short while they gazed out together on the heaving skyline. Then Heriolf Merchantman said, 'This is the second time. And the dog this time also. Have a care that you do not find yourself living in a circle and getting nowhere.'

It was said half in jest, but something in the words struck home to Bjarni all the same. He had had such dreams at the outset; stupid, boy's dreams of carving a path for himself with his sword. He might as well have dreamed of becoming Emperor of Byzantium. But it seemed all the time other men were laying his course for him: Dublin and the King's bodyguard,

Heriolf beside him here. The nearest he had come to choosing his own seaway was the night he had sold his sword-service to Onund Treefoot. But now Onund had cast him out.

'Why did he do it?' he demanded.

'Do what?'

'Everything – I don't know – lame Hugin – throw me out?'

'For the first,' said Heriolf, 'it was the quick and sure way to save him from Asmund. When the wound is healed it will but take the edge off his speed. In some lands they do it to dogs to stop them chasing the king's deer. Would you rather have had him hanging from the god's tree with the corbies and the black-backed gulls pulling at his carcass? For the second, he will have trouble enough to make his own peace with the priest kind, without you on hand to make the thing yet harder. For the third – how long think you it would have been, after last night's work, before death, disguised as the wrath of the gods, came upon you?'

'I had not thought of that,' Bjarni said after a silence filled with all the voices of a ship at sea; he found an odd comfort in the merchant's words, an easing to the sense of rejection.

'Na,' said Heriolf, 'I did not think you had.' His face creased into its slow reflective smile. 'You could do worse, I'm thinking, than take sword-service with Thorstein the Red.'

The weather was worsening, and they had to lie up storm-bound for three days in the lee of Coll, so it was fine before *Sea Cow* came wallowing past Calf Island into the sheltered harbour of Mull; and all was not well with Hugin. The rags that bound his injured paw were beginning to be stained with evil-smelling brownish pus, and he was increasingly restless, his eyes cloudy and his nose dry and warm.

'There must be a wise-woman, a healer of some kind, in the settlement,' Bjarni said in response to Heriolf's 'Whither away?' He was scrambling ashore and hauling the big dog up beside him as soon as they had tied up to the timber jetty.

'There will be,' the merchant said, turning from the orders that he had been giving to his crew. 'Bide while I see to the cargo; then come up with me to Thorstein's Hall. After, we will find her.'

'No,' Bjarni said, Hugin's hot head under his hand and the dog's tongue curling round his thumb. 'First I find the healer. Thorstein can wait.'

Heriolf looked at him, on the edge of hard-held patience. 'Aye well, you know best what things come first with you. Go you up to the Hall, all the same, but make for the Women's House behind it. The Lady Aud keeps her own bower apart from the main Hall, but it is open for all comers. I reckon there'll be someone among the women with the skills you are looking for.'

So Bjarni slipped the bit of rope he kept for the purpose through Hugin's collar, and set out alone save for the great hound limping three-legged at his side. Up from the ship-strand with its tall ship-sheds and slipways, rope-walk, smithy and timber stacks, into the warm huddle of the settlement. Up from the cold sea smells of fish and salt and pitch and timber into the warmer reek of the settlement, dung and hearth smoke and the fatty goodness of evening meals and the fainter inland smells of fern and heather coming down on the evening wind from the high moors, and he saw ahead of him further up the glen the unmistakable whale-backed mass of the Chieftain's fine Hall standing guard, as it were, over all.

Here and there faces turned to look at him as he passed, men seeing to a broken harness strap, women spinning in a house-place door, bairns driving home the family pig from its daylong rooting. But strangers coming up from the sea were common enough in the settlements of Thorstein the Red.

The hurdle gate in the quickset hedge of the Hall garth stood open and unguarded in the usual way and Bjarni looked in. A man mending a leather byrnie on the bench before the high-gabled Hall jerked a thumb over his shoulder when the stranger with the black dog checked to ask where he could find the Lady Aud.

'The Women's House is up there beyond the cookhouse apple tree, by the doorway. You can't miss it.'

Bjarni rounded the end of the Hall and found himself in the usual huddle of outbuildings, stables and byres, cookhouses, store-sheds and guest lodgings, and then the bower, the Women's House, lowset under its thick heather thatch, and the windshaped apple tree at the gable end, the small russet apples catching the westering light among the saltburned leaves. On the rough grass beneath it three saffron-haired girls were gathered about a creel of freshly-dyed wool; the eldest two, perhaps twelve and ten, hanging out the damp brown hanks to dry on lines strung between the lower branches, while the youngest sat close by, humming tunelessly to the saffron-striped kitten in her lap. They looked round at Bjarni as he passed, then went on with what they were doing.

Beyond them the doorway stood wide on warm shadows and a flicker of firelight; and Bjarni came to the threshold and paused, looking in.

The westering light lanced in through narrow horn windows under the thatch to mingle with the light of the fire on the central hearth and show what he knew must be the main chamber of the bower. It was full of quiet movement that had nothing of restlessness in it. A woman was weaving some patterned stuff at an upright loom set under the western windows where the light was good, and two girls sat spinning close by; another, her hair falling all about her hot face, was turning little flat barley-cakes on the bake-stones of the hearth at the heart of it all. A fifth, older and seemingly cast in a larger and richer mould than the rest, was sitting in a low carved chair beside the fire, seeming to be mending a tear in the shoulder of a great wine-red cloak lined with wolfskin. Her own gown was of some rich stuff the dark almost sullen green of hill-juniper, held with a glint of gold at the neck, and a pair of beautiful brindled deerhounds lay beside her in the folds of it. Her head was bent over her work; the hair, drawn-back and knotted like any country woman's to be out of the way, must have been crow-black in her youth, but looked now as though somebody had raked ashy fingers through it.

Easy enough to tell which was the Lady Aud; Aud the Deep-Minded, who had once been Queen to King Olaf the White of Dublin, by that rich gown and the fact that hers was the only chair. But Bjarni, standing on the threshold and looking in, felt that he would have known her in a room of women wearing the same gown and seated in the same chair.

The thrum of the spindle and the lazy chatter of women's voices fell silent, and one of the hounds growled softly. Bjarni felt the vibration of an almost silent growl in answer pressed against his own leg, and gave a small jerk to Hugin's leash. He could do without a dogfight at this moment.

'Peace, Vig! Peace, Asa!' said a voice, deep for a woman's. The Lady Aud looked up, and Bjarni found himself meeting the gaze of the darkest eyes he had ever seen, faintly slant-set in an old and beautiful broad-boned face. He had heard it said that the Lady Aud had skraeling blood, the blood of the far North, in her veins, and that was maybe where her wise-powers came from . . .

'Come your way in, stranger, and tell the thing that brings you here.'

And keeping a light hold on Hugin's collar, Bjarni advanced into the broad chamber to stand beside the hearth. 'Lady, I am Bjarni from the ship of Heriolf Merchantman in the haven. It was told to me that I might find here someone with the skill and kindness to mend my dog of a wound to his paw that he took five days ago?' He looked anxiously into her face. 'He's a good dog – worth the saving.'

'As most dogs are to those that love them,' said the Lady Aud, and her hand rested lightly for the moment on the head of the great brindled bitch beside her. She turned and looked up to the woman at the loom. 'Muirgoed, leave the weaving, it is your skills in leech-craft which we need here.'

The woman let her shuttle fall and came to kneel beside the hearth. 'Let you show me,' she said, the faint lilt that she gave to the words showing that the Norse was not her native tongue.

Bjarni kept his hand on Hugin's collar, watching anxiously as she took a little knife from her belt and began to cut away and fold back the stained rags. Hugin whimpered and tried to pull his paw away but made no attempt to bite, seeming to know that she meant no harm against him.

When the last fold of rag fell away she drew in her breath at the sight of the mutilated paw, hot and swollen and with an ugly weeping mess where the ends of the two midmost toes should have been. She put her hand under Hugin's chin and lifted it to look into his eyes. '*Mai, mai, mai,* here's a sorry thing,' she said to the dog alone; and then to Bjarni, 'Keep him still, I will fetch the salve?' Rising, she disappeared through a door behind the painted hangings that enriched the walls.

By the time she returned, the other women had drawn closer to watch. The three children had come in also, the youngest still clutching the saffron-striped kitten; and even the Lady Aud had paused in her stitchery and was leaning forward for a closer view.

'Who did this?' she asked as the woman Muirgoed dropped to her knees again, setting down her remedies and the bowl of water she carried, and fell to bathing Hugin's hot and angry paw.

'Onund Treefoot,' Bjarni said.

'So-o! Onund Treefoot. Was the dog chasing his deer?'

'There's not many deer on Barra.'

'Why then?'

Bjarni was silent a moment, then he began carefully to try to explain. 'There was a girl – '

'And you wanted her?' said the Lady Aud gravely.

'No. She wanted me: and I grew weary of pretending not to see . . . It was at Onund's bride-ale, and we were dancing.' He wondered what in the name of all the gods of Asgard had possessed him to try to tell the whole confused and ugly story to this unknown woman, simply because she had asked. But he ploughed on, trying to get the thing sorted out in his own mind as he went along; trying to tell it true. 'She came at me out of the ring-dance, seeking to pull me in with her. I was drunk, I suppose. I pushed her on to the man beside me, and reached for another girl out of the circle to dance with, and she – the first girl – was daughter to the Odin Priest; later, I think she told a lying tale of me to her father. There was thunder, and I think she put it into his mind that the Lord of Thunder was angry because there was no sacrifice on his altar – Odin and Frigga had the black ram and white ewe that wedding custom calls for – and that he demanded a black dog.' Bjarni stumbled and checked for the moment; the story was growing confused, running out of hand, but having begun it he could not stop until the end. The woman Muirgoed had finished bathing Hugin's paw and was spreading strong-smelling green salve on the wounds.

'Bad girl,' said the bairn with the saffron kitten into the top of the little creature's head. She seemed to find the story quite clear so far anyway.

Bjarni took a deep breath and struggled on. 'After, when we had taken the bride home to Onund's hall, the Priest came demanding Hugin – my dog – for a sacrifice. There was fighting. Onund came out to see with his sword. He did that to Hugin to settle the thing quickly.'

'I am thinking that Onund Treefoot was never one to waste time picking at knots,' said the Lady Aud as though to herself. Then to Bjarni she said, 'And after that?'

'Nothing after that, Lady. You asked me why, and I have told.'

'So now I ask you what happened after. Tell me how the bedraggled pair of you come to my threshold.'

'After – Onund bade me go from Barra. I had sold him loyal sword-service through two summers. He said that himself, and gave it back to me with honour, to take elsewhere. Heriolf Merchantman was in the harbour.'

He made a small gesture of finish with his free hand across his knee. Then he added one thing more.

'Heriolf said that after that night's work, there'd have been but a short life left for me on Barra.'

'I think Heriolf Merchantman may well have been right,' Aud said gently.

The woman had begun to rebind Hugin's paw with a clean linen rag. 'Groa,' she said to the eldest of the three bairns, 'let you bring some milk, and a flask of the green fever-draught.'

The girl rose and slipped away through the inner door. When she returned Muirgoed had made fast the bandage. She took the wooden stopper from the flask and sniffed at it, then poured a little into the milk and held it under the dog's nose. 'Drink, Dark Brother.' Hugin hesitated, then flicked his tongue into the milk, and having got the taste of it, dipped his muzzle and lapped until the bowl was empty. 'That should cool the fever,' the woman said, her hand on his head. 'Bring him back to me here tomorrow.'

Then, as though suddenly remembering something, she looked up at the Lady Aud, who had returned to the cloak that she was mending. 'I have your leave?'

'Do you not always have my leave?' said the Lady. 'As one queen to another.' Clearly that was a long-standing jest between them and Bjarni, getting to his feet, wondered what it was. Men had small hidden jests between themselves, but he had not known that women did.

Heavy steps came thumping up through the garth and something loomed like a bear in the doorway. Swinging round, Bjarni saw a big man broad-built and already inclined to paunch, and got the impression, though he could not see clearly against the yellow sunset light, of big blunt features and a badly broken nose amid a bush of fiery red hair – not the dark fox hue that was Onund's, but a lighter, fiercer colour, almost the colour of molten iron.

He did not need to be told that he was looking at Thorstein the Red, sea lord of a great fleet and many islands and a man to carry fear with it along the mainland coasts.

He was grumbling as he crossed the threshold: 'That moon-calf Kadir has let the brood mare out again.'

His mother cut the thread with the little knife at her girdle and held up the heavy folds of wolfskin and thick Roman-red cloth. 'Has he? I make no doubt that Erp will have all things in hand . . . See, I have finished mending your cloak.'

The man came tramping round the hearth to take it from her; and brought a hand like Thor's Hammer down on her shoulder by way of thanks.

And Groa, the eldest of the three children, standing with the empty milk-bowl in her hands, clearly felt that the newcomer amongst them was in danger of being forgotten, and put in a little breathlessly, 'O my father, see – here is a stranger with us. He was with Onund Treefoot until his dog – '

Bjarni, standing by with his hand in Hugin's collar, wondering how to make his own thanks and get away, or maybe get away without making them at all, grew rigid. Fool that he had been to tell! Now it was all going to be told again, and he had a sick feeling that Aud in her lovely kindness was going to offer his sword-service to this huge son of hers as though he were some stray bairn to be befriended. And if she did that, even if Thorstein would take him, he must refuse. Whether or not he wanted to, he must refuse, or know that yet again his life was being shaped for him by other hands than his own . . .

But the Lady Aud had dropped her spool of thread, and was commanding, 'Groa, help me rewind my thread, your fingers are so neat.' And then over the bent red-gold head to Thorstein, 'Heriolf Merchantman is in the haven, maybe you have seen him? Bjarni Sigurdson here is with him, but his dog has an injured paw, and he has brought him here for Muirgoed's tending.'

And a wave of relief and gratitude broke over Bjarni.

Thorstein was looking at him out of a pair of tawny golden eyes, the kind that having met their gaze, it is hard to look away from. 'You do not look like the merchant kind.'

Bjarni shook his head. 'I leave that to Heriolf. He has fine silks and good hide ropes – the usual. Oh, and a jewelled cup with a cross on it that he thinks may interest the Lady Aud.' This with a glance toward the mistress of the house, who looked up from her granddaughter and her spilled thread to meet it with a smile.

'For myself I have only my sword-service for sale.'

8

Easter Faring

So Bjarni became Thorstein's paid man as he had been Onund's and he was well enough content, though still there was an ache in him somewhere like the ache of an old wound when the wind is from the east.

And with Hugin also, all was well. With Muirgoed's salves his paw mended cleanly and before the next moon had waned and the yellow birch-leaves were falling, he was running on four paws again, and only limped on three when suddenly he remembered to.

The gales blew up from the west and the year darkened towards winter. In the sheltered crop-lands the ox-ploughs were busy and the winter wheat was sown. The bees which could not be kept through the black months were turned out of the hives, and the woods rang with the sound of axes felling timber for the raising and mending of farm buildings and the slim war-keels down at the ship-strand.

For the most part the farm work of the settlement was done by thralls, while the free men of the Kindred, the ship-carles and hearth companions, threw in their lot with the shipwrights, and rode hunting red deer and wild pig, for the most part not so much for pleasure as for meat to add to the slaughtered cattle for the winter salting down. But at times – harvest, sheep-shearing, the round-up when the horses were brought down from the summer pastures – thrall and free, farmers and seamen and warriors (they were mostly the same thing), came together, working side by side.

On the evening of one such day, a day of flying cloud and changing lights in which Ben Mhor, the Great Mountain as the Gael folk still called it, would be clear enough one moment to pick out the high corries and the screes scarring its sides, and the next time one looked it would be gone into empty sky and trailing storm cloud, Bjarni was standing with his elbows propped on the long wall of the colt-garth, watching the ragged, slender two-year-olds, whom he had been all day helping to get in for their breaking. Hugin sat pressed against his leg with lolling tongue and half-closed eyes. And beside him, also watching the colts, leaned a man whom he had seen often among the horses, but never spoken with or met eye-to-eye with before now; a tall young man with a quiet face, not unlike a horse himself, and the glimpse of an iron thrall-ring showing at the neck of his rough wadmal sark.

The colts were uneasy, the wind setting their manes and tails flying as they wheeled and fidgeted with wide eyes and up-flung heads. The young man spoke to the nearest in a tongue that Bjarni guessed was no tongue known to men, and the mealy-muzzled colt swung its head to look at him and whickered softly as one horse greets another before it remembered its fear and arched away.

'Were you born in a stable, that you talk to the horse kind in their own tongue,' Bjarni said, 'with a mare

97

for a mother, who could cast her skin like a seal-woman?'

'No stable of Red Thorstein's, anyway,' said the other and, glancing round, Bjarni saw that he had turned his head from the colts and was gazing away south-easterly along the dim blue line of the mainland, with the look of someone seeing beyond the range of mortal sight.

'From that way?' he said.

The man nodded. 'From Argyll – a land of the horse people. But that was long ago. My mother too. She is Muirgoed, chief among the Lady Aud's bower-thralls.'

Bjarni looked at him in surprise. 'Then I know your mother. She tended Hugin's paw when it was scaithed.'

'That sounds like my mother.'

'But I did not see any thrall-ring on her neck.'

'Not now, not for a long while. But the mark is still there, hidden by the silver chain the Lady Aud set there in place of it.'

'You were bought together, then? Or was it war?' Bjarni asked after a pause, not prying, just taking a friendly interest.

'War,' said the other man, seeming to take the thing as it was intended. He brought his gaze back out of the distance. 'You will not be knowing? No one has told you?'

Suddenly and a little bitterly, he laughed. 'Ach well – good it is for the soul to find our own unimportance. Ten – twelve years ago, Jarl Sigurd of Orkney came summer-raiding along the Islands and my father the King called out his spears to withstand him and his war-bands, but they were too strong. They slew him and his warriors around him, and my mother and me – I was not yet old enough to be with my father among the dead – they carried off into thralldom.

Others also – they sold them in Dublin market but
my mother and me, the Jarl kept. We were a year on
Orkney, and then he gave us both, together with a
fine stallion and a gold cup, for a friendship gift to
Thorstein the Red.'

Bjarni was silent, taking this in, thinking back to
the woman with the Lady Aud in her bower while
Hugin, growing bored, nosed at his hand.

'You are not believing me?' One eyebrow gently
quirked.

'Why would you tell me such a tale if it were not
true?' Bjarni said. 'Na, na, I was thinking now there
is an odd thing, Bjarni Sigurdson, that you took your
dog to a queen for tending, and she salving the wound
as though she were none but some old herb woman
of the woods.'

'The princesses of Erin are many of them herb-wise,'
said the man. 'There was one called Iseult. Muirgoed
my mother was wise in herbs and healing before ever
she came to be a queen.' He pushed off from the turf
wall. 'It grows late, and I grow hungry if you do not.'
But as Bjarni turned also, he said, 'I have your name
now, Bjarni Sigurdson. Let you have mine in fair
exchange. I am Erp Mac Meldin of Argyll.'

And he went swinging off to his own place, while
Bjarni whistled Hugin to heel and headed for the
Hearth Hall and supper. He understood now that
small jest that had passed between the Lady Aud and
her bower woman, understood also something of the
bond that must have grown between them over the
years, before they could share that particular jest
without bitterness.

There was good rich witty talk in Thorstein's Hall in
the winter nights between the harp-songs and the
horseplay after the women had gone from the cross-

benches. Travellers' tales to listen to from the farmost
edges of the world. Thorstein counted a good few
mercenaries among his hearth companions; men as
far-flying as the wild geese, to whom the Iceland run
and the long haul around the North Islands and on
to Norway were no more than a river crossing.
Andred, who had been far south to the Hot Lands
and into the mouths of great rivers to trade with men
whose skin had been burned as black as bog oak by
the sun, while other men hairy all over swarmed
among the branches of great trees overhead and threw
strange fruit over them. Leiknen One-eye, who knew
the Mid-Land Sea as other men knew their own back
garth and had walked the streets of Miklagard and
swore they were paved with gold. And among them,
Bjarni had his own tale to tell when the harp of story-
telling was handed round, for though he had been no
further afield than when he first came west-over-seas
to join the settlement of Rafn Cedricson, no one else
in that company had been with Onund Treefoot in the
narrows of Bute when the great stones came whistling
out of the sky.

They worked and slept and fought and feasted
together, and as the dark months went by he formed
an easy comradeship with them, though nothing that
could not be easily broken. The only real friendship
that he formed on Mull remained the odd crooked
friendship he had struck up with Erp Mac Meldin on
the day they brought the horses down from the
summer pastures.

Winter passed, with its black winds and bitter rain
and the wild seas pounding on the coast. Amid all
the wild weather, suddenly there began to be signs
of spring; catkins lengthening on the hazels down
the burnside and a fluttering of small birds among
the birches that were flushing purple. The first of

the greylag geese that had grazed on the *machair* all winter long took off for the North one wild night, yapping like a pack of hounds through the storm clouds overhead.

And down on the ship-strand there began to be a swarming activity, as the lean war-keels were run out from their sheds, and their crews set to pitching their sides and overhauling spars and rigging and sails in readiness for the summer sea-faring. And newly run out onto the slipway from her own high-gabled shed where she had lain in slings all winter, the Lady Aud's own galley was being made ready for the seaways ahead of her sisters, for it was the Lady's custom to make a sea-faring of her own at Easter, to spend the few days of the fast and the feast with the brothers on the Holy Island of Iona. Bjarni, returning from the nearby drift-wood fire with a pitch pot, saw the ship lying there, almost ready for the water, in the early spring sunshine, though mast and gear all lay still in the brown-shadowed shed behind him, and he felt a pang of delight at sight of her. She was so beautiful, the unbroken sweetly-running line of her from stem to soaring stern. She had no dragon-head but her carved and freshly painted stern post ended in a curve that was faintly like a shepherd's crook, or maybe the arched neck of a swan. He had been told that her name, *Fionoula*, had something to do with a swan – an Irish maiden who had been turned into one, long ago.

Despite all the difference between them, she called to something in Bjarni that *Sea Witch* had called to before ever he was one of her crew, and he reached up and laid his hands upon the curves of her bows, thinking that it would be good to be taking an oar among her rowers for this springtime sea-faring in honour of the White Christ.

The White Christ was not quite the stranger that he had been to Bjarni last autumn, for there were many of his followers in the settlement. A fine free mixture of old faith and new, Thorstein himself had been born and bred a Christian, but had loosened the ties somewhat as he grew older, and thought it quite enough to have added an altar to the White Christ to the ancient axe-hewn figures of Thor and Odin in the God-House where Thor's Ring lay on his altar and the smell of old blood rose darkly from the earthen floor. The Lady Aud grieved for that; she prayed for him daily and never ceased to hope that her prayers might mark a change, and meanwhile loved him as he was. She had her own little stone-built chapel further up the glen where she and her women and a few of the menfolk went every Sunday. The rest of the settlement shared their worship – when they worshipped at all – between the church and the God-House. Bjarni did nothing about either of them. He had lost his own gods, as they had lost him, on the night that their priest had demanded the death of Hugin, but he felt no call to cross over to follow the Lady Aud's god. And it was certainly no wish for her Holy Island at Easter that drew him now, but simply the longing to which he could give no name to have some share in the thing that would be *Fionoula* at sea . . .

'Hi,' barked a voice behind him, 'stop looking at her as if she was your first girl and get on with pitching that seam!' and he came back to himself and looking over his shoulder saw old Hrodni the master shipwright, and with him, wrapped in a sealskin mantle against the chill wind, the Lady Aud come down to see how the ready-making of her galley went forward. She did not say anything to the men at work along her curving clinker-built sides, but for a splinter of time her eyes met Bjarni's, and as he got back to his pitch pot and *Fionoula*'s seams, he had the oddest idea that he could feel them still, resting thoughtfully on the back of his neck until, deep in talk with the master shipwright, she moved on.

It was the custom in the settlement long since agreed to by Thorstein the Red that each year the Lady Aud might name her own rowers, who also served her as bodyguard, for the Easter faring. For the most part she chose the same men year after year, but three days later when Verland Ottarson, who was always her captain and ship chief, called in the chosen ones, Bjarni was amongst them.

At first he did not believe it. 'You have got the wrong Bjarni. There's more than one of us on Mull.'

'Only one cack-handed swordsman who sold his sword-service to the chief last harvest end, and him with a black dog lame in one paw.'

Bjarni looked about him at the chosen crew, knowing them all: a Christian crew for a Christian sea-faring. 'I am not of the Lady's faith,' he said. 'Tell her – she'll have forgotten.'

'Tell her theesen,' growled Verland, 'I've better things to do.'

He found the Lady Aud in the herb plot behind the bower, sitting on a turf seat and watching the first bees among the physic herbs that Muirgoed was tending, the two brindled hounds lying at her feet.

'Lady,' he began when he stood in front of her, and then checked, not quite sure how to go on.

She looked at him, her beautiful old hands relaxed in her lap. 'Bjarni Sigurdson. There is a thing you wish to say to me?'

'Verland, your shipmaster, called my name among your chosen crew for the Easter faring.'

She nodded in the way that she had, with her head a little to one side, with a trace of a smile. 'That would be because I bade him.'

'But, Lady, you are forgetting.'

'What am I forgetting?'

'Lady, all the other men that you have chosen are of the Christian kind; a Christian crew for a Christian feast-faring.'

'It so happens, for this time,' said the Lady Aud. 'Yet there is no rule carved like runes in stone that says that I may not have a follower of the old gods amongst my rowers, and surely a man who has helped to make her ready for sea should have his place among *Fionoula*'s crew when they run her down from the landing-beach.'

Bjarni swallowed. He had to make sure that she understood, get the thing quite clear.

'Lady, I do not feel any call to follow your god.'

'Not now,' the Lady agreed. 'Time can change many things, but that will be for you to choose.' Her face in the shadow of the sealskin hood lit into its rare, slow smile. 'I never order any man to row my galley; I have had no need to. Instead, I ask – let you come as one of my rowers on this sea-faring.'

They took *Fionoula* out for sea trials next morning. And in squally weather two days later they hove out from the haven, bound for Iona, following the inshore waters between Mull and the mainland, for the sake of the women under the awnings that had been rigged to give them some privacy and shelter from the wind and spray. Even so, Muirgoed was direly sick, and the Lady Aud not much better; and only Groa, the eldest granddaughter, being brought for the first time, seemed quite unaffected by the pitch and toss of the galley in the short steep seas, and came out with her kirtle bunched to her knees and her hair thrust back under a blue and russet striped kerchief, to scramble and balance her way between the rowers toward the bows.

She checked beside Bjarni, holding on to a stay to steady herself. 'Where's your dog?' she asked, and glanced down as though half expecting to see Hugin at his feet.

He looked up at her through the hair that the wind was blowing across his eyes. 'I left him to run with the hound-pack. He got used to that way of things these two past summers on Barra.'

Groa was silent awhile, gazing ahead into the squally distance. 'This is so good,' she said at last, 'I wish we could sail on and on – round Iona and out between the islands to the open sea, beyond Ireland – beyond Iceland, maybe . . .'

'Careful, tha'd have to be,' Bjarni warned her. 'Nobody knows what happens out there: we might fall off the edge.'

'But how if there isn't an edge?' Groa said, seemingly more to herself than to him. 'The sea might be like the Mid-Land Sea that Leiknen One-eye talks of, only much, much bigger with more land on the far side of it, and another great city like Miklagard, waiting to be found – and good farming land . . .'

It was not the first time that she and Bjarni had talked together since the day that he had brought Hugin to the Lady Aud's threshold, but he had never known the bairn launch out into this kind of daftness before. Maybe it was the effect of being at sea. If so, he wished she would just go away and be sick like the other women; it wasn't lucky, this kind of talk, not on ship-board.

'There's other islands out there too, so they say – St Brendan's Isle, with trees covered with white birds instead of blossom, every bird singing like the evening star. If I were a man I'd build a ship of my own, and go to see.'

'And if you were a man, I'd come with you,' said Bjarni, suddenly, not caring whether the talk was unlucky or not. Certainly this Easter faring had a strangeness to it not like any sea-faring that he had known before.

'Lift her! Lift her!' came the voice of Verland at the steering oar, giving the rowing time.

Next day, after a night passed at one of the fisher-villages along the coast, they had a fair wind and were able to raise sail as they came coasting down the Ross of Mull towards the low green shores of Iona.

9

The Bay of the Coracles

The Lady Aud, her granddaughter and Muirgoed were housed in the gull-grey stone beehive huts of the guest lodgings, a little apart from those of the Holy Brothers themselves, and the crew of *Fionoula* made their own camp under the ship's awnings rigged in the lee of the white sand dunes that fringed the landing-beach. And there they passed the first of the four nights that they were to spend on St Columba's Isle. The next day was a day of quiet before the fasting and the mourning of the White Christ's Friday. For the Lady it was a day of retreat and prayer and quiet ready-making; for her crew a rest day of nothing much to do but sprawl in the long dune grasses or around the ship, telling stories and playing fox and geese with pebbles on a game-board finger-drawn in the sand. At noon they fed on salt fish and barley stirabout from the monastery kitchen, washed down with thin ale, and not much of it.

'Best make the most of it,' Verland told Bjarni. 'It's all tha'll get today, and tomorrow will be leaner still.'

And another man, with his mouth full, added, grinning, 'Doesn't seem fair, does it, that you should go empty-bellied for a god that's none of yours, hanging on his tree.' And there was a general laugh.

It was all perfectly good-natured; the men of Thorstein's ships and settlements were too well used to the mingling of faiths to worry too much about it in these days when, if the Northmen raided a Christian holy place, they did it not because it was Christian but simply because it was rich.

But it made Bjarni feel shut out from their company, all the same.

'Odin hung on a tree for nine days,' he said to the world at large. Pushing his last bit of fish into his mouth, and chewing on the dry saltiness of it, he got to his feet, and strolled off to keep his own company.

He wandered southward along the coast until in a while he came down to a cove at what looked to be the southernmost end of the island. And there, for no good reason – he had passed other coves and inlets whose sand was as white and whose rocks were as warm in the sun – he sat down. There were small dark sheep, ring-straked and dappled, grazing on the *machair* behind him. He could hear the shrill bleating of a lamb, and the deeper call of its mother in answer. The dunes at his back kept off the wind, and it was warm in the sunshine. It was not always like this, he knew; Iona had its fair share of wild weather. Haki, whose oar was next ahead of his, had told him how a couple of years ago a black squall had blown up just as they had lost the shelter of Mull, and the seas breaking over them amidships as they came in to land, so that it had been all they could do to get *Fionoula* safely beached, and the Lady and her women ashore, drenched but not actually drowned. But today the tide crooning and creaming among the rocks and fingering the sand was green glass in the shallows, deeply blue farther out. Kingfisher's colours. And the light was not quite like the light he had known anywhere else. Maybe such a light would lie on the Islands of the Blessed, far out towards the sunset, where the Old People believed that their souls went after death. Maybe over Groa's isle with the trees of white birds, each singing like the evening star . . .

He was half asleep, when there came a flounder of feet and slipping sand over the dune slope, and someone in a brown habit sat down rather wearily beside him. Glancing round, he saw a thick-set man of middle years, his face broad and bony under the bald dome of his tonsured forehead: a warrior's face, Bjarni would have said, rather than a monk's, but with something extraordinarily peaceful in the gaze of the very blue eyes.

'I saw you go by,' said the newcomer, 'but I was busy with the sheep. They'll do well enough, now. You looked as if you had things to be thinking about. But you will have had a while for thinking and will not mind if I come to share the bay with you.'

'It's your bay, and none of mine,' said Bjarni. He had not meant to sound so surly, but he was not yet in any mood for company.

'It is nobody's, and all the world's,' said the man, his gaze drifting out to sea. 'This is the Bay of the Coracles, the place where St Columba and his few monks landed when first they came from Ireland.'

Bjarni had heard something of this holy man from Ireland who had brought the new god to Scotland, but he had not really listened. Now, in this place of quietness and light, he suddenly felt that he would only have to look up to see the monks landing on the sand, and the interest quickened in him. Not wishing any misunderstanding with the brown-clad man, he said, 'I am one who holds by Thor and Odin, but on Mull I have heard much of this holy man, and of the settlement he planted here. That would be a long time ago?'

'More than three hundred years.'

'And there have been holy men following after him here, all that while?'

'Almost all that while: there have been times when the raiders came, and afterwards for a while there was no one here but the sea birds. Once, more than a lifetime ago, the relics of St Columba, which had lain here since his death, were taken back to Ireland for greater safety than we could give them here and housed for a while in our mother abbey of Kells. But later, we brought him home. We have had quieter times of late with the cloak of Thorstein Olafson for our shelter. But there is a savage wind blowing among the islands, a restlessness that can be felt even here – a load of good land for the taking in Ireland – the Northmen have ever been a folk with their eyes on any farther shore.' He sat silent a few moments, trickling white sand through his fingers. 'One day Thorstein will be gone from us, in one way or another, and then the raiders will come again.'

'So what will you do when that day comes?' Bjarni asked, thinking in terms of underwater stockades and maybe even a bought bodyguard of men like himself. Everybody said that the abbey was rich, despite the brothers' simple way of life.

'Die, as our brothers died before us,' said the man beside him, the monk who looked like a warrior.

Bjarni opened his mouth as if to say something and then shut it again.

And the man brushed the last of the sand from his fingers, and turned toward him with a wary smile. 'But all this can have little interest for you. Tell me of yourself, how you who follow Thor and Odin come to be one of the Lady Aud's rowers this Easter faring?'

From some people it might have seemed too probing, but from this man Bjarni took it for honest interest, and did his best to answer truthfully. 'I think the Lady Aud hopes that you – the brothers – this place – might make a Christian of me.'

The monk sat thoughtful a few moments, then asked, 'And how would that seem to you?'

'I don't know,' Bjarni told him. 'Sometimes I feel one way, sometimes the other. Sometimes I still feel in my belly that I am Thor's man, Odin's man, sometimes I feel that they are finished with me and I am finished with them.' Trying to explain, he found himself telling the old story yet again, to another total stranger – and when the story was done, sitting with hands round updrawn knees, staring at a small yellow sand-flower, and wishing that he had not told it. Because now of course the man would try to show him that his old gods were not good for following, and drag him over to the faith of the White Christ, and something in him flinched from that as from some kind of invasion that he had left himself open to.

But seemingly the man knew it: for he said only, after a long pause, 'Remember it was not Thor who demanded the life of your dog, but his priest. Priests are but men. This one was a man with a daughter, foolish and vengeful but probably much loved.'

And there was a trace of a smile in the voice, though his face was grave when Bjarni looked round at him. 'Surely you are not like most of your kind? I thought that you were supposed to hate the old gods, not defend them.'

The man returned his look, the smile that had been in his voice creeping into his eyes. 'The thing is not so plain as that. I made my prayers to Thor in the God-House when I was a boy, before I followed my foster-brother west-over-seas. We came to raid, and stayed awhile as raiders sometimes do. I fell sick, and so came under the hand of a solitary holy man who had healing skills . . . I had hopes that my foster-brother would stay, too; but he went back to Norway and his own kindred, his own gods who were no longer mine. Yet when we parted, he swore for my sake that all followers of the White Christ would be safe within his boundaries for all time; so there was something gained after all.'

Bjarni had an odd feeling in the belly as though something had jolted him there. Yet he had no sense of surprise. In this island of the clear light, nothing, no wonder, could be really surprising. 'What name was he – your foster-brother?' he asked.

'Rafn – Rafn Cedricson. I have often wondered what the pattern of his life has been.'

Bjarni was silent a short while, looking down at his linked hands. Then he said, 'This much I can tell you. He is – two years ago, when I last saw him – he was Chieftain of a settlement far to the south of here, where the three great rivers of the Lake Country come to sea.'

He was aware of a sudden great stillness beside him, but he did not look round, feeling that whatever he might see in the face of the man beside him was no affair of his. 'Your settlement,' the monk said quietly, out of his stillness; and nothing more.

'Yes,' Bjarni said, and was silent. There was a long, slow-passing silence, while the knowledge grew in him that he must tell this story also. 'Until two years ago,' he said at last. 'Then – there was a holy man – not like you. He kicked my dog – that was another dog – and I tipped him into the horse-pond and held his head under for a while to teach him the unwisdom of that. He was old, and I suppose I held him under too long.'

'And so he drowned,' said the man beside him.

Bjarni nodded. 'I had been only a few months there. I did not know – or I had forgotten, it did not seem a great matter – about the Chieftain's oath. So I made him an oath-breaker. He gave me a sword and bade me out of the settlement for five years, until he could bear to see my face again.'

A sea bird swept close above their heads, its wings warmed with sunlight, and they both watched it bank, and swing out over the bay.

'When the five years are up and you go back, tell to your Chieftain that Gisli his foster-brother forgives him the oath-breaking,' the monk said simply.

'I will tell him,' Bjarni said; and surprised himself by asking, 'But what for me?' scarcely knowing what he meant.

'For you? The five outlaw years shall have earned you your quittance.'

Far off, borne on the wind, Bjarni caught the faint shepherd clang of the church's bell, and Gisli drew his legs under him and got up. 'It is time for Vespers. I must go my way.'

When he was gone, Bjarni sat on, arms crossed on updrawn knees, gazing out over the white sand and the creaming shallows, thinking more deeply than ever he had thought in his life before. He had come on this Easter faring with half an idea at the back of his mind that he might do as the Lady Aud would have him. Now he took the idea out, looked at it and was not so sure. It was the sensible thing to do. At least going halfway and getting prime-signed was the sensible thing to do; many of the merchant kind and the mercenaries had found that. Once prime-signed by a Christian priest you were accepted into the following of the White Christ, which made life much simpler if for instance you wanted to take sword-

service with a Christian chief; but you were still free
to turn back to your own gods in time of real need. It
was a thing quite easily done. At least, he had thought
so. But now suddenly he was seeing it as something
that could not – should not – be easily done at all.
This whole matter of which gods one held to ... In
his inner eye he saw Rafn and Gisli tearing their lives
apart from each other over it. A thing that mattered
as much as that ...

After a while he got up and turned back to the
camp by the boat-strand, still thinking.

He went on thinking a good deal through the days
that followed; the day of fasting and mourning, the
day of waiting, the day of rejoicing. He had no part
in any of it, but he went hungry with the rest on
God's Friday, there being nothing to eat anyway, and
with the gathering of *Fionoula*'s crew before the open
door, watched what went on in the little stone and
wattle church bloomed with the light of honey-wax
candles on Easter morning. And, watching and listening, he learned more of the White Christ to add to
what he had learned already during the months on
Mull.

And then in the midst of the night after Easter, the
last night that they would spend on Iona, he woke
quickly and quietly as a man wakes to the old hunter's
trick of a thumb pressed below his left ear, but there
was no one near him. He had rolled out from under
the ship's awning, and now lay staring up at the sky
of dappled cloud, pearl-coloured, drifting across the
moon, hearing the sounds of a calm sea and the
breathing – snoring – of the other rowers under
the awning. He had an odd feeling of having arrived
somewhere that he had been searching for. As though
in his sleep all his confused thinking of the past few

days had sorted itself out, and now he could be still and see where it had got him.

He knew quite clearly that despite the night when the priest had called in Thor's name for the death of Hugin, he was not ready to leave his old gods yet. Maybe he never would be. Yet something in him reached out to this other god, who was Brother Gisli's, and Erp's and the Lady Aud's. But the step was too great to be taken with loyalties divided. Brother Gisli had shown him that. He could not go all the way. But he could go part of it... He found that he was thinking of prime-signing no longer as just a sensible thing to do, but as a kind of threshold: and surely the White Christ, who knew the ways of men's hearts because he had been a man himself, and died for other men, would understand if he could only come as far as the threshold.

In the first green light of morning with the shore birds crying, he went in search of Brother Gisli and found him in the home pasture behind the grain store, squatting with a cade lamb between his knees, which he was feeding with milk from a leather bottle. He squatted down also, and waited until the little one was full fed and, with the alder teat plucked from its milky muzzle, had gone wobbling away. Then Brother Gisli looked up at him with his slow quiet smile. 'A fine morning, and a fair wind for the Lady's homeward faring.'

Bjarni came straight to the point. 'I would be prime-signed before we leave Iona.'

'So-o!' Brother Gisli shook the last drops from the bottle onto the grass beside him. 'This is a thing left somewhat late in the day.'

'I had much thinking to do,' Bjarni told him. 'I had to be sure.'

115

'And now you are sure.'

'Now I am sure. I would be prime-signed before I leave Iona.'

Brother Gisli looked at him with great kindness, a little sorrowfully maybe. 'Ach well,' he said, 'it is a beginning.'

Bjarni gave him back his look, straightly. 'It's as far as I can go.'

'I dare say Christ won't mind the waiting.' He got up. 'Come then – '

'Shall I kneel here?'

The monk shook his head. 'This is a matter for Father Faremail, our Abbot, and there must be two to see it done and stand surety for you.'

'Will you stand surety for me, foster-brother of my Chief?'

'I – and another. Now come, for the tide will turn before Nones, and there is little time to spare.'

And so in a short while Bjarni Sigurdson was kneeling before the Father Abbot in the doorway of the little church, with Brother Gisli and the Lady Aud herself kneeling on either side of him, with the brown-clad brotherhood, and the crew of *Fionoula* looking on. There had been no ready-making, no questions asked. Prime-signing had no need of such things.

The Abbot was bending over him as he tipped his head back, saying something that had the sound of welcome in it, though he did not know very clearly what it was; making the sign of the cross on his fore-head with water which felt very cold and trickled down between his eyes.

He got up, and the Lady Aud's arms were lightly round him for a moment, then Brother Gisli's fiercer hold. And the thing was done; very quickly, for the tide was already on the turn.

10

Council on Orkney

Off the southern shore of Hoy, three longships lay at
anchor, waiting for slack water and safe passage
through the western end of the Pentland Firth and up
into the great floe that sheltered the fleet of the Jarls
of Orkney; Thorstein Olafson's great *Sea Serpent*, *Wild
Horse* and *Star Wolf*, their crews taking their ease
before the last long pull that would take them up to
Jarl Sigurd's landing-beach.

On the fifth starboard oar of *Sea Serpent*, Bjarni sat,
elbows on knees, chewing his way thoughtfully
through the lump of ship's bannock that he had saved
from the hurried morning meal.

A year and the half of another year had gone by
since he had been prime-signed, kneeling before the
door of the little grey church on Iona, with the tide
just on the turn. Odd, now, it seemed, looking back,
to remember all the tangled thinking of the days
before he had made his mind up to that kind of
halfway baptism. It didn't seem to matter all that
much, now. The Lady Aud had been pleased, and he
felt more at one with the Christians among his fellows;
and at feast time he went, for the most part, to the

altar to the White Christ that Thorstein had set up among the altars to the older and darker and more familiar gods in the God-House. But that was about all. Maybe it would have gone on as meaning more if Brother Gisli had been still there under the skies of men; but when they had taken *Fionoula* back to Iona this spring, Brother Gisli had been gone from the island, only a small grey stone in the monks' burial ground to tell that he had ever been there, and another of the brethren looking after the cade lambs.

Sitting with his mouth full of dry bannock, Leif Ketison beside him playing knuckle bones right hand against left, he let his mind drift back, past Brother Gisli, over the four summers since Rafn had given him his sword and slung him out of the settlement. Four sea-faring summers that had made of him a seaman who knew the ways of ships in all weathers and in all their moods. Four summers that had grown his beard for him, short but thick, a young beard still, but the captain of the Dublin garrison would scarce have found it lacking now. Well, he would sooner have been Onund's man and Thorstein's and had the free-ranging years among the islands. They had been good, for the most part, those years. He realised suddenly that he was looking back on them as something that was over – almost over – and gave his shoulders a small angry shake as though to rid himself of the unlucky thought that had come upon him out of nowhere . . . no, not quite out of nowhere. There was a new wind blowing among the islands, as Brother Gisli had said, a restlessness. Many chieftains, even Aflaeg the Lord of Barra and father of Aesa, had already up-anchored and spread sail for Iceland; there was good farming land on Iceland, or so it was said, to be had for the taking. Word was carried on a colder wind, too, of stirrings in Norway; King Harald Finehair was on the move again. Too many men remembered all too well the last time that he had come west-over-seas to make his powers felt among the islands. And Onund himself, so it was said, was away back to Norway with Thrond his sword-brother whose father had lately died – some trouble over the inheritance with Harald laying king's claim to the land. The old Barra roost was breaking up and would not be the first of its kind.

Maybe that, the breaking up and outward drift among the island chiefs, was the reason for this council called between the most powerful of them, Thorstein the Red, and Jarl Sigurd of Orkney.

High in the bows of *Sea Serpent*, Thorstein raised one arm; the anchor came in and the great blue and red striped sail went lurching up the mast, followed by the sails of *Star Wolf* and *Wild Horse* lying astern. To Bjarni, hauling at the anchor cable, there did not seem to be much difference between sun-bright water now and as it had been fifty breaths ago. But Thorstein was one – Onund was another – who could navigate in thick fog by the wave-patterns, the sound of the sea that tells of the sea-bed shapes, as familiar to him as the shapes of stack and headland above the sea. Both men knew the secrets of deep water through eyes and ears and the soles of their feet.

The sails filled and billowed out, and the three long-ships slipped forward, the south-west wind behind them, into the perilous waters of the Pentland Firth. Presently they came about in a swath of flying spin-drift, and were heading north, tacking up into seaways between Hoy and South Ronaldsay. For a while Hoy took the wind from them, the water quietened and grew deeply green. The sails came rattling down once more and again they took to the oars, to bring the little fleet into the haven below the Jarlstead.

For three days and another, Jarl Sigurd and his son Guthorm, Thorstein the Red, and the wisest and most powerful of their chiefs spent much time deep in council together where the land arose onto open moors beyond the in-take boundaries and no man might come close unseen to hear what passed between them. Not on the Moot Hill within the circle of willow wands, but in the main Standing Stones left by an older people, for this was not a moot council, but a stranger-gathering, and amongst them were strangers of another breed from the Viking kind, men from the mainland, not like the Old People of the West Coast and the Islands, but men of a harsher build, and with blue tribal patterns pricked on breast and forehead, and whose tongue, when they spoke alone together – though they could speak the Norse tongue well enough to the Jarl and his people – had a dark sound to it, a sound that made Bjarni, hearing them at a distance, think of the spatter of thunder-rain on the broad leaves of summer.

And while the great ones held their council among the heather-washed stones of an older people, the lesser folk of the settlement and the ships' crews carried on with the daily business of living in the harvest fields and cattle yards and along the boat-strand, and in between whiles amused themselves with any means that came to hand. There was little hunting to be had on the low bare windswept isles of Orkney, with no forest land to shelter deer or boar, only seal hunting, which was a thing done for meat and skins, dangerous, but without pleasure. There was also hawking after grouse and ptarmigan, but not much more. But something that was almost a fair had sprung up among the scattered bothies between the settlement and the haven, as always among the Northmen when there was any kind of gathering, a meeting of traders and craftsmen. In the open ground between, men raced and wrestled and strove which could throw their spear the furthest or split the toughest log with one throw of a war-axe, and feasted and drank from the ale-booths and wagered their silver on a string of cock fights behind the sail-shed, where the high turf walls gave some shelter from the never-ending wind.

But rumours of what the chiefs were discussing drifted down on the wind in the way of such things to the rest of the settlement. Bjarni, returning from some errand that had taken him down to the ship-strand, and heading for the nearest ale-booth to spend the silver that he had won by a wager on the red cock earlier in the day, noticed more men than usual gathering at the armourer's smithy, a tendency to gather in knots and fiddle with the weapons in their belts. 'Is it a war-trail, then?' he asked of the world at large, flinging himself down on a bench at the ale-house entrance. 'I had thought maybe it was an Iceland faring.'

A man whetting his dirk on the stone door sill looked up, testing the blade on his thumb. 'Even for an Iceland faring, it's as well for a man to have his weapons keen.'

'It is Iceland then?' Bjarni pressed, flinging up an arm to capture the attention of the snotty-nosed potboy. 'Drink, here!'

The other shrugged. 'Who can tell for sure, save the wind that blows through the heather up yonder.'

And a man sitting close by with a young goshawk on his fist put in, 'None the less a man might hazard a guess – with those painted Pictish lords up there with the Jarl, I'd say more like Caithness and maybe the southern land beyond.'

'So, a war-trail.' Bjarni took the ale-jar from the potboy's hand and took a good deep swallow.

The man with the hawk, who was older and seemed to be more of the thinking kind than the rest, gentled its neck feathers thoughtfully. 'Not at first, I'd be thinking, not with their embassy up there. There's a great emptiness all over Caithness, hunting runs, wide moorland with good land under the heather, too much land for all the tribes of the Painted People. We could do with more land ourselves . . .'

'You have been there?' Bjarni asked, looking out over the green lands of Ronaldsay and the blue mountains of the mainland along the southern sky.

'Every autumn. The Jarl hunts there each autumn, and counts the hunting runs as good as his own. The gods know there is no hunting, save seals, on Orkney.'

'Aye,' someone else put in, 'there's emptiness to spare on Caithness, and what people there are might well be glad of our swords, with Harald Finehair readying his ships on every strand in Norway, for a coming against the Scots coast.'

The man whetting his blade on the door stone seemed satisfied with its edge at last, and looked up again, thrusting it into his belt. 'And yon's another reason, good as any and better than most, for a Caithness faring. Harald in Caithness and Sutherland would be a deal too close in our midst for comfort by way of the Great Glen or the Pentland Firth . . . Better to be there first.'

It all seemed good sense, but . . .

The goshawk suddenly spread its wings with a harsh cry and bated violently from its master's fist. The man quieted it and got it righted, then got up and carried it outside, away from the peat-reek and the crowding faces.

And Bjarni, looking after them, saw the mountains

of Caithness suddenly grown shadow-thin, rising out of a faint sea mist that had already blotted out the coast.

By dusk the sea *haar* had thickened and came rolling up from the south-west, a heavy clinging sea-smelling murk that blanketed sound and crept even into the Jarl's great Hearth Hall to mingle with the reek of the peat fires and make ragged smears of light around the torches.

And with the mist came one of the coast wardens, bringing with him a stranger in a rough seaman's cloak. From his place among *Sea Serpent's* crew at the guest end of the hall, Bjarni saw him as he passed within arm's length and caught his breath in surprised recognition. Sven Gunnarson! He told himself not to be a fool; his mind had been running on the Barra days, and this cursed mist was enough to set a man imagining things. But it was Sven Gunnarson!

The two men made their way up the hall together to stand before Jarl Sigurd in his High Seat with the dragon-carved fore posts. And the warden, leaning on his grounded staff, reported, 'Messenger from three ships just come into the haven.'

'In this murk?' said Jarl Sigurd, fondling the ears of a great hound sitting propped against his knee.

'Jarl Sigurd is not the only seaman west-over-seas,' said Sven.

'I can think of others, not many; which of them lies in my haven this night?'

'Onund Treefoot, of *Sea Witch*.'

'So. And what is the message he sends?'

'He asks leave to water ship from your springs.'

The Jarl's thick brows shot up, and his flat-backed head on its long neck thrust forward, making it look even more than usual like the prow of a galley. 'Since when has Onund Treefoot had need to fill his water casks from another man's springs, unless it were done without the asking?'

Sven gave his familiar one-shouldered shrug. 'We are on the whale's road north-west. An Iceland faring – a peaceful faring; we have women and bairns on board, and roped cattle. Therefore we have no wish for fighting.' Bjarni knew how he must hate saying that. 'To have carried enough water from the outset would be to carry fewer cattle and less grain and seed-corn.'

'And so you thought to refill your bags from mine.'

'Orkney is the furthest landfall on the Iceland run,' said Sven.

'Lewis is further,' said Jarl Sigurd.

'Aye, but between Barra and Lewis there has been ill blood these many years.'

That was a story well known to all in the hall, beginning with a raid made by the Lewis chief on Barra when the Barra fleet was away raiding elsewhere.

The Jarl nodded. 'And the sharing of water is a matter for friends and kindred.' He grinned into the carefully wooden face of Sven Gunnarson. 'There has never been friendship between Barra and Orkney.'

Sven swallowed. 'That is the message that you send back?'

'That is the message that I send back. Yet I turn no man hungry from my hearth. Now that you are here, eat before you take it to him.'

'Not under this roof,' said Sven, and turned away, swinging his salt-stained cloak behind him.

As he passed Bjarni their eyes met, and Sven's widened for a moment. Then he went on, with no word spoken between them.

Bjarni took a bannock from the bowl in front of him, but sat staring at it, with, for the moment, no

wish to eat. So – of a surety there was a new wind
blowing among the islands, and Onund Treefoot
filling his sails with it, setting his keels with all those
others on the Iceland run ... Onund down there in
the fog-bound harbour, almost within walking distance. And that was all, nothing more ... Bjarni took
a savage bite out of his bannock and dug his horn
spoon into the nearest of the large communal bowls
of eel stew. What had he to do with Onund Treefoot,
that he should be waiting now like a hound for his
master's whistle?

He did not have so long to wait. The eel stew and
the baked seal meat were gone, but he was still busy
with bannock and curds; and the ale-jars were going
around. The Countess and her women were not yet
gone from the cross-benches; and the harper on his
stool at the Jarl's feet was scarcely launched into *The
Fight at Finnsburg*, when the second stranger came
through the doorway, the mist making a silver bloom
on the great cloak that he wore huddled about him,
the hood pulled forward over his face, and seemingly
something under his arm, bundled under the thick-
ness of it.

The dark sodden folds hung almost to brush the
bracken on the floor, giving no sight of the man's feet,
but the familiar swinging walk with a sideways lurch
of the shoulders at each step told Bjarni instantly who
he was, and told him also that the old wound was
giving trouble.

How in Thor's name had he contrived to come up
from the harbour unseen? Well, the mist was thick
enough, and it was said that Onund could put on a
cloak of invisibility when he chose ...

The harper broke off his tale, one hand still poised
above the harp strings; men looked up from their ale
or a bout of arm wrestling or a game of fox and geese

to follow the cloaked figure with their eyes as he stalked up the Hall to where the Jarl sat in his High Seat with his sons and his guests around him. Guthorm's hand half went to his dirk, the movement echoed by more than one of the Jarl's house-carles, then fell away, back onto his knee. There was no menace in the dark figure, at least none that could have withstood cold steel. The stranger had reached the High Seat and come to a halt before it. As he did so the thing under his cloak stirred, as though roused by the ceasing of the movement, and began to bleat like a lamb.

Onund Treefoot flung back the folds and, stooping, set the thing on the Jarl's knees, saying as he did so, 'Sigurd of Orkney, Onund of Barra claims fosterage to his son.'

The creature – it was certainly no more than a year old, though wrapped already in a sealskin jacket and breeks of scarlet cloth – seemed to be newly waked from sleep. It looked about it at the strange place in which it found itself, and the strange faces crowding in the firelight and, shutting its eyes and opening its mouth, burst into a string of shattering roars.

Jarl Sigurd looked at it blankly, then thrust out a hand to keep the thing from rolling straight off his knee again. There was a ring on the hand, a great slab of amber set in gold; the bairn saw it, the yells ceased between one and the next, and it put out its own hand with a wet sucked thumb, to cling to it. The bellowing died into a contented snuffling.

The Jarl's face combined fury and astonishment as he glanced from the bairn to its father and back again. For a moment he seemed inclined to simply take away his hand and let the creature fall. But it was too late for that. Once a bairn had been set on your knee and fosterage formally claimed for it, there was nothing you could do, though its father were your bitterest enemy.

Onund had flung back his cloak, and stood looking on, the devilry dancing in his lean white face in the way that Bjarni remembered well. 'So! Now there is a foster-kinship between Barra and Orkney. And between kindred, water should be free,' he said. 'Therefore I claim the right to water ship from your springs.'

11

Foster-Kin

The Jarl's face gathered darkness like a storm cloud. In the chief guest seat opposite him Thorstein Olafson stroked his fiery bush of beard and looked on through the peat smoke with the air of a man judging the mettle of two stallions before a horsefight. The Pictish envoys looked on with the more remote interest of men watching the tribal custom of a people not much known to them. The whole Hall seemed to be waiting, as though they had seen the lightning flash and were waiting for the crash of thunder.

For a long moment the silence held, and then Jarl Sigurd flung up his head with a roar, but it was a roar of laughter, not storm. 'Now by Thor and Odin, here is one after my own heart!' He rocked to and fro, heedless of the bairn on his knee, who would have ended on the floor after all if Guthorm, who sat beside him, had not reached out a long arm and caught it into safety like a puppy by the scruff of its neck, and handed it over to one of the Countess's women who came out of the shadows to take it from him. The Jarl beat his fists on his knees, laughing still, and the laughter was caught up and ran and swirled like a racing tide among the crowded benches.

'Ill would it be for foster-kin to deny his wells to foster-kin! Water ship tomorrow. See now. I will send men down to bring up your people for it is a dreich night to be huddled under canvas. Meanwhile, sit you, and eat!' He let out a bellow fit to fetch the old swallows' nests out of the thatch. 'Food! Bring more food for our guests!'

Onund remained standing before him. 'My men will do well enough, but I'd be glad to get the women and bairns under cover for the night.'

'Sit then,' said the Jarl again. 'Here at my side while I send for them.'

'I will sit, and gladly I will eat and drink under your roof when I return, but first I go to fetch my people, for I am thinking that they will not come for a stranger's bidding,' Onund said. 'The bairn, your foster-son, I leave in your keeping, this tide.'

And he turned and stumped away down the Hall, gathering his cloak about him as he went, paying no heed to the laughter and thumping of ale-jacks on trestle boards that went with him, nor to the wailing of his son, left alone among strangers.

Bjarni, who had been watching him, still half under the old spell, got up, flinging a leg over the bench, and went out after him. The fog wafted like wet smoke into his face as he came out through the fore porch door and ahead of him he saw a blurred figure moving with the familiar lurch in a saffron haze of torchlight.

On the edge of the garth he caught up with him. Onund looked round at the pad of footsteps behind him. And by the quick movement under his cloak, Bjarni judged that his hand had gone to the dirk in his belt.

'Slippery going, on the harbour path in this wet

witches' brew,' Bjarni said. 'My shoulder is the same height as ever it was.'

There was a loosening in the cloaked figure; unseen hand came away from unseen dirk, and Onund Treefoot flung back the shoulder fold of his cloak. 'Broader than it used to be, though,' he said, setting his arm across Bjarni's shoulder in the old familiar way. And that was all, no more of strangeness or startlement than if they had last spoken with each other the day before.

They went on together down the rocky path that snaked between furze and rough grass to the shipstrand and the scarce-seen ghosts of ship-sheds and jetties that loomed to meet them through the grey half-light. Water as grey and lightless as the mist lapped upon the shore, and along the ghost of the main jetty, the yellow sheen of mast head and storm lanterns told where two longships were made fast, with the thicker-set shape of what looked to be a merchant vessel between.

Peering down into this vessel, from which a good deal of noise was coming, Bjarni made out the huddled shapes of women and bairns, one of them crying, roped cattle, a barking dog, faces that seemed to belong to the mist, looking anxiously toward the hollow sound of their feet on the timbers of the jetty. And among the men who surrounded them, here and there the glint of torchlight on knife blade.

'Get the women and the bairns ashore,' Onund shouted. 'We have the Jarl's word. We water ship in the morning.'

All along the line of tied-up vessels, crouching men unfurled themselves and some came scrambling onto the jetty while others set to handing the women up to them, and a few of the Jarl's men, who had been standing by to keep a wary eye on the strangers' fleet, came forward to lend a hand. A short while later Onund had gone lurching forward to speak to someone aboard *Sea Witch*, and Bjarni was being thumped about the shoulders by old comrades, Sven Gunnarson among them.

'I'd ha' thought you were a ghost up there in the Jarl's Hall if you hadn't had your mouth so full of bannock,' Sven said, fetching him a buffet that all but sent him sprawling into the belly of the merchantman among the roped cattle.

They were getting the women up onto the jetty. One would not come, but stood in the prow, looking up and calling in a voice sharp-edged with fear and anger, 'What of my bairn?'

Onund turned from *Sea Witch* to answer her. 'All's well with the bairn, as I promised. You shall have him in your arms again before the tide turns.'

She made a small sound that was almost a sob, and came to the shipside, and Bjarni, reaching down to catch her hand and swing her up onto the jetty, saw in the white and weary oval of her face that she was still angry, but no longer afraid. She knew him, just as Sven had known him, but she had other things on her mind, and instantly turned away, thrusting between the other women to come at her lord. 'How do I know that you speak the truth?'

'Woman,' Onund said, 'I make few promises, but have I ever yet failed in a promise made to you?' And he swung away from her about other matters that had to be seen to.

It might be no sweet and easy thing, Bjarni thought suddenly, to be Onund Treefoot's woman.

Soon all was sorted out and, carrying the weary bairns among them, the women had turned to the track snaking inland towards the Jarl's Hall; a few of the men going with them for escort, while the rest, left behind, began rigging the usual night-time shelter of ship's awnings. The Jarl's coast warden led the way, and Onund brought up the rear, Bjarni again beside him with his shoulder under the other's armpit, feeling the familiar weight and balance as though there had been no two years between.

In the firelit Hall more food had been brought up in readiness for their coming, and there was warmth and a kind of rough-edged welcome; bannock and curds and laverbread, raw salt fish and porridge sweet with honey-in-the-comb, all things that could be quickly made ready while fresh supplies of seal meat were cooking.

They were gathered in by the women of the household on the cross-benches. Onund's son had gone back to sleep, and lay curled up in the Countess's lap, as though it were the lap he had known all his life, his thumb in his mouth and her arms about him. Aesa his mother saw him there, and started towards him, her arms held out, but she met the Countess's gaze and a faint warning shake of the head. She glanced questioningly round to find Onund, and received from him the same signal. She let her arms fall empty to her sides, and let herself be settled into the place that had been made ready for her, close beside.

Red Thorstein being already in the chief guest seat opposite the Jarl's, Onund was given a place of honour at the Jarl's side, and Bjarni, lacking bench space to sit, settled himself among the hounds near by.

'It was thought among the Islands that you were sojourning in Norway,' Thorstein said across the hearth, when the newcomers had had time to take the edge off their hunger.

The women and bairns had been carried off to the bower by that time, and the men were left to pass the ale-jars among themselves, and when Onund held out his horn for refilling, Bjarni, gathering his legs under him, and reaching for the nearest jack, poured for him as he would have poured for his own chieftain. Onund drank deep, and sat with the horn on his knee. 'A long story that is.'

'The night is before us.' The Jarl drank also. 'Tell on.'

And Onund told, pitching his voice for the whole hall as the harpers do, and making of it a story indeed; a long story full of weapon-ring and burning thatch. And the hall listened to it happily as to any new story. Thrond's father had died back in Norway, and Harald Finehair had claimed his land, since Thrond had up-anchored and gone west-over-seas. Thrond's grandfather, with a warrior heart still inside his ancient body, had counter-claimed, and the thing had come to fighting, and the old man sent word to his grandson. So Thrond and Onund had taken out their longships and with a fair wind had reached the Norwegian coast and the grandfather's house before any of the King's men knew of their coming. Some kind of agreement had been patched up with the King, and Thrond had taken the value of the homesteading in goods and gear, and set sail for the Iceland settlements. Last spring, that had been.

'He would have had me go with him, but I had hearth-friends and kinsfolk in the south,' Onund said, 'and I was minded to hunt in their runs for a while. So to the south of Norway I went, to Rogaland, not noising it abroad, and lodged for a while with an old shipmate who I made the Mid-Land Sea run with more than once when the world was young. While I was there, one brought me word that King Harald, knowing that I had been with Thrond, had taken land of mine – farmed by my kinsman, it was – and given it in charge to a man of his own, Harda by name. So

I gathered my crew and a few men from round about who were younglings with me, and went to Harda's house and slew him and took his goods and gear and burned his Hall to the ground. But that same moon, another of the King's men went to my grandfather's house and mishandled the old man so that he died of it. See how one thing flows from another . . . We went to his house also, and burned the thatch over his head, killing him and thirty more. They were holding a great ale-brewing, and that made it easy.' He sighed. 'Almost too easy. Then came Jarl Anders with his own carles and a gathering of the country folk, and there was a fight – something of a fight – before we took him. I was somewhat weary of killing, just then, so I demanded of him wergild for my grandfather's death – with a spear at his throat, I demanded compensation. He paid none so ill, with a couple of fine horses, three gold arm-rings, and the velvet mantle off his back, and we let him go. But after that it seemed that maybe the time had come to be away from Norway.'

There was a general nodding of heads and muttering of agreement.

'So I headed back to Barra and picked up the women and bairns and those of the men who would be coming with me. And now the keel-road is for Iceland in the wake of Thrond and the rest of the Barra brotherhood.'

'I have heard that there is good land to be had for the in-taking in Iceland,' said the Jarl. 'I have seen fine cattle grazing, and the blow-holes of hot water from the earth's heart, that in some places keep the frosts at bay.'

'Also it is not on Harald Finehair's door sill, and a man may get on with his own living without the King of Norway breathing down his neck,' added Onund.

'And what of Barra? Yon's too far to be keeping for

a summer keel-strand,' Thorstein said, gazing into the depth of his ale-jack.

'All the kings of Ireland may hunt the deer on Barra, as they did before my coming.' Onund glanced with a quirking brow from Thorstein to the Jarl and back again. 'Unless either of you would be for making your hunting runs there.'

'For myself,' the Jarl said, 'my runs are closer to hand. Good hunting I have already each autumn across the Pentland Firth.' He paused reflectively, again pulling at the ears of the hound against his knee, and his eyes flicked sideways at the Pictish envoys, drawing them in. 'Good land there is there also, and in many places too few men to hold it, if Finehair brings his keels and his firebrands that way, as seems like enough he may.'

There was a little silence, and again Onund looked from one to the other, the beginning of a smile narrowing his eyes. 'Ah-h! I was wondering what brought Orkney and Mull under one roof this end of summer, to say nothing of the lords of the Painted People.'

The silence closed in again and he shifted a little to find an easier position for his aching stump. Bjarni knew the signs. The three sea lords seemed for the moment linked together in understanding of what was not said between them, while their men looked on; and into the silence came the sounding of the sea, and the faint haunting note of the seals, who always sang in misty weather.

'It is in my mind – almost – to wish myself with you on this new hunting trail,' said Onund; then shook his head like a horse with a fly in its ear. 'Na, na! It is the far North and West, a new life in a new land, for me and mine.'

The night wore on, the men of three islands and

three fleets, who had fought each other before, and would like enough be at war again if they were to meet in open water, mingling together, sleeping safe alongside each other by the laws of fosterage and guest right when the sleeping-rugs were spread on the benches and the bracken-strewn floor. Only, Jarl Sigurd slept in the Hall among his guests and his house-carles instead of going to his own bed in the Women's House, in a way which Bjarni thought might have some reason to it.

Next morning early, with the last rags of mist rolling away before a stiffening east wind and the light lying long and clear and level across the islands, Onund set his crews to watering ship. The women reappeared from the Women's House, Aesa still empty-armed, while one of the Countess's bower women followed after carrying the bairn, content enough now, on her hip. But maybe Aesa had had him to herself through the night, for a chunk of raw turquoise hung on a cord around his neck, that had not been there before.

When the water-kegs were refilled and safe aboard, with other stores which were gifts from the Jarl, they shared the morning meal together in the Hearth Hall, the babe now tumbling among the hounds at Jarl Sigurd's feet. And, the meal over, Onund and his companions rose to go their way. Leave-takings were going on among the women, but through it all Aesa had her eyes on the bairn that she might not yet touch.

In the last breath of time – it was as though his son had been a hostage for the peace between them since last night – Onund said to the Jarl, 'All good go with you on your hunting runs ... I'll be taking the cub with me now, not leaving him for a squalling burden to your Women's House; not this tide. But if one day another tide should bring him back to you, do not be forgetting that he is your foster-son.'

For answer, Jarl Sigurd bent and scooped the bairn from among the hairy grey shapes. 'Surely I will not forget.' He set the creature on his knee for a moment, then handed him over with something of haste to his father, leaving a damp patch showing on the saffron colour of his breeks. 'The gods grant that by that time he may be able to hold both a sword and his water.'

Onund took his son, and handed him on, also rather hurriedly, to Aesa, who had come up beside him.

She and the Countess had kissed each other tenderly at parting; but outside in the keen wind, huddling the damp baby under her cloak, she said in a bleak whisper to her lord, 'I hope the water is worth it?'

'You will think so, by the time we come to Iceland,' said Onund Treefoot, turning his face to the way down to the ships.

Bjarni took the harbour path with them the one last time, his shoulder under Onund's in the old familiar way.

'What of the dog?' Onund asked at the very end, when he was about to board *Sea Witch*.

'Well enough,' Bjarni told him, 'though something lacking in speed, as you said he would be.'

And with nothing more said on the matter, the old grief was left behind.

'Thara is safely wed to a mainland farmer, and the priest her father, Asmund, bides with his sacred wood and the Barra folk who remain,' Onund said after a pause filled with the voices of men calling to each other, and the crying of the gulls. 'Come with us, then.'

Something tugged at Bjarni, a two-way pull deep within him. Then he shook his head. 'If I were to come with you, I would come, Asmund or no Asmund. But my sword-service is sold to Thorstein Olafson, at the least to the end of the next summer faring.'

'Ach well, the Iceland road is open for all men to follow, and at all times,' Onund said.

He swung himself over *Sea Witch*'s side, and Sven put up a hand to steady him as he made his way aft towards the steering oar.

Standing on the salt-caked timbers of the jetty, Bjarni watched *Sea Witch* cast off, watched the rise and dip of the oars as they were swung out, followed by the big, deep-bellied merchantman with the women and bairns and livestock on board, and *Star Bear* bringing up the rear. He saw the seas begin to take them out in mid floe, and the sails bloom out from the masts. Saw them heel a little before the wind . . .

He turned and went back up the looping track towards the settlement and the Jarl's Hall.

'The doubt was on me that I should be seeing you again,' Thorstein said to him later that day, grumblingly, through the red bush of his beard. He had come down to the harbour again, to watch where his crews were readying *Sea Serpent* for the next morning's homeward tide.

'My sword is sold to you, at least for another summer,' Bjarni said, not looking up from the rope he was coiling.

12

Summer Faring

Mull and the lesser islands of Thorstein's ruling thrummed like a hive that was about to swarm. The armourers' hammers rang early and late; while down at the ship-sheds of the main settlement there was a new war-keel on the slipway, and the rest of the fleet being made ready for sea; and the smell of pitch and paint, hot metal and raw new timber hanging over all. It was the hum of activity that broke out every year when the birch buds thickened and men began to talk of the seaways by day and dream of them by night. But this year it had been going on all winter long, growing more urgent as the time for launching the longships drew near.

Worn sails and rigging were renewed; dried and salted fish made ready, and on every hearth in the settlements the women were baking the flat round ships' bannocks that never went stale. And it was said that in the Women's House behind the Hall, the Lady Aud and her bower women were making a new banner of poppy-red silk from foreign parts worked with a great spread-winged raven, stitching into it seven black hairs from her own head, and the ancient spells for victory that women weave at such times.

No harm in a spell for victory, even though the enterprise had been agreed with the Pictish envoys; no embassage could speak for all the tribes of Pictland.

In full spring, with the grey geese flighting northward to their nesting grounds, the small birds busy in the forest fringes and the lambs crying in the sheltered pastures, the time came to be launching the longships.

On the last night before sailing the crews gathered, some to the Lady Aud's little stone chapel, the rest to the God-House where the altar to the White Christ stood beside the altars to more familiar gods. And there in the torchlit dark a young boar was slain, and the Priest dipped the sacred whisk into the blood and sprinkled the gathered warriors and smeared the waiting altars, all the altars, lest the White Christ should feel himself unfairly used.

Afterwards the war-bands swore faith to Red Thorstein on Thor's Ring, the great arm-ring that lay with his Hammer on the tallest of the altars; the great brotherhood oath of the war-trail, on ship's bulwark and shield's rim, horse's shoulder and sword's edge.

Bjarni swore with the rest, but he had a sore and angry heart within him. He was not the only one – for along with a good few others, including *Fionoula*'s crew, he was not to go with the war-bands, not as yet anyway, but bide on Mull to guard the settlement, the Lady Aud and her granddaughters against all comers while the Lord of the island was busy elsewhere.

'It was not for this that I sold him my sword for another year,' he grumbled to Erp, squatting against the stable wall and pulling too hard at Hugin's ears until the big dog growled softly in protest.

And Erp looked up from the broken headstall that he was mending. 'And there was I, thinking that you sold it in the way of these things, for whatever use he chooses to make of it.'

'If he thinks so little of me, I wonder he would be wasting good silver on me at all.'

'There is a thing maybe you have not noticed,' said Erp. 'That you are not the only one, and that among the others are some who all men know to be his foremost warriors. Are you thinking that Red Thorstein would leave the guarding of his womenfolk to the dregs of his war-bands?'

'Aye, you're in the right of it,' Bjarni agreed. Then with a rush of rage and misery, 'But it's easier for you to talk wisdom, like a grey-beard whose fighting days are past, because you – ' He heard what he was saying, and broke off.

'Because I am no fighting man? Because I have never been a fighting man, since I was too young to carry a sword when the raiders came.'

'I had forgotten,' Bjarni said. And then, looking round at the man beside him, 'Have you never thought to run for it?'

'Where does a man with a thrall-ring on his neck run to? My own land is lost to me, and I am not one of the Viking kind whose home is wherever there is salt water. Also I could not be making my own escape and leaving Muirgoed my mother here unfree.'

Bjarni had gone back to pulling his hound's ears, stripping them through his hands like a pair of gloves, but more gently this time. He heard the ache in the other's voice, but there did not seem anything more to say.

And Erp breathed on the bronze buckle of the head-stall and rubbed it with a bit of rag. 'Comfort yourself with the thought that you may have raiders to beat off while the Lord of Mull is away on his own war-trail.'

The summer passed, while the men left on Mull fidgeted and fretted, went hunting, and gambled the sarks off their backs and picked quarrels among themselves for lack of anything better to do. There was always the chance that the Old People of the fisher-villages might seize the chance to rise, but they did not. Once, raiders came, but the headland watch gave warning of their coming, and the cattle had been driven far inland before they beached. So they never got the shore-killing that they had come for, and left a few of their own kind dead on the shoreline behind them, and at summer's end the thatch was still on the roofs of the settlement.

Then just as the late northern harvest was being got in, *Wild Horse* put into the harbour with the news that they had been waiting for so long. Haki the ship chief went up to the Women's House to speak with the Lady Aud, and before the evening meal the word was running like heath fire through the farms and villages.

Thorstein and Jarl Sigurd had come together, the one by way of the Great Glen, the other across the Pentland Firth and down from the north. There had been fighting in Caithness, as all men had guessed that there would be, despite last year's meeting of Northmen and Picts on Orkney. But now there was peace of a kind in Caithness, and Thorstein left to hold the foothold that they had gained, while Jarl Sigurd turned south once more to deal with the Pictish tribes that were still skulking in their wake. Also the messenger had brought word from Red Thorstein to his mother that she should bring over to him his daughter Groa, for her marriage to Dungadr of Duncansby, one of the northern Pictish chiefs of Caithness, a marriage that should help to hold the peace together, and gain the Northmen time and space to plant their settlements.

What passed between Aud and her granddaughter on the matter, no one outside the inner circle of the household ever knew. Some, who saw her afterward, said that Groa looked as though she had been weeping. But when *Wild Horse* and *Fionoula* were run down into the water three days later – Aud, who was not called the Deep-Minded for nothing, had been making certain preparations of her own through the summer, so that now there need be little delay – she followed her grandmother aboard, walking with her head up, and the look about her of knowing that she was fifteen and a marriageable woman, the look too of knowing that she was a king's granddaughter with a princess's duties. And Bjarni, seeing her come, thought for a moment of the bairn she had been three springs ago, wishing to sail on and on into the West to find a new world or St Brendan's Isle with the trees full of white birds and all of them singing like the evening star.

Her younger sisters came also, round-eyed with excitement, for it would be too dangerous to leave them at home in a settlement that must be so thinly defended in the months ahead.

'Will it not be as dangerous for them, this faring into unknown Pictish lands?' Muirgoed had asked her, anxious for the bairns who had been her nurslings.

'At least, whatever the danger, they will be under my own eye. Under yours, too,' the Lady Aud had said, and then more lightly, seeing that the young ones were listening, 'And who knows, we may find bold bridegrooms for all of them, though they are something young as yet.'

So now they were packed all together with the kists and creels containing the wedding gear in the cramped space under the awnings and the after-deck of *Fionoula*, while Erp, whom the Lady had bidden to come along as her household thrall, sat before the dark entrance much like a hound on guard.

Bjarni, hauling on a hide rope as the striped sail broke from the yard, tasted the spray salt and cold on his lips after the whole summer spent ashore, felt *Fionoula* keel a little to the wind, and the life leap within him.

They did not follow the water-line of the Great Glen as the springtime fleet had done, for that would have brought them in too far south of Thorstein's base; too much Pictish territory to cross with the tribes still unsettled, maybe on the war-trail.

Instead they ran northward, keeping to sheltered waters as far as might be for the women's sake, even running the narrows between Ellan Skyaine, the Winged Isle, and the mainland coast before they came out into the open sea with nothing between them and the world's end save, for a while, the dim blue cloud bank of the Outer Isles.

At least, with women on board and the garland of greenery at the masthead which signified a bride being taken to her new land, neither they nor *Wild Horse* following in their wake were likely to have trouble from others of the Viking kind, unless of course they met with the likes of Vigibjord and Vestnor.

They did not have altogether plain sailing, all the same, for the seas were as wild as usual up the West Coast, and worsened as they ploughed their way up toward the great headland at Cape Wrath – the Ness of the Turning, men called it – where the coast changed direction to face almost north. And though *Fionoula* was a good sound little seaboat, she had been built for inland waters and rolled like a farrowing sow in the steep western seas, and most of the passengers were in a sorry state. 'Better it would be for them if they might pull at an oar or handle the sail with the rest of us,' Bjarni thought. 'Less time they'd have for the wave sickness then.' But at last on the fifth day out from Mull they sighted the three limestone stacks that marked the mouth of the Pentland Firth, and a while later the ship chief brought them into the quieter waters of a broad bay, guarded by cliffs as tall as the stacks had been, loud with the crying of sea birds, then, riding the in-flowing tide, up the estuary of a river that came looping to meet them between rock ledges and skerry-fingered shoals and shallows, out of the wide wastes of moor and bog. On either side of them as they rowed stretched a wide-skied misty land, full of the crying and calling of shore birds, a land of coarse grass and winding waterways and sky-reflecting pools, and far off the dark cloud-line, like another shore, of distant forest, a land which seemed to Bjarni to have too much sky for comfort, as the sea never did.

13

Bride-Ale in Caithness

Thorstein's camp was some way inland, much like any other winter camp of the Vikings, a headland taken and fortified. This was no sea headland, though, but a low hill shoulder guarded on three sides by looping river and on the fourth, where it ran out from the main mass of the hill behind it, by a ditch and a roughly thrown-up turf wall. In the enclosed space was a confused huddle of turf and hurdle-walled bothies, mostly still roofed with ships' awnings. The ships themselves were drawn up like stranded sea beasts on the marshy river bank, and the blue reek of hearth smoke lay over all.

Fionoula and *Wild Horse* had been sighted by lookouts at the river mouth, and all the last stretch men on small shaggy horses had kept pace with them along the banks, while others raced ahead with news of their coming. And when they came toward the makeshift jetty Thorstein, with a great arrow-breasted goshawk on his fist, and a knot of his hearth companions, was there to meet them. They shipped the oars and came alongside under their own way, to the shouts of a greeting going to and fro across the

narrowing water. *Fionoula* settled with a faint bump
and scrape of timber against timber, and men sprang
ashore with ropes to make her fast. The women and
bairns had come out from their quarters a while back,
to see and be seen as they came up the last stretch of
the river, and the jolt as the *Fionoula* touched the jetty
caught Lilla the youngest bairn off balance, so that
she fell over backwards, bumping her head, and began
to cry, but was picked up and comforted by Muirgoed
of the gentle horse-like face. Now the bairns and then
the women were being got ashore to the helping
hands of the men on the jetty. Erp lifted the Lady Aud
ashore, and Bjarni, who was nearest to her, caught up
Groa and clambered ashore holding her high against
his shoulder, her arms round his neck as cold as oar-
thresh to the touch, like something that belonged to
the sea. Maybe a seal-woman would feel like that,
to the mortal man who stole her skin . . .

For one instant, as he would have set her down, he
felt her arms tighten round his neck, and saw her
frightened gaze going out past her father to someone,
something, beyond. And looking the same way, he
saw the strangers who had come down with Red
Thorstein and his hearth companions. Men of the
same kind as the envoys of last year on Orkney, with
the blue patterns on their foreheads and their beards
cut long and narrow. And foremost among them was
a tall raw-boned man in a cloak of magnificent
freckled lynx skins over his darkly checkered breeks,
dark eyes looking out from either side of a great beak
of a nose which, together with the rough grey-brown
hair that sprang from his forehead like ruffled
feathers, gave him a look of kinship with the great
gyrfalcon he carried on his fist. At least he was not
old. Bjarni had been afraid of that. He was much
older than Groa, which was to be expected, but much

younger than Thorstein Olafson. Bjarni was surprised to find out how much that mattered to him.

'You have made good speed, my mother,' Thorstein greeted the Lady Aud. 'And see now, here stands Dungadr of Duncansby, lord of many spears, my friend, eager for a first sight of his bride.'

The Lady stood on the weed-grown jetty, looking from her wet feet to her braided hair the Queen of Dublin. 'Groa is in no state to be seen by any bridegroom, still drenched and emptied from the wild seaways from Mull. I would have thought that might have struck home to even your wooden wits!'

Thorstein frowned. Clearly he was afraid of what she might say next. 'Peace, old mother. He is used to the coming and going of traders, and knows something of our tongue.'

But the Lady Aud, old and weary and seasick as she was, was bestowing upon this Pictish princeling the slow and beautiful smile that had won many men to her way of thinking. 'Then he will understand what I have just said to you.'

The Pict bent his head to her in courtesy, and put in swiftly, speaking the Norse well enough, though with a strange dark lilting accent, 'Lady, I do not see the maiden: I shall not see her until you give me leave,' and lifting his free arm, he held the folds of his cloak before his face.

'That is prettily done and prettily said,' the Lady Aud told him. 'Though not after the manner of our people.'

Thorstein said between laughter and growling impatience, 'So be it, then, but let it not be too long before our two people are bound together by marriage peace.'

'I will speak the word as soon as I see fit. Meanwhile I and my granddaughter and my bower woman have the need upon us for warmth and food and shelter, and quietness to gather our scattered selves together again.'

A long heather-thatched bothy had been made ready for them, and when the Lady Aud's treasure kists and the wedding goods that they had brought with them had been carried up from the ships, they settled in to recover from the wild seaways and make themselves ready for Groa's bride-ale. And while they did so the Painted People and the Northmen ate and drank together and went hunting for the fresh meat that would be needed for the feasting, returning from the forest at evening with the carcasses of red deer and grizzled boar slung across the backs of the hunting ponies. It was a pleasant time, Bjarni found; a time for greeting old friends and exchanging the summer's news. There was news from the men of the war-bands of fighting and the making of treaties, of Jarl Sigurd in Sutherland talking peace with Melbrigda Tusk, the *Mormaor*, or ruler, of those parts. From *Fionoula's* crew there was news of a smaller and more friendly kind; of harvest and the seal hunting, a son born to a man, an old man dead after a glorious drinking bout and a cliff-top fall, a quarrel between neighbours, a litter of pups born to someone's favourite bitch . . .

Then on the fourth day, the day before the new moon, which seemed to please the Picts mightily – Bjarni wondered if the Lady Aud had known that among them, the new moon was the time for a wedding, for the start of all things – meal and honey were brought from the store, and new milk from the little black cattle, hardly larger than faery cattle, that grazed the hill pasture. A fire was made within the Women's House, and soon the smell of baking stole out through the camp, telling the waiting men that

Groa the daughter of Thorstein the Red was making her bride-cake, and word was sent to Dungadr in the hunting camp that he had made a short way down-river.

Next morning, while the shadows still lay long through the camp and across the river marshes, Groa came into the Hearth Hall, clad in a gown of once-brilliant eastern striped silk that had been worn by the Queen of Dublin before her, and with her hair braided under a silver-gilt wedding crown. She walked beside her grandmother to the freshly made-up fire where her father and Dungadr with his groomsmen and the brown-robed Christian Priest waited for her.

Thorstein joined their hands together above the leaping flames in the sight of the mingled gathering of Picts and Northmen that filled the smoky Hall. And Groa and Dungadr, who had had only that one passing sight of each other until now, looked at each other steadily through the drifting peat-reek, while the sealskin thong was tied and re-tied and the drops of bright sacrificial blood fell into the fire. Afterward, the brown-robed Priest stood forth to sign them both on the forehead with the Cross in token of blessing. It was a good way to let the White Christ into the bride-making, though of course all men knew that it was the hands above the fire that in truth made the marriage bond, that and the carrying the woman home to her new hearth . . .

The huge flat bride-cake was broken up and the fragments piled into the hollow of a shield for sharing among all comers; and the crowd spilled out on to the open turf before the Hall, where the smell of baking meat was already wafting from the cooking pits. The day passed like most other feast days, the young men running and wrestling and showing off their weapon skills against each other, Pict against Pict, Northman against Northman, Northman against Pict; and in between, returning hungry for more of the roast boar meat and venison and the great bowls of oaten bannock and wild honey.

Bjarni, sprawling beside one of the fires with his mouth full of the black pudding that had been his prize in a wrestling match, found his thoughts wandering back over the years to that other wedding feast on Barra, and how the day had ended for him. Well, Hugin was safely out of it this time, anyway . . . Safely out of what? He sat up sharply; safely out of what? Then he relaxed; safely out of nothing. It was the two-year-old memory that had given him that sudden sense of change in the wind; something coming to an end. No more than that. He laughed at himself, and crammed his mouth with the rest of the black pudding, and the feeling faded. But it did not quite go away.

The day had moved on towards evening; a day of sunshine and clear distances, which was rare in those parts. And in the mouth of the rough timber Hall, Thorstein sat with Dungadr, and between them the Lady Groa, her wedding finery laid aside for the little sisters to be wearing when their own days came. Her farewells were over with them and her grandmother and Muirgoed who had been her nurse, and they were away back to the Women's House. She was the only woman now in all that company, and waiting, as they were all waiting, for the next thing that must happen.

Meanwhile the bride-ale still went round, and the warriors sprawled at their ease around the fires, drinking to all things under the sky, gnawing the last sweet shreds of meat from the stray bones and tossing the remains to the hunting dogs, asking long complicated riddles, while Thorstein's harper strolled among them, declaiming the long saga of Wayland Smith to any who cared to listen.

The sun had scarcely slipped below the rim of the moors, leaving a smear of brightness in the north-westward sky, when somebody set up a shout and, looking where he pointed, all men saw the first faint nail-paring of the new moon afloat in the bright after-wash of the sunset.

Next moment turmoil broke out, as the Picts, who had begun melting away for some while past, came pouring round from the rear of the Hall where their small shaggy horses had been tethered in readiness, flinging themselves astride them as they came. The chief's horse they led among them, and on the instant Dungadr was up on his feet, laughing. He caught Groa and, slinging her up onto his trampling beast, mounted behind her and swung his horse toward the gate-gap in the camp's turf wall, his sword companions closing up around him with much laughter and eldritch shrieking to the new moon as they streamed through. They had all known what would happen, but it was all so sudden, like something in a dream.

Bjarni caught one glimpse of Groa's face looking down, white and startled, from the hard curve of her new lord's arm. Then he was racing with others of *Fionoula*'s crew for the place where their own horses were waiting. It should have been for the bride's brothers to give chase, but since she had none, it must be for the youngest of the men who had brought her to her bride-ale to take their place. And indeed, remembering that glimpse of her white stricken face, Bjarni, slipping free the tether of the nearest horse and swinging a leg over its back as they in turn headed for the gate-gap, felt as though he were indeed her brother, and this a real marriage by capture instead of a ritual pretence.

The marriage party were well on to the moor by the time he and his fellows were clear of the gate, skeining out like wild geese as they headed for that sheen of brightness in the north-west. They settled down to ride. Presently they began to gain on the group in front. That was part of the pattern of things, for Pictish custom demanded that the brothers should come up with those who carried off the bride, so that there should be fighting for her. But both chiefs had given their orders that the fighting was not to get out of hand, for a sham fight could be dangerous between one-time enemies who might yet become enemies again. So the struggle, when the Viking leader caught up with the tailmost of the Painted People, swinging his horse to meet him, was not too deadly; a flurry of blows at the outset, becoming a running fight with the stray blow between riders leaning towards each other, the stray attempt, half-laughing, to pull each other from their horses' backs as they headed on through the heather and the white tufted bog grass toward the crescent moon. The fight was a good one, with some heart in it, all the same; few of the riders came off from it unscathed. Bjarni had broken knuckles and a black eye to show for it when they came up the rising ground to the headland fort of Dungadr, high on its sheer sandstone cliffs above the Pentland Firth. The entrance to the great turf ramparts was ablaze with torches to light the way with welcome, and draw them in, Bjarni thought: but it seemed that they were not to enter the stronghold yet. Something else had to happen first. The torchbearers were leaping down the slope to meet them; men brought marriage cloaks for bride and groom, a head-dress of golden eagle feathers for Dungadr.

Other Picts were taking the riders' bridles as they dropped from the horses' backs. 'What now?' Bjarni shouted to the man who took his horse.

The man shook his head. 'Nothing to fear,' he said. 'Nothing to fear.' But clearly they were the only three words of the Norse tongue that he possessed, and must have been taught to him for the occasion. They were in a narrow furze-grown cleft that dropped away between the thrusts of the cliff edge, the leading torches ahead now, then Dungadr with a hand reached back to Groa behind him, and the rest of the wedding party, Pict and Northman following after with the remaining torches strung between. Bjarni found himself next to *Fionoula*'s captain and demanded of him, 'Where are they taking her? What is all this about?'

The other shook his head. 'I would not be knowing. It is my guess that they have to pass the marriage night in some special place.'

The defile ran out on to the cliff face, and became a path snaking steeply downward, to end at last in a grey pebbly shelf above the tide-line. And there, only a few galley-lengths off shore, rose the nearest of the three stacks that marked the mouth of the Pentland Firth with the hills of Hoy to the northward.

On the seaward side the stack rose sheer with scarce as much as a lodgement for a sea bird's nest between the surf at its feet, and the rough grass at the flat crest; but here on the inland side a track much like the one they had just come from leapt and straggled upward among ledges and steep grass slopes, the course of it shown by torches already set along the way; and a curragh, a skin boat, lay leaf-light at the edge of the water, nuzzling at the pebbles.

It was all so strange that it seemed to Bjarni afterwards like a dream that he never quite forgot. The

yellow sparks of the furze flowers among the dark
pelt of the bushes, the hot resin smell of the torches
mingled with the cold reek of the sea murk as the tide
went out; the faint soft throb of a drum somewhere
high overhead, that began as Dungadr lifted the Lady
Groa into the curragh and the boatmen took up their
poles.

All the short late summer night the skin drums
throbbed on the cliff top, with sometimes a thread of
pipe music woven in and out among the pulse of it,
while the men of the wedding party spent the dark
time as best they could on the sloping pebbles, making
sure that no one else should come to the crest of the
stack under the new moon. At dawn the curragh came
back out of the curls of sea mist that had begun to
rise, and the Chieftain lifted his woman ashore, and
they turned their faces again to the cliff path. Then
the drumming stopped, and the morning felt curi-
ously light and empty without it.

This time the crowd in the gateway, Dungadr's
womenfolk foremost among them, were there to draw
them in. And that day there was feasting in Dungadr's
Hall as yesterday there had been feasting in Red Thorstein's, all for the strengthening of the peace-bond
between the two peoples. And Bjarni for one began
to feel that there had been enough of feasting and
merry-making, and to be glad that they would be
returning to their own camp the day after.

The women of the Painted People did not eat with
their men at feast times, but later and apart in their
own hall. And meanwhile they served the men,
carrying round the jars of mead and heather-ale to
keep the drink horns brimming. Groa had not been
seen for most of the day; but she was back now and
foremost among the Chieftain's women, with silver
apples weighting the ends of her braided hair, and a

kirtle of some dark forest-green stuff, pouring for her
new lord, then moving up and down the hall among
the small tables to pour for any man whose cup was
low.

Bjarni, seeing her come towards him, held up his
cup for refilling and under cover of the harp-song and
the usual evening uproar, asked, 'What shall we tell
the grandmother? Is it well with you, my Lady Groa?'

She finished the pouring, careful not to spill any
drop, before she lifted her eyes. She was changed from
the Groa he had known. He wondered if she still
remembered St Brendan's Isle. She had the look of
someone taking herself and life very seriously; but
she did not look unhappy or afraid. 'Tell the grandmother it is well with me. Tell her that I wish I might
come home; but I remember the thing she told me,
how she hungered for her father's Hall when she first
was Queen of Dublin, and was not comforted until
her first bairn, my father, was born.'

She flashed him a swift smile and moved on with
her mead jar to the next empty cup.

Next morning the little band set out on the ride back
to camp. They rode cheerfully. The peace was safely
made with the Painted People. Soon it would be time
to replace the ships' awnings with thatch. Soon it
would be time to bring in wives and bairns, clear the
land-takes for ploughing and planting barley,
breeding cattle for the rough moorland pastures, dogs
to herd the cattle. Jogging along with legs comfortably
trailing in a very different manner from the way they
had ridden the other way two nights ago, Bjarni began
to think how he should get Hugin up from Mull –
unless of course he was to return to Mull himself, in
which case better to leave him there. Oh! but it would
be good to feel the black fluttering ears under his

hands again . . . There had been fighting earlier in the summer – Jon Ottarson riding beside him had an ill-healed scar below his shoulder to show for it – but now, all things seemed to have gone almost disappointingly smoothly.

Yet when they came within close sight of the settlement that would one day be the heart and soul of the Norse settlement of Caithness –

'Something's wrong,' said Jon, and hitched at his arm, which still bothered him.

The whole hill slope was swarming with movement, throbbing like a softly tapped drum. Horses were being brought in from pasture, men were gathered about the armourer's bothy from which came the red flare of the forge fire and the ring and clatter of hammer on anvil, while others waited their turn at the weapon store in the midst of camp, where spare weapons and bundled stores were being brought out and set beside the horse-lines, ready for loading the pack beasts.

'What's amiss?' Orm Erikson asked of one of *Sea Serpent*'s crew, who squatted within the gateway burnishing his war-cap with a rag of greasy wadmal.

'Word from Jarl Sigurd, that's what's amiss,' said the man. 'The peace-talking has gone up in flames, and swords are out again. So Thorstein gathers in the war pack; three ships' crews of us, heading south with tomorrow's sunrise.'

No one was much surprised; it was the kind of thing that happened. 'Which crews?' someone asked.

'*Sea Serpent*, o'course, *Walrus*, *Fionoula*.'

Bjarni caught in his breath with a little hiss, as he urged his horse fast with the rest. Life was good, and he was not going to get left behind with the bairns again.

A little later, having got his war-sark out from his

sea-kist and found the stitching of one of the horn shoulder plates worn through, he was heading for the store-shed in search of waxed thread; and so came upon the Lady Aud overseeing the issue of ship's bannock and dried meat for the war-bands while Muirgoed, helped by the two remaining grand-daughters, dealt with wound salves and bandage linen.

She beckoned to Erp, standing near, to take her place, and stepped aside for the moment. Bjarni was seemingly the first of the wedding party she had seen since their return.

'Is it well with the bairn?' she asked.

Bjarni nodded. 'It is well with the Lady Groa. I had word with her before we left and she bade me tell you that, and also that she wished she might come home to you, but that she remembered that you told her once how you hungered for your father's Hall when first you were Queen of Dublin, and were not comforted until your first bairn, her father, was born.'

'My first bairn . . .' said Aud, and her gaze went out for a passing moment to follow where Thorstein the Red strode through the camp, with his war-axe on his shoulder and the late sunlight making a bonfire of his coppery beard.

She brought her gaze back to Bjarni. 'She will do well enough, the little one, if all that this mating has been for does not go up in a shower of sparks and fall to ruin, after all.'

14

The Making of Treaties

In the green light of early morning with the plovers calling over the moors, the war-bands rode out through the gate-gap in the turf rampart; a moving darkness of men and horses heading south. Thorstein Olafson with yesterday's messenger beside him and his own sword companions close behind and, behind again, the men of the three longships' crews, with the pack beasts among them. And beside Bjarni, rather surprisingly, rode Erp, to act as horsemaster and maybe scout.

'A horsemaster you will need; and like enough one to spy ahead for you,' he had said, standing before Thorstein the night before.

'And how shall I be sure that you will not lead us into a trap?' Thorstein had asked, as one reasonable man to another.

'If this were Argyll and my own land, I might well do that thing,' Erp had returned in the same manner. 'But these are not my hills and the people are not my people, though I can pass for one of them more easily than you could do. Also our tongues are kin, though not the same. Did I not serve you well enough in the turning of tongue to other tongue when you had need, in times before this?'

And Thorstein the Red had thought on the question a moment, pulling at his fiery bird's-nest beard, then said, 'Sa, sa – ride with us, then, and if you have earned it, and live to ride back again, the first thing that Grim the Smith shall do after our return is to cut the thrall-ring from that scraggy neck of yours.'

They rode south at speed, a three-day ride, checking for a few hours at night, and a short break at noon to feed and rest the horses; for themselves scarcely any rest at all. And they rode with their swords sitting loose in the sheath.

More than once they halted while Erp scouted ahead, where a river bend or steep glen mouth or deserted rath might shelter an ambush; but even when they drew toward the Dornoch Firth and the Sutherland boundaries, the country seemed empty, and surprisingly quiet for a land locked in battle. Burned homesteads and slaughtered cattle, yes, but of warriors, living or dead, scarce a sign and no sign of women or bairns about the ruined steadings, who must all have taken to the wildwood.

'This is a land that has been at war, but one way or the other, I am thinking that the war is over,' Erp said, sitting with Bjarni beside their horses as they ate their noontide bannock on the third day.

They had begun by that time to find bodies. Bodies of their own kind and the Painted People, sprawling among the heather or beside a river ford, from which the horses shied, wild-eyed and snorting.

And not long after, cresting the ridge ahead of them, they came in sight of Jarl Sigurd's camp, the usual rookery of turf bothies and ships' awnings, and saw here and there the scars of burning, and beyond the grey sheen of the firth, and dappled mountains far to the south. And from then on they rode through a spent battlefield, with the smell of death lying over it, from which the ravens and black-backed gulls burst upward at the last moment from beneath their horses' hooves.

But when Thorstein set the great curved oxhorn to his mouth and sounded a long hollow call, it was answered; and the two calls echoed to and fro, setting the echoes flying along the shore.

'Seems there's one man left alive, at all events,' Thorstein shouted back to the men behind him, as they headed on for the gap in the stockade. They saw the dark shapes of many men, it seemed, gathering there to meet them and draw them in.

Whatever had happened there, a strong company of the Jarl's men had come through it alive, and seemingly having had the best of it.

But not the Jarl himself.

Sigurd of Orkney lay on his great bearskin cloak, his galley prow of a nose tipped starkly towards the striped wadmal overhead, in the turf bothy roofed with his own ship's awning, which his men had rigged up for him to die in when the wound fever seized him four days ago, and the threads of redness that carry death had begun to spread upward from the small wound above his knee towards his heart. His great sword lay beside him, and before the entrance of the shelter, up-reared on a spear shaft, was the hacked, shaggy and blackening head of a Pictish warrior, with the huge dog-tooth sticking out from the side of the mouth, that had given the Mormaor of the Sutherland tribes his name, Melbrigda Tusk.

Just inside the entrance stood Guthorm, wearing the dragon-coiled arm-rings of the Jarl of Orkney, and the heavy amber ring sitting somewhat loose on his sword hand that had been his father's.

'It was a good fight while it lasted,' he said in answer to Thorstein's grim questioning. 'I am thinking that there will be no more fire in the furze in these parts, not for a while and a while anyway. My father rode back from the fighting with the Tusker's head swinging by its hair from his saddle bow. The wound on his leg seemed a small enough matter then.' He glanced up at the grizzled trophy on its spear shaft and gave a short crack of laughter. 'They will say, I suppose, given time, that Melbrigda's hacked-off head bit him, and the wound sickened from the venom of the bite.'

'Like enough, like enough. There have been strange tales told of the deaths of heroes before now.' Thorstein rested a kindly hand for a moment on the young man's rigid shoulder.

The Orkney men were already raising a death pyre for Jarl Sigurd, big and high with fallen branches from the dark low woods inland, with drift-wood gathered from far and wide along the shore, and with logs hacked from an ancient pine that had been struck by lightning in some long-past summer storm. They built it where the land rose above the firth, where the cairn, or howe, that they would raise afterwards would make a future sea-mark for longships coming and going that way. In the green late summer gloaming they brought him out from the bothy and carried him down to it, his hearth companions close around him and Guthorm to support his head and shoulders as a son should do. Pine-torches were carried before him and behind, their smoky flames teased out by the light sea wind, and all the men of the war-bands save the few left on guard streaming after.

There was no moon that night, only a blurred brightness in the drifting cloud-roof, and the sea sounded loud and faintly hollow under the bowl of the sky.

They laid his body, still wrapped in his bearskin cloak, on the crest of the pyre and the head of Melbrigda at his feet. They cut the throats of two captured bullocks by way of sacrifice, and flayed the carcasses and stacked the hides with the fat still on them around the pyre, with the champion's portion from each beast, setting aside the rest for the funeral feast (meat was too precious, just then, to be given recklessly to the flames).

Then Guthorm, with a torch in one hand and the dead Chief's sword in the other, mounted onto the pyre, laid the sword in its accustomed place beside him and, leaping down again, plunged the spitting torch deep into the base of the pyre.

A great shout went up, and torch after torch was thrust into the brushwood and piled logs. Fire kindled and ran in red seams through the pile, to meet and flow together and flare up in sheets of flames, the crests bending over in the sea wind. There were no women to keen for the dead man. That would come later, round hearths far to the north. But the warriors started up a slow heavy death-chant, leaning on their spears around the pyre. And the flamelight lipped the tide-edge of the firth with wavelets of fish-scale gold.

The flames were at their height when there was a shout, and some kind of distant scuffle broke out and drew nearer on the fringe of the crowd, and out of the night shadows two men who had been left on guard appeared, dragging a third man between them. The death-chant grew ragged and fell away, and a murmur ran through the Northmen as his captors hauled him into the full red glare of flames and torches, to where the new Jarl stood with Thorstein beside him.

'This is a matter that cannot wait until we have howe-laid my father?' demanded Guthorm in a voice that flayed like an east wind; a strange voice for so young a man.

'Maybe, maybe not,' said one of the guards. 'We found him behind the woodstack, and were not liking the pattern on his forehead. Stand up, you!' He wrenched the man back against his shoulder, and spiked up his head with the point of his dirk under the chin.

Bjarni, standing close by, saw that he was very young, the crescent-arrowhead patterns on his forehead that would have been pricked there in woad when first he came to manhood showing still clear-edged with newness in the torchlight; the long oval of his face as smooth as a maiden's amid a tangled mane of dark hair.

'Canst speak my tongue?' Guthorm demanded.

'Somewhat,' said the young man. He was panting like a deer that has been hard run, but his eyes, long and dark, were steady on the new Jarl's face.

'Then what brings you lurking behind the logstack in my camp?'

'I came to fetch away my father's head,' said the young man.

There was a small harsh silence, and men crowded closer to watch and listen.

'You come too late,' Guthorm said. 'Your father's head has already gone to the flames.'

The next thing happened so fast that it came and went and was done with in the time covered by five beats of a racing heart. The young man gave a strange snarling cry, and sagged forward in the grasp of the men who held him; and next instant, as, taken off guard, they slackened their hold a little, he writhed clear with the speed of a striking snake; his hand whipped to the torn breast of his jerkin of fine jay-marten skins and came away with something small and bright and deadly in it. And snarling still, he sprang at Jarl Guthorm's throat.

The new young Jarl had not slept for four nights, and was slow in his reactions, and it was Thorstein whose dirk stopped the attacker in mid-leap. Others, Bjarni among them, sprang in from all sides. There was a flicker of bare blades in the flamelight; and the young Pict lay among their feet, his life pumping out of him from a score of wounds. But it was Thorstein whose blade had struck first, and Thorstein who had a small deep stab wound in his own upper arm to show for it.

A couple of warriors stooped to haul the body away. 'Onto the fire or over the cliff?' someone said.

Thorstein stood with a hand clapped over his upper arm, a little blood oozing between the fingers. It was for the Jarl to say.

Guthorm, breathing a little quickly, shook his head. 'Neither. Carry him up to one of the tents, and leave him. Likely his own kind will come for him, and for talking of – other matters – before my father's howe is raised.'

Sure enough, next morning when the flames were quenched and the ashes cooling, and the war-bands, gathering stones from the long tidal ridge and the country round, had begun to raise the long boat-shaped howe, a knot of horsemen riding under the Green Bough came to the gap in the stockade, seeking to renew the treaty talks that had broken down before.

Guthorm met them, his cloak flung back to show the Jarl-rings above his elbows, his face hard and steady under the worked rim of his father's war-helm and Erp beside him to turn his words to and fro. 'The last time we talked peace together, little came of it

save the death of many men, my father among them,'
he told them. 'Yet we had the winning of that fight,
and your hunting runs have not returned to you. How
then shall it serve either of us to talk peace again?'

'If an arrow fail to find its mark, shall it serve no
purpose to loose another?' returned the foremost of
the riders, an old man in a cloak of fine red deerskin
with the gold and amber torc of a chieftain about his
neck. 'You come seeking living-space in Caithness and
Sutherland; and indeed there is room, maybe, for both
of us, but only as a thing agreed and freely sworn to
by both of us. Without that, though we be not free of
our own hunting runs, how shall you be free of them
either? Free to ride abroad without fear of an arrow
between the shoulders; free to sleep at night without
fear of our fire in your thatch; free to let your women
and bairns out of your sight when the time comes that
you bring them from over-sea to warm your hearths.'

'That is a true word,' Guthorm said after a moment.
And then, abruptly making up his mind, 'Down with
you then, and we will talk, in hope of a happier
outcome than the talking had before.'

And so in a while, when the horses had been led
away, the chiefs and elders of the Painted People, with
their escort of young braves behind them on the one
side, and Jarl Guthorm and Thorstein Olafson with
the captains of their war-bands on the other, sat confronting each other across the newly kindled Peace
Fire in the midst of the camp. And there they set up
the Green Bough lashed to its spear shaft, and talked
of peace between their peoples for the second time.

Thorstein, his own peace talks past and ended in a
wedding feast, seldom spoke, but remained pulling
gently at his great beard and listening, his tawny eyes
moving from face to face as one way and another the
tangles and confusions were unsnarled or cut through,

points stubbornly argued, demands and counter-demands resisted or yielded to, and agreement drew slowly nearer. At last the thing was done, even to the promise of an exchange of foster-sons. It sounded better that way than to talk of hostages. And the peace oaths were sworn on sword blade and barley bread and salt: and so the treaty was made for a second time, with maybe something more of hope for its holding power.

And then, the light westering and the time drawing on toward evening, food was brought, and great jars of brown cloudy heather-ale. But before they set to feasting, the old chief in the deerskin cloak, who all along had acted as spokesman for the rest, looked up from the fire and said, 'There is another thing.'

'Aye,' said Jarl Guthorm, 'I was thinking there might be,' and his tone had a guard on it.

'Now that there is foster-kinship promised, and the bonds of friendship between our two peoples, let you give back to us the head of Mormaor Melbrigda.'

'You are too late in that asking,' said the Jarl after a moment. 'The head of Melbrigda Tusk has already gone to the flames, and the ashes have been laid with all honour.'

There was a moment of crackling silence.

And into the silence Jarl Guthorm said, 'But we can give back to you the body of his son who first came seeking it.'

The silence dragged on, full of the crying of shore birds and the hollow sounding of the tide, the stamping of a pony in the picket line; but in the heart of it, just silence, dragging on and on.

'So-o,' said the old chief at last. 'That was the hunting trail that he would follow alone.'

Low-voiced, Erp translated.

'Who killed him?' the old chieftain asked at last.

And Red Thorstein, speaking almost for the first time, said simply, 'I killed him.'

The chieftain took his gaze from the young Jarl. 'Why?'

'He made to kill the Jarl Guthorm, and my blade was the nearest.'

'Sa, sa. It is a reason that holds water,' the old man said, with an air of detached judgement. And he leaned forward and took a gobbet of meat from the dish that was cooling in front of him. 'Yet it is glad I am that the friendship was sworn between us before this thing came into the open; for there are those, especially among my young braves, who might mis-understand.' He took a piece of barley bannock to go with the meat.

Bjarni, setting another dish down in the ashes of the fire, guessed that he had deliberately waited until the oath-taking was over, before bringing up the matter of the Mormaor's head.

15

The Shadow Among the Trees

The elders of the Painted People went back to their own place, carrying with them their dead, wrapped in skins and roped onto a hurdle drawn behind one of the horses. And next morning, leaving the new young Jarl and the new-made cairn behind them, Red Thorstein and his war-band headed north again.

Towards noon on the second day, they came down off high moors into a shallow wooded glen through which a burn ran in a chain of pools strung together by stretches of swift-running water. And there they halted, as they had done on the way south, to water the horses and turn them loose to graze.

The trees that grew down to the water's edge were not the dense oaks and dark whispering pines of the wildwood, but birch and rowan and alder, thin leaves making a threadbare summer's-end dazzle of sunlight and dapple-shade, and there were open spaces of coarse grass underfoot, so that the grazing was none so ill.

The air was shimmering with dancing midge-clouds; and Bjarni, itching from their stings on every bit of himself that was open to the air, strolled upstream to above the pools where they had watered the horses, drawn by the idea of cold water on his burning skin: but coming on a small backwater just above the horse pool, and kneeling down to plunge his head into it, he saw something that made him forget his midge-bites. A fat brown trout was lying close under the bank, nose upstream, the current making ripple patterns along its flanks. Something to add savour to the evening bannock!

Careful not to let his shadow fall across the water, he slipped down full length along the bank, and with infinite care and slowness, slid his hand and then his arm into the cold peat-brown water. Time passed, while slowly, slowly, he edged his hand upstream, till his faintly curving fingers were almost under the fish. A little more, a very little more . . . No sound in the heavy noon-tide save the whine of the midge-clouds that he had forgotten, and the lap and purling of the burn. Once, for a moment, he was half aware of a moving darkness among the trees, but no sound; then it was gone. Probably it was no more than the faint web that one may see in certain lights out of the tail of one's eye. He had not moved: already his fingers sensed the living flank of the trout. He was not even breathing now. Another instant . . .

And then, from somewhere downstream toward the noon camp, the silence was snapped by the twang of a released bowstring.

Bjarni whipped his hand from the water, the trout flicking away as he sprang to his feet. He was racing back toward the camp. Ahead of him there was a great stillness in the woods; a stunned stillness only just breaking into uproar as he reached the clearing, a snarling surge of voices and the snatching up of weapons, and in the midst of it Thorstein Olafson, a war-arrow flighted with red kite feathers between his

shoulders, lay coughing up his life into the coarse
burnside grass.

Coming so quickly after the quietness of the trout
in the backwater, the thing burst over Bjarni like a
dream. In the dream men were running, and Bjarni
was running with them, in the direction from which
the arrow had come. The direction of that dark flicker
among the trees. His dirk was naked in his hand,
though he did not remember having pulled it from
his belt. The tumult had sunk away and they ran in
silence, spreading out, questing like hounds stubborn
on a half-lost scent.

He had no idea how long the dream lasted, but
afterwards he thought not long. In the dark shadows
and crowding undergrowth of the wildwood the
bowman would almost surely have got away; but here
among the open woodland of wind-shaped birch and
rowan and alder it was another matter; and afterwards
Bjarni wondered if the man was really not much
interested in getting away, once he had done the thing
that he came to do . . .

There began to be a changed smell in the air, a chill
rooty smell, and the trees were thinning out as the
glen broadened, the hills on either side falling away;
and suddenly before him was open country, coarse
grass and furze, and beyond a rich and wicked green-
ness feathered with the white tufts of bog grass. And
ahead, not more than a bowshot away, was the quarry.

Bjarni let out a shout with all the wind that was yet
in him, to gather in the scattered flanks of the hunt
and, free of the tangle, somehow lengthened his own
stride.

The man had lost speed and there was an uncer-
tainty about him. He swivelled as he ran, losing still
more ground – it must be that he was off his own
hunting run and had not known of the bog, or at least

was unsure of the ways across. Still in the dream Bjarni was aware of the rest of the hunt gathering to his shout close on his heels, breaking out of the woods on either side, but himself still in the lead. There were short throaty cries around him, the cries of the pack when it sights the game. Ahead of him the man had turned at bay; he saw the drawn bow and jinked to one side as he ran, and felt the wind of an arrow whistle past his cheek.

There was no time for another, or maybe no more shafts in the man's quiver. He flung his bow aside and crouched, his knife in his hand, the bog behind him, as Bjarni hurled himself forward over the last short distance between. The ground was beginning to feel soft and hungry under his feet, but he was not aware of that; not aware of anything save the man waiting for him, dirk in hand, and the dirk in his own hand and the high red killer-singing inside his own head. Only the two of them in the dream; even the rest of the hunt had ceased to exist. For an instant he saw the bared teeth and widened eyes of the man who had killed Red Thorstein, his lord, as he dived in under the snake strike of the Pictish blade. He felt the dull shock, and grating of blade on bone as his own blade went in above the collar bones into the taut throat. And the thrust burst the dream and let in reality. Let in the faint shiver of cool air off the bog, and the sharp cry of a raven sweeping overhead – and the man still rocking on his feet for a moment before sagging to his knees, twisting over as he fell, so that he lay face up among the bog grasses.

And the face was the face of the young Pict he had seen three days since, hacked down beside Jarl Sigurd's funeral pyre. Staring down at it, Bjarni felt the hair lift on the back of his neck, as old winter's night tales of slain warriors returning from the dead flickered through his mind. The same long narrow face, still almost beardless, the same dark hair springing back from the same warrior-patterned fore-head, the same look in the wide eyes and snarling back-drawn lips. And then he saw that one thing was different; the twisted silver arm-ring above the right elbow, the same but worn on the other arm; and no white mark on the other, as there would have been if for any reason it had been changed. Brothers, maybe twins! The twin sons of Melbrigda Tusk. And the thing, which for a splinter of time had been nightmare, became Blood Feud.

There was a great deal of blood, pumping from the red gash in the man's neck, then from other wounds on his breast and belly and flanks, as others of the hunt came crowding round, each fiercely eager to have a share in the kill. Bjarni, stooping to clean his dirk on a grass tussock, realised that his feet were half gone into black ooze, and hurriedly pulled up first one and then the other.

'Best get him onto solid ground before we all stick in this putrid mess,' he said, quite casually, as though it were a deer that they had brought down; but now that the dream was gone from him, his heart was lurching oddly over the cold sickness in his belly.

They hauled the body of the young Pict back from the salt ground, bound his ankles together with his own quiver strap for easy hauling – no particular point in getting back to the rest of the war-band looking and smelling more like a slaughter house than need be – and set out over their hunting trail, dragging him behind them.

When they got back, the noon camp was breaking up and making ready to move off, horses being saddled, men gathering up weapons and gear, and over all, tangible as brewing thunder, a sense of sullen anger that was more than the anger of men whose lord has been slain, and in the midst of all, Thorstein Olafson lay wrapped close in his striped silken cloak, with Erp squatting beside him, with the remains of the arrow that he had drawn out still in his hands. Close by, the captain of the war-band stood watching the final lashing of a hurdle of saplings and branches that had been made ready.

He looked round when the hunters tumbled the hacked body of the young Pict at his feet, and said, 'The hunting was good?'

'The hunting was good,' they agreed, breathing hard.

'And it seems that the kill was the work of many.'

Bjarni was not going to claim it. He was not at all sure that he wanted to claim it. But Ottar Erikson, giving credit where it was due, said, 'Bjarni Sigurdson was first blade at the killing.'

'I am thinking he was kin to the man who came seeking Melbrigda's head and would have slain Jarl Guthorm,' Bjarni said in explanation, as though explanation were needed.

'Aye,' said Egil the captain, looking down at the battered body at his feet, 'if yon's the way of it, Blood Feud it would be.'

Bjarni said, only half in question, 'So we turn south again to collect the blood price,' and heard eager agreement from the young men around him.

'Blood Feud, I said, and you, it seems, have already collected the blood price. But even if it were not so – ' Egil's voice took on the weary growl of one who has said the same thing before, and more than once – 'still it is for us who are the war-band of Thorstein Olafson to hold on northward to raise the shield ring round the Lady Aud his mother in case of further trouble, and to follow her ruling in the matter afterwards.'

Then Bjarni understood the atmosphere of sullen resentment, of revolt only just held in check, that he had felt throughout the camp.

'She is only a woman,' Ottar Erikson spluttered. 'It is not for her – ' and his protest was echoed by the rest of the hunters. Other men were gathering round them, men already leading their horses, men hot-eyed and sullen, fiddling with their weapons, as the thing that had been settled once began to unravel again like a frayed cloak.

Egil let out a roar like a mountain bear. 'Name of thunder! She is the woman of Red Thorstein's fleet and war-bands and settlements, whom men call the Deep-Minded, for the wisdom that is in her!' He fetched a deep breath, and went on more quietly, 'Hast forgotten that we came into Caithness not as raiders to fire a few farms and carry off the church gold, but to make new homes, new settlements when the fighting is over, which is a matter as much for the women as for the men? Therefore, whatever comes later, for this time we ride on north.'

And a short while later they rode on north, the huge body of Thorstein the Red, Thorstein Olafson, borne on its hurdle in their midst, and the body of the young Pict left lying behind them for the wolves and the hooded crows.

But Erp and Bjarni, riding two of the war-band's fastest horses, were away ahead of them, their orders to make the winter camp with all speed, and carry the black news to Aud the Deep-Minded.

They rode hard, halting only for a few hours in the darkest part of the night. They haltered the horses and turned them loose to graze. It was then, while they gnawed their way through their dry bannock, that Bjarni came out with the question that had been nagging at him since noon. 'He must have come tracking us all the way. That time when the horses were restless for no reason ... Why did he come so far? He cannot have been waiting his chance; there were other chances just as good. He must have followed us clear off his own hunting-ground so that the country was strange to him; which is why we got him, on the edge of a bog that he didn't know was there.'

'If it was Blood Feud,' Erp said slowly, 'a thing only between him and Red Thorstein, and having nought to do with the rest of his people, then he would have no wish to make war-fire in the heather again. He would do his killing well clear of his tribal territories.'

A light wind had begun to rise, hushing through the heather, and a spattering of rain blew into their faces. 'That is what you would do?' Bjarni said at last.

'That is what I would do if I were free and taking vengeance for a brother slain.'

Well before dawn they had saddled up and were on their way once more. A low dawn and a day of worsening weather; and way past noon with a wind roaring down from the north-west and the rain-mist driving in great swaths across the hills, they came up the slope from the river marshes and in through the gap in the camp stockade, and dropped from their weary horses in the garth.

'Where is the Lady?' Bjarni demanded of a man who came to take the horses.

'What news?' the man demanded.

'No news,' Bjarni said, 'until herself has heard it first.' But his voice told well enough.

'In the bower,' somebody told them out of the gathering crowd. The air was full of urgent questioning, but no one asked again. Maybe because no one needed to.

In the Women's House Aud sat beside the turf fire, stitching at a garment of dark green wool, Muirgoed also stitching beside her, and at their feet the two remaining granddaughters squatted, spinning somewhat lumpy and uneven thread with deep concentration, Lilla, the youngest, with her tongue stuck out of the side of her mouth. They had all looked up, hearing someone coming, and for a moment as he checked on the threshold, Bjarni saw the whole scene caught like a fly in amber. Then Muirgoed said in a high chill whisper, 'Did I not say I heard his voice in the wind, passing out over the sea? Aiee! Aiee! – '

And the two spinners dropped spindle and distaff and broke out into a frightened wailing.

'Muirgoed, take the bairns into the sleeping place,' Aud said very quietly, her lips scarcely moving. And when they were gone she spoke only one word, 'Dead?'

'Dead,' Bjarni said heavily.

There was a moment's pause, and he heard the wind and rain hushing across the thatch.

Then she said, 'In battle? But of course in battle.'

Bjarni shook his head. 'Not in battle, the fighting was over when we got to the Jarl's camp. An arrow out of the trees on our way north again.'

Aud drew a long shuddering breath. But she was so used to being responsible for the well-being of men that when she spoke again, she said, 'You are as two drowned men dripping on the threshold. Come you closer to the fire.' And when they had done as she bade them, 'Sit now, while you tell me what there is to tell.'

And they obeyed her, the warmth of the burning peat feeling good to their sodden and weary bodies. And with Erp, who had never in all his thrall years sat in the Lady's presence before, putting in a word where needful from time to time, Bjarni stumbled through the whole dark story, of Jarl Sigurd's death and howe-laying, and the Peace Fire afterwards, of Melbrigda's head, and the two young Picts, his sons. Of the arrow out of the birch woods by the ford. 'There is no more,' he finished. 'They are bringing him back – by tomorrow's noon they should be here. But the Captain bade us ride ahead to bring you the word.'

A gust of wind beat like great wings across the thatch, and a flurry of rain spattered hissing into the fire. And the Lady Aud, who had remained silent, her eyes fixed on his face the while, gave a small shudder. 'Cheerless lying he will have tonight,' she said.

'They will find shelter for him,' Bjarni said. How stupid that sounded; but it was the best he could do.

And Erp with a kind of heavy gentleness said, 'There will be many cloaks gladly given to shield him from the rain.'

The Lady Aud bundled up the green garment that she had been sewing, and got up. 'Go now and get food and then sleep,' she said as they lurched to their feet after her. And that was all.

But Bjarni remembered afterward how for that one instant she stood holding the bundled cloth in her arms and looking down at the dark green folds exactly as a woman holds a bairn in her arms and looks down at the small face turned against her breast . . . Then she turned and went to deal with the sounds of grief and fear beyond the curtain of the sleeping place.

Erp and Bjarni looked at each other a moment, then turned and went out into a wild grey world, to look for food and sleep as she had bidden them, and answer the demands for news of the men who came crowding round them.

*

Some while after noon on the following day the war-band returned, bearing Red Thorstein on his branch-woven litter in their midst.

The bare earth of the Hearth Hall floor had been strewn with fresh bracken, yellow-tipped with the first fires of autumn in readiness, and the Lady Aud his mother stood dry-eyed on the threshold to receive him. And there, with torches to light the gloom, and the storm still beating its wings about the roof, she and Muirgoed, the only grown women in the camp, did for him the ancient work of womenkind, making him fair and decent for his howe-laying.

And all the rest of that day, in his striped silken cloak and a great black bearskin over all, he lay by torchlight, with his hearth companions taking turns to guard him, while out on the hill shoulder above the camp where the land looked toward the sea, other men built his funeral pyre.

The rain had ceased, but it was hard to find wood dry enough for burning; and there was no lightning-struck tree to hand, as there had been for Jarl Sigurd, six days ago. They gathered drift-wood from the estuary, scoured the nearer fringes of the forest for dead branches and brushwood, and the open hillside for furze. Pitch they brought up from the boat-strand. And in the dark of the night Dungadr and a handful of his companions came riding over from the head-land rath, with a couple of farm sleds piled with dried peats and great jars of the fiery rye spirit. News travels fast in the wilderness.

All that night and the day after, preparation for the Chief's last rites, his arval, went on, while Thorstein lay in his Hall with a dish of salt on his still breast and torches burning at his head and feet; the pyre growing high on the hill shoulder, the hunting parties out in the woods after deer and boar for the cooking pits that were already heating behind the Hall.

At evening on the third day, they bore the chief from his Hall, up the open hillside to where the fire-stack waited for him. The sea wind blew his red beard all one way and made zigzag partings in the fur of the black bear as they lifted him up to the flat top. There were no beasts for sacrifice this time, but Brother Ninian, the Lady Aud's Priest, standing out at the head of the pyre in his brown habit with his bell and his staff, speaking words for a Christian burial. Bjarni did not hear the words; he was thinking, 'Two pyres in nine days. This is an ill harvest time.'

The torches were thrust deep into the base of the pyre, and the flame ran hesitatingly at first in threads of brightness among the stacked peats. Bjarni watched a red tongue licking round a pitch-daubed branch, delicately as though savouring it, then bursting into a greedy rush of flame. The fire began to crackle as the flame took hold, and the smell of burning pitch rolled inland in a choking cloud, flecked with flying sparks. Somebody shouted and pointed, and Bjarni, looking that way with the rest, saw across the wild swinging waters of the Pentland Firth, fire on the high headland of Hoy, answering theirs like a beacon, and knew that Orkney, left without its own Jarl, was sending a wordless message.

In the grey dawn with the shore birds crying all about them, the pyre fell in over its own glowing heart. And when the heart had ceased to glow, they raked in the speckled ash, and began to pile stones and rocks and turf over the fire scar on the hill shoulder, so that here too, as above that other firth away to the south, there should stand a sea-mark for passing ships in the years to come.

*

In the open garth of the winter camp other fires were
burning as the day drew in to the long northern twilight. But these were fires for the living. All day the
arval had been going on, as men trailed back from
building the howe for a draught of ale and something
to eat, and then went back to add a few more stones to
the growing pile. But now the cairn building was over
for that time and men were gathering more and more
thickly to the space before the makeshift Hall. The
cooking pits had been opened and the fatty reek of
baked meat filled the air. A pile of peats had been
made into a seat for the Lady Aud before the entrance
to the Hall, and she sat there on a spread silver sealskin. Lilla and Signy sat huddled against her knees
and Muirgoed, her bower woman who had been a
queen herself in her day, in her usual place in the
shadows behind her.

Dungadr and his companions had gone, back to the
headland fort and his new young bride. Bjarni had
thought to see her with her sisters; but her place was
at her husband's hearth now, and no longer at her
father's. He thought it might have been a kindness all
the same, both to her and the Lady Aud, even more
of a kindness than sled-loads of peats and rye spirit.

He said as much to Erp, but Erp had said only,
'Other peoples, other ways. It would have been the
same in Argyll.'

The night was far spent, the feasting was over and
eyes were growing brighter and tongues looser as the
ale went round. Laughter woke and spread through
the crowd, mingled with boasts of vengeance and of
mighty deeds in the past or not yet actually done –
here and there the sudden spitting flare of a quarrel
that for the most part died away as quickly as it had
risen. Here and there a man reached for the Hall harp
as he felt a song coming upon him – whether or no

anyone wanted to listen was beside the point, the thing that mattered was the urge to give tongue.

Then Egil the Captain rose in his place, his ale-horn in his hand; and the men nearest to him drew closer to listen, then others beyond them, and so on, until the whole camp – and those of the war-bands still sober enough to know what was in the wind – were shifting, closing in through the firelit dark.

The Captain looked about him, then drank off his ale-horn and shook out the last drops upon the ground. Then he began in a loud sing-song voice, the storyteller's voice, to tell the death-tale of Red Thorstein Olafson. He had told it all before, briefly and level voiced to the Lady Aud, but this was another thing, this was the Death Telling without which no chieftain should be howe-laid, the telling which later would be reshaped and enriched by the harpers and woven into the sagas of the folk.

Better it would have been if Thorstein had died in battle and not of an arrow loosed from hiding, but Egil did his best with the story. And the Lady Aud listened, her eyes unwavering on his face, as she had listened to Bjarni, four days ago.

When it was over, she said, 'That was a fine telling, Egil, and from my heart I thank you for it.'

But there had begun to be a murmuring among the crowding warriors, and their Captain, still standing with his empty ale-horn in his hand, said, 'Lady, there is another thing.'

'Speak it then,' said the Lady Aud; and there was a faint bracing of her shoulders, a tightening of all the lines of her face, to tell that she knew – and had known for four days – what thing it was.

'There are those among us, the younger men for the most part,' Egil said, 'who were for turning south again at once, to exact the wergild, the blood price, for Thorstein Olafson in split skulls and burned thatch.'

'Yet you held on north,' said the Lady. 'That was well done.'

'We came to bring the Chief's body back for howe-laying, and to form the shield ring for his mother and his bairns if need be. We came also, Lady, for your ruling in this matter.'

There was a raw, rebellious muttering here and there. The Lady Aud was the Mother of the Folk, but this was man's work, and she was only a woman, after all.

The Lady heard it, and rose a little stiffly to her feet and stood confronting them in the firelight; and little by little the muttering died away.

When she had the war-band silent, she spoke to them, partly as though she were a man herself – she had always had a man's eye for the shape of events, and a man's ability to weigh one thing clearly against another – partly as though she were the mother of them all.

'Out of all that I have heard in the four days that are past, two things stand clear, and the first of them is this: that the death of the Chief, my son, was no killing on the war-trail, but a slaying carried out in Blood Feud, even as Egil the Captain tells, and the debt has already been repaid. There is nothing more that is called for, in all honour!' She was silent a moment, holding them all with her gaze. Then she spoke again. 'The second thing is this, that you came here following your Lord, as the men of Orkney came following theirs, not for a raiding summer, to make a shore-killing of black cattle, and carry off a booty of gold and slaves, and sail home at harvest leaving the smoke of burning thatch behind you. This was in part a war-trail, true, but a war-trail meant for the gaining of a foothold that should lead to peace talks and treaty making, for settlement in a new land. Now the fighting is done – for the main part – and the time for settlement is come; and peace is better held together by marriage bonds and the ties of fostering – I am told that there was talk of the giving and taking of foster-sons, in the south – than by the death of more and always more men.'

'This is strange talk for the Viking kind to be listening to,' growled an old ship chief, 'and I am one that's had enough of it.'

But the Lady Aud singled him out with a half-smile for an old friend. 'Maybe so, Ranulf Ormson, yet listen to it, none the less, and remember it well, for the sake of the settlements that will grow up in river mouths, for the sake of women and bairns brought from old hearths grown cold to sit by new ones that are not yet lit, baking bannock from harvest not yet sown. In the name of the White Christ, listen to me, and remember when I am not here to say it all again.'

A startled breath ran through the crowd. She had been a part of their lives so long ... and Egil said hotly, 'Lady, you are not yet old!'

She looked at him, and then round at the startled faces in the light of the arval torches, and laughed, very softly, as at the foolishness of men. 'Na, na, not that. Yet I feel myself suddenly too old, and without the heart in me, for the building of a new world. I have no place nor kin here in Caithness, no place nor kin back in the Islands; but in Iceland I have kinsfolk still, brothers whom I have not seen for many years. Therefore in the spring when the voyaging season starts; when certain other plans of mine are worked out, I shall go to join them.'

And the men of the war-bands knew that there was no more to be said.

16

The Ship and the Dark Woods

The inland forest of Caithness was like nothing that
Bjarni had ever known before: a dark whispering
fleece of wind-shaped pines islanded with stunted
dwarf oak and ash and tangled masses of thorn. Dying
trees were propped up by those still living, while
underneath both were the trunks of dead giants that
had fallen and rotted away to timber, where an
unwary step might send one crashing through into
an ants' nest. And always there was a sense of the
forest having a life of its own, eyes of its own,
watching, unseen menace among the trees.

Through the forest a peat-brown river, deep enough
to float a merchant ship though too narrow for her to
be worked in any way save by ropes from the shores,
looped its way down towards the rocky coast below
Dungadr's stronghold. In one place on the western
bank, the trees fell back into a ragged clearing and
there, as the last lees of late summer turned to full
autumn, a stockade camp was coming into being, a
camp of turf and timber bothies squatting round
a low-roomed oddly boat-shaped longhouse that was

to be winter shelter for the Lady Aud and all her household.

There was no reason as far as the men raising it could see why the ship her heart hungered for should not have been built on the ship-strand back at the main settlement, while the Lady remained safely among the rest of the Mull men. But no, on the very day after the arval she had decreed that *Seal Maiden* should be built in the forest, where trees for timber were close to hand; and furthermore she herself would spend her winter with the builders, that she might watch her ship come to life.

It did not seem reasonable. Bjarni said so to Erp as they worked side by side, making fast the ropes to bind the turf roof on the longhouse through the winter storms.

Erp spat on his hands to get a better grip on the rope he was securing. 'Not reasonable, maybe no,' he said thoughtfully. 'But none so hard to understand all the same. Likely she hates and even fears the settlement; that smells of her son's death. Maybe she wants the darkness and the wild, as a sore-hurt animal wants them – a place to be away with dignity in her grieving.'

Bjarni looked round at him a moment in surprise, then turned back to the work under his hands, saying nothing more.

With the stockade built and the longhouse finished so that there was shelter for the Lady Aud, there was less urgency about the rest of the camp. Some tasks were done in the shipwrights' bothies, but it was on the river below the camp that the real work was going on as the length of open bank, cleared of scrub, became a ship-strand, and in the forest the felling-axes rang early and late as men searched out and felled curved and crooked trunks and branches that would best serve for the curved ribs and cross-pieces of a ship. And already, the first thing of all, the heart and centre of all that was going on, between securing-piles on a levelled stretch of the bank, lay a great edge-hewn oak trunk that would be the keel of the ship which, in the spring, would carry the Lady Aud on her Iceland faring. Soon the curved stem and stern posts were in place, giving to *Seal Maiden* something of herself, something of the pride and grace that would be hers when she took to the water.

All along the bank as the autumn drew on and the river ran gold with fallen birch-leaves, men with adze and chisel were splitting and shaping the green timbers into planks, and the planks were being steamed over pits of hot stones and clamped into the curves of the ship's sides, and the smith had set up his forge and was working on the iron bolts that would presently hold her together in the northern seas.

For the most part the work was done under the eye of a couple of skilled shipwrights from the main fleet by the men who would presently sail her, and by the crew of *Fionoula*, which lay in the lower reaches of the river below the white water, with only a skeleton crew on board, ready for whatever need the Lady might have of her.

By day, the sounds of camp and ship-strand kept the noises of the forest at a distance, but at night when man-made sounds fell silent, then the voice of the forest woke and the forest itself seemed to draw nearer in the darkness. Wolves cried closer beyond the stockade as the dark and cold of the year drew on, so that they kept torches burning at the corners of the camp, and men sat up with axes across their knees, anxious for the small scrub horses corralled within the stockade.

Winter came stalking them like a white beast

through the trees, with gales and rain giving place to the stillness of deep frost; then the white smother of snow, then back to gales and rain. Shipbuilding went on whenever the weather was open enough, and every shipbuilding day the Lady Aud came down, wrapped to the eyes in her warm hooded seal-skin cloak, to see how the work went forward. It was a harsh winter, but a changeable one, with times when the river iced up under the bank – the churned mud of the camp was solid ice under foot, and the hunting was hard, so that despite the oats and the salted meat in the store-shed, everyone was wearing a lean and hungry look before the end of it. But there were patches of open weather, and the seaways were never quite closed. Twice, *Fionoula* put to sea, and from time to time messengers came and went between Orkney and Shetland and beyond and the clearing in the Caithness forest where the graceful skeleton of *Seal Maiden* grew daily more like a ship. And by winter's end the Lady Aud, never one to turn from the thing that needed doing next, had completed marriage treaties for Lilla and Signy, one in Orkney and one in the Faroe Islands. The blood-line of Thorstein Olafson would run strongly in the island world through the years to come.

When the ice broke up for the last time under the banks, and the black alder catkins had begun to lengthen, *Seal Maiden* was nearly ready for the seaways, a clinker-built merchantman to carry women and goods and gear on the Iceland faring, and deep in the draft and broad in the beam accordingly, yet with something of a longship's grace about her none the less, and with the seal-head of her prow up-reared as though she craned her neck to glimpse above the tree tops the seaways that waited for her.

And the five years of Bjarni's outlawing would soon
be up.

Through the long winter moons while *Seal Maiden*
grew on her slipway among the trees, Bjarni had not
thought about that at all, he had not thought about
the outside world, nor the passing of time. It had not
seemed as though there was anything beyond the
winter and the trees, but now with the first stirrings
of the still-distant spring, the changed smell of the
wind, the fluttering of the small birds among the riverside scrub, there began to be a restlessness in him as
though, with the waking of the forest, his own sap
was rising too, a restlessness that was one with the
wild geese in their northward flighting. But he did
not know his direction as the wild geese seemed to
do.

The day came when *Seal Maiden*, her sides painted
and her seams caulked, was ready for her launching.
They set rollers under her and then, shoulders to her
flanks, ran her down the bank, shouting at the feel of
her grow live and buoyant as the river took her.
Already her sails and cordage had been brought from
the main winter camp, and soon they would be loaded
along with the stores and the women's kists onto
the sleds that had been used for timber hauling all the
winter, and her crew would pole her down-river, por-
taging her past the white water where the salmon
were already leaping, to the broader, quieter waters
where she would be finally readied for the open sea.

The wolves no longer cried so close about the camp
as they had done in the moons of full winter, but they
still cried close enough from time to time and it was
better to be safe than risk the loss of a pony. The
watchfires burned night-long at the corners of the
camp. On the night following the launching, Bjarni
and Erp took their turn on guard, as they had so many

nights before, at the corner close to the pony corral that reached towards the river and the boat-strand, where the new ship which last night had been a dark shape on the chocks now rode, a thing new-come to life, waiting for her mast to be stepped and her great sail to blossom out on the paleness of the water.

Erp had a broken piece of hauling-harness on his knee, and a length of fresh rope to mend it. In the passing of those forest months, he had come more to be a kind of steward to the Lady Aud; not that there was much in her household that needed a steward's overseeing; but anything that had to do with the needs of the horses, it seemed, was still Erp's affair.

It seemed to Bjarni that the wolves were howling closer again tonight, with a new note, almost a note of triumph in their crying. In the corral behind him, the little scrub horses were restless.

'You'd think they knew,' he said.

Erp looked up from the rope he was splicing by the light of the watchfire. 'Who? And knew what?'

'The wolves – that soon all this will be theirs again. And the wildwood will come creeping in again over the fire scars, and the turf walls will shrink away, and it will be as though we had never been here at all.'

'You sound like a harper,' said Erp, smiling a little at the rope in his hands. 'Also you sound a shade regretful. Has life been so sweet, here among the trees?'

'Na, na, it's not that, it's – my five years are almost up.'

'Surely that is a matter for rejoicing, you can go back to your own settlement and your own Chief.'

Bjarni threw another branch on the fire and gave a baffled shake of the head. 'Aye. Yet it seems a poor-spirited thing to do, as if I had spent the whole five years since I was cast out waiting to crawl back at the first moment.'

'Aye, and you had thought to be the Emperor of Byzantium by now,' Erp said without mockery. He let the half-spliced rope fall on his knee to give Bjarni his full attention. 'There are other ways open. I am very sure that you can go with the Lady Aud on this Iceland faring, or you can remain in Caithness with the new settlements, or return to Mull – or simply take your sword and look for another sword-service. Plenty of markets for a good reliable blade.'

Bjarni was silent, gazing into the watchfire. Again, far off in the trees, a wolf howled in the darkness. Somehow none of Erp's suggested ways seemed the right one, not even the last, or rather there was nothing to tell him which, if any, was the right one.

'I was wondering, I might try the Dublin garrison again. The captain bade me go and grow myself a beard.' He rubbed his hand against the crispness of hair on his chin. 'I don't know – it's as though I were waiting for a wind to rise . . .'

Erp sat quietly for a while, working on his rope. 'I will tell you a thing,' he said at last, speaking so seriously that Bjarni, who had been sitting with his arms around his knees, staring into the fire, sat up straight and looked round at him with an altered gaze. 'You are not in truth the stuff that mercenaries are made of. Some men can sell their sword-service like a new saddle or a bale of hay – strike a fair bargain and abide by it, to the death if need be, needing nothing more. You are not one of them. For you there needs to be another kind of loyalty. You're one of those fools who needs to follow your way for reasons of your roots behind you and the heart within your breast. Your five years are up. Go back to your own settlement.'

Bjarni stared at him in surprise. 'Three summer months' trading or raiding, and the rest of the year sweating over the in-take land to bring it to harvest?'

'Why not?' said Erp easily. 'It's the life you were looking for before you held your holy man's head too long under water.'

Anger rose in Bjarni's throat, while at the same time he knew that what Erp said was true. 'That's the kind of advice you might expect from a thrall!' The words seemed to burst out of their own accord. He heard them hanging in the air, and would have given everything he possessed, little as it was, to call them back again. For a moment there was an odd look in the other's face. Then, still more angry and not altogether sure what about, he reached out and grabbed the breast folds of Erp's cloak. 'I didn't say that! You hear? I didn't say that.' He started to shake him to underline the words, and the shoulder brooch tore away and the loosened folds fell open. There was something lacking, something that had always been there was not there any more . . . It was a moment before he realised that it was the iron thrall-ring; and the light of the watch-fire showed the band of thickened white skin round Erp's neck, where it had been. He raised his eyes to the other's face, and for a moment they looked at each other in silence, while Bjarni forgot his anger in this new thing.

'When?' he asked.

'This evening after supper,' Erp said lightly as though he spoke of some small and passing matter. 'On the day *Seal Maiden* took to the water.'

'And so you're free from the Iceland faring,' Bjarni said, an idea beginning in his head. 'Your mother too?'

'My mother will never leave the Lady Aud.'

'But you,' Bjarni persisted, 'you're free; we could head for Dublin or the like, together!'

Erp shook his head. 'There could come a day ...
but meanwhile, free or no, I am the Lady Aud's man
still, while she has need of her own about her.'

And looking at him still in the glow of the watch-
fire, Bjarni was making a discovery, and his face
cracked slowly into a smile. 'You're another of the
fools who needs to follow your way for reasons of
the heart within your breast!' he said. And he thought,
but did not say, You might be worth listening to, after
all!

In the next few days, Bjarni thought a good deal on
Erp's advice, though he still lacked the thing that led
the wild geese: he was still waiting for the wind to
rise. But it was worth thinking of, all the same.

He was still thinking, two days later, as he came up
the newly-cleared portage way towards the camp. The
Lady Aud had wished word of some sort taken down-
river to *Fionoula*, as she had wished it more than once
during the winter when milder weather opened the
forest ways each time, and as before, Brother Ninian,
her chaplain, had gone as her messenger with a couple
of the ship-carles to see him safely back again.

This time it was Bjarni and Orm Anderson. They
had been late starting back, for Brother Ninian had
been seized with the desire to pray with *Fionoula*'s
crew, and when the need for prayer came upon
Brother Ninian he lost all sense of the passing of time.
So the day was fading fast, the still-wintry twilight
lying like smoke among the trees, and the white water
of the salmon leap was gathering a faint light of its
own. The three men walked in hunting file, Brother
Ninian in the lead, his head bowed and his crossed
hands lost in the sleeves of his habit, probably still in
prayer, Bjarni thought, following a little behind, and
last of all, Orm, the biggest of the three, to cover their
rear. They should have had Brother Ninian in the

middle, but the chaplain was, as he said himself, not a man to follow other men, but only the light of God. Well, as long as he did not fall into an ants' nest, or blunder down the bank into the river . . .

The dusk was crowding in on them more closely now, the night-time sounds of the wildwood beginning to wake. At least, Bjarni hoped they were the ordinary night-time sounds of the wildwood; they sounded not quite the same out here as they did from within the stockade. The great forest of Caithness was no place for mortal men to be abroad in the night, for there were other and darker dangers than wild beasts among the trees . . .

The camp was not far now; once he thought he heard one of the hunting dogs bark on the farmost edge of hearing; but the bark did not come again to hold the other sounds at bay. It was good at least to hear the brush and tramp of Orm coming along behind him, and feel that there was someone at his back. Then a new thought came upon him, lifting the hairs on the back of his neck. How did he know that it was still Orm behind him, and not some nameless horror that had taken Orm's place? Calling himself all kinds of a fool, he snatched a quick glance behind him. Difficult to see in the dusk and among the riverside scrub, but certainly the figure lurching along in the rear had the familiar large and slightly lumbering shape of Orm Anderson.

With a quick breath of relief, Bjarni turned face forward again. But almost in the same moment he heard a stumbling crash and a curse from the man behind him. 'What's amiss?' he called back.

'Broken my shoe-thong – keep going – I'll catch up with you – '

Bjarni hesitated. A man stooping to mend a broken shoe-thong here would be open to any attack that

might come upon him. But Orm could look out for
himself well enough – his task was to get the chaplain
safely back to camp.

He went on, after the dark hooded shape that was
beginning to blend into the twilight; listening all the
while for the sounds of Orm coming up again behind.
But all he heard was the faint panting sound that was
the breathing of the forest itself – or his own fear.

Then with a kind of coughing snarl, a giant blackness arose from the undergrowth straight ahead. For
a splinter of time it was just blackness without shape,
one of the troll kind, the terrors of the wildwood,
eaters of men and the souls of men. Then it reared up
roaring, taller than a man, and showed its proper
shape; the shape of a great forest bear, newly woken
from its winter sleep, famished and savage and in
red-eyed mood to kill anything that came its way;
maybe heading for the salmon run, until men had
crossed its track.

Bjarni saw the massive up-reared head and huge
powerful forefeet raised. He saw Brother Ninian fling
up his arms in a futile attempt to protect himself. He
was not aware of whipping out his dirk, but it was
naked in his hand as he sprang forward. He hurled
the chaplain aside into a hazel bush, drawing back
his arm to strike. The great head with gaping jaws
towered above his own, the fetid stink of the huge
brute was in his throat. The snarling roar seemed to
shake the forest as he drove in the blade; and in the
same instant, a blow from the huge forepaw on
the side of his head sent him reeling, the curved claws
raking down his cheek and shoulder. Bjarni, his head
instinctively drawn sideways into his shoulder to
protect the place where the life-blood runs through its
channel close beneath the skin, heard through the
furious roaring of the bear and his own yelling, Orm's

voice behind him and the sounds of the other man crashing through the undergrowth. Next instant the mighty forearms were around him, and the life was being crushed out of him against the hot hairy body. Somehow he managed to drag his arm free, the dirk still clenched in his hand, and drove in a second blow. The creature's roaring changed to a kind of coughing snarl – blood began to come out of its gaping jaws; then another dirk struck in beside his own, the crushing grip about his ribs slackened, and the whole hairy mass sagged forward like a mountain falling.

Bjarni was underneath the fallen mountain and its blackness was flowing up, up through him. There was blood everywhere, the smell of it hot and rank, his own or the bear's, he did not know which. He did not know anything very clearly. But the great twitching weight was being heaved off him, and he was being dragged clear. He had no idea of time passing, nor of the order in which things happened, but he heard voices, Orm's and the chaplain's, without any idea of what they said. He felt the chill of river-water sluicing over him, and his shoulder being lashed up with strips from somebody's sark, probably his own.

And then somehow he was on his feet on ground that lifted and fell under him like the deck of a galley in a swell, with his arms across other men's shoulders so that they took most of his weight, which reminded him of something but he couldn't think what. His head felt as though there was a swarm of bees in it, and he couldn't think through the buzzing that they made.

'The bear,' he mumbled, 'just a bear after all.'

'The bear's dead,' someone said. 'We'll fetch it later if the wolves don't get it first. The thing now is to get you back to camp.'

He had no clear remembrance of getting back to

camp at all; but a time came when he was back within the stockade, and there were faces around him in the light of a torch that someone had brought, and a smother of voices. And then the Lady Aud's voice clear among the rest, bidding him be brought into the store-room behind the longhouse.

Then he was lying on piled skins in the midst of a pool of torchlight and Muirgoed, with her patient horse's face bent close above him, was tending the gashes to his neck and jaw and shoulder, while Erp kneeling beside her held his arms tilted outward to keep the wounds open for thorough bathing. There had only been a kind of numbness in his shoulder, but now he felt as though he had been branded with hot irons, and quite suddenly the bee-buzzing in his head became booming darkness that swallowed up the torchlight . . .

The next thing he saw was the ash-coloured light of morning beyond the outer door-hole of the bothy. He had the kind of headache that came of drinking too much heather-ale, and breast and ribs and shoulder felt as though a galley had been launched across him. Exploring with his free hand, he found bandage-linen, and the memory of the bear came back, and close behind it the memory of Brother Ninian with his arms flung up against the huge darkness with the snarling jaws.

Something, someone, moved beside him, and for a moment his heart lurched into his throat. But it was only Muirgoed with fresh bandage-linen in her hands. 'Brother Ninian?' he croaked.

It was the Lady Aud, standing behind her, who answered. 'It is well with Brother Ninian, and he is even now giving thanks to God for his preservation.' A faint note of amusement crept into her voice. 'I also give thanks to God for my chaplain's life; but it is in my mind that something of my thanks is due also to you.'

Bjarni mumbled something in reply, but scarcely took in what she said, leaving it, as it were, to be taken out and looked at another time.

Later in the day, when Muirgoed had tended his raked flesh and fed him barley-gruel with something bitter-tasting in it, and he had slept again, he woke again to a feeling of great quietness not unlike the quietness he had known that last morning on Iona. There was a small seal-oil lamp burning in the corner of the bothy, and beyond the door-hole the dusk was blue, with a first star hanging above the dark shape of the wildwood. A wonderful blue, deep and yet translucent as though the light were shining through it from the other side. Bjarni had never seen such blueness, and yet – it reminded him of something – somewhere – a long time ago. He lay wondering what it was: and then suddenly he had it – his blue glass dolphin that he had left in the glen where he had buried it, five years ago. Every detail of the glen, the birch trees and the narrow brown brawling beck, was suddenly clear to him. Five years, and at either end of them a holy man, one dead because of him, one alive because of him. And now the quietness; and the blue beyond the store-shed door . . .

Afterwards he wondered whether it was because he had quite nearly been dead himself such a short while ago that he had the quietness and the feeling of one skin less than usual between him and the next life; and of having come to the place for staying quite still for a breath of time and then making a fresh start. But most men came close enough to being dead a few times in their lives: more likely it had been something in the gruel that Muirgoed had given him. At the time he did not wonder about it at all, but just accepted it.

Sleep took him back again; and the next time he
awoke, the world had returned to its familiar
everyday self. But he did not quite forget . . .

He lay in the store-shed for four days, sleeping a
good deal of the time, tended by Muirgoed and by
Erp, while the last preparations for the Iceland faring
went on all about him. He began to sleep less, the
claw marks on his cheek and shoulder were healing
cleanly, and the raging headache he had first woken
with had faded to an echo of pain somewhere just
inside his skull. On the fifth morning he began to be
restive and started demanding his spare sark so that
he could get up. 'Not yet,' Muirgoed said. 'Bide one
more day.'

And Bjarni subsided, grumbling. Later he would be
alone, then he would get up and wrap the sealskin
rug around his nakedness and go and find his spare
sark for himself. But maybe Muirgoed, who had
nursed other young men in her time, recognised the
rather too sudden giving-in, and knew what it meant.
At all events, Bjarni found himself very seldom left
alone in the hours that followed. Some while after
noon, men arrived from Thorstein's settlement, and
Aud must go to welcome them and discuss the
matters that had brought them there, with Muirgoed
to get food and drink for them, while Erp was away
seeing to some trouble amongst the sled horses. Bjarni,
gathering something of what was happening, was just
about to take his chance when the small figures of
Lilla and Signy appeared through the door-hole, and
squatted down on their heels side by side at the foot
of his makeshift bed. They had been in and out a few
times in the past days, bringing his food and holding
the wound-salve for Muirgoed when she came to
dress his shoulder, for they were of an age now where

they must become used to such things. But this was different. This time they had come to stay.

Bjarni glowered at them. 'And what is it that you do here?'

'Muirgoed and our grandmother bade us come,' Signy, the elder of the two, explained clearly and kindly. 'We are to bide here until someone comes back, to make sure that you do not get up – because you are to bide still one more day, Muirgoed said.'

'And if I get up all the same, you will stop me?'

'But you will not do that, will you?' Signy said.

And Lilla put in beseechingly, 'Please, let you not – because you are in our care.'

Bjarni drew his knees to his chin under the sealskin rugs, and sat looking at them while they sat and looked back. For the moment it was in his mind to get up all the same. But to do that would make the bairns look small and foolish, not able to carry out the task that had been given to them. And fool that he was, he couldn't do that – which was exactly what the Lady Aud and her bower woman were relying on.

Lilla, who had something bundled in her arms, pushed back the folds of her cloak and took out a harp. 'We brought this. We thought maybe you would tell us a story or make us a song, to pass the time,' and she leaned forward and propped it against his knee.

Anything, Bjarni thought, would be better than sitting and staring at each other until rescue came. He took up the small well-worn instrument and settled it as well as he could onto his knee and into the hollow of his good shoulder. He could handle a harp as well as the next man, no better, but as well as most; and even with one arm not much use to him, he could probably make some kind of strumming. But any song or story that he knew they would have heard over and over again.

'Tell about trolls,' demanded Lilla.

'Tell us about you, when you were our age,' said Signy, clearly seeing his problem and willing to help him out of it.

So, striking the odd flight of notes from the badly-tuned harp from time to time, when the points in the story seemed to call for it, Bjarni told them about the time when he was a boy in Norway, before ever he came west-over-seas; told them about the time that he and his friend Arva had decided to make their fortunes by breaking into the ancient burial house on the moors above the settlement where it was said that a king lay buried with his treasures of gold and fine weapons all about him. In actual truth, the adventure had not been very exciting, for all they had found, after many spells of secret digging where a warren of gorse bushes hid their work, had been a pot full of charred bones and an ancient dagger eaten through with rust. But with the eager faces of Lilla and Signy before him, he found himself improving the story as he went along. He added a battle with a troll-woman for Lilla; he added a storm that made the sky seem full of rushing black wings – and the bones and rusted dagger became a kingly skeleton clad in a sark of ring-mail as fine as a salmon skin and a helmet with a face-mask set with garnet eyebrows, and all about him cups and swords and horse gear all of solid gold, so much gold that they had had to fetch a ship's awning to carry it away in. The story grew and blossomed as it went along, as Bjarni discovered more and more that he had the story-telling skill in him that he had not known he possessed before, with the story-teller's ability to improve on the truth.

'What happened to the treasure?' Signy asked when the story was done.

'Ah now,' Bjarni said slowly, to gain time. And then the answer came to him. 'Harald Finehair, the King, got to hear of it; and that was the end of the treasure so far as we were concerned.'

His listeners nodded sadly. They knew Harald Finehair's reputation among the men who had come west-over-seas to get clear of him. And Lilla said, 'Even the blue glass dolphin?'

Bjarni had not been aware of putting his blue glass dolphin among the story treasure. He must have done it without thought, simply because it was there, although he had scarcely thought of it for five years, a small private image. 'Er, no,' he said, 'I hid the dolphin and when I came west-over-seas I brought it with me.'

'Have you got it still?' Lilla said, while in the same breath Signy demanded, 'Show us!'

Bjarni shook his head; he was tired and the lovely brightness of invention was leaving him. He went back to telling more or less the truth. 'I have not got it with me. When I took my sword and left Rafnglas, I buried it for safe-keeping in a place I would not be forgetting, a little side glen below the moors – good farming land it would be – and left it behind me.'

'But you'll go back for it, one day?'

'Maybe,' Bjarni said and made a flighting of notes on the harp.

A small movement in the door made him glance that way. Erp stood there with a piece of hauling-harness in his hand and his head bent at a faintly listening angle.

On the last evening before they set out to get *Seal Maiden* down-river, when the sleds were already laden, an evening of squally rain and a west wind blowing through the tree tops, Bjarni sought word with the Lady Aud in the longhouse. His shoulder was stiff and he still felt as though a galley had been launched across him, but the ground was steady under his feet once more, and he could stand before her without swaying.

She sat beside the fire, the last of the kists and bundles around her, waiting for the morning. Muirgoed and the two granddaughters were moving about journey tasks in the farther shadows, but the Lady Aud sat on her stool gazing into the fire, her hands palm-up and empty in her lap. It was almost the first time that he had seen her sit beside a fire without something in her hands.

She looked up after he had stood waiting before her a few moments. 'Bjarni Sigurdson, you have something that you would be saying to me?'

'Lady,' Bjarni said, 'I have carried it to the best that was in me, I will carry it still until we come to the coast, but on the day you sail for Iceland, let you give me back my sword-service, that I may carry it otherwhere.'

The Lady Aud looked at him with her strong brows raised a little. 'The hunger for strange seas is on you?'

'No, the hunger for land – a land-take of my own.'

'There is good land to be had in Iceland – or are you wishing to bide with the Caithness settlement?'

'My five years are up, and I am free to go back to my own settlement,' Bjarni said.

'So-o. The homing hunger. It comes to many of us, from time to time.'

'Also, I have a dog waiting for me on Mull, and a message that I have carried with me undelivered these three years past.'

'And these be all good reasons,' said the Lady Aud.

'So, come to me on the tide-line on the day *Seal Maiden* sails for Iceland, and you shall have back your sword-service and your pay.'

A few days later, on the landing-beach below Dungadr's stronghold, where the Lady Aud and her women had sheltered while *Sea Maiden* and *Fionoula* were provisioned and made ready for sea, a sizeable crowd was gathered, Picts and Northmen. Dungadr himself had come down with his hearth companions for the final leave-taking, and with him Groa and the women of the household. Groa, with her striped cloak flung back despite the thin spring wind, carrying herself proudly like a ship with the wind filling her sail. Before summer's end there would be a new young one at the Chieftain's hearth.

And then for the last time Bjarni stood before the Lady Aud, where she had called him a little apart from the rest, to receive back his sword-service. 'Are you still of the same mind?' she asked.

'I am still of the same mind, Lady.'

'So, then take your pay.' She gave him a small pouch of soft crimson leather that jingled pleasantly as it passed from her hand to his.

'My thanks, Lady,' he said, and would have stowed it in his belt, but she stopped him, smiling. 'Open and check it. Never take your pay unseen.'

Bjarni opened the purse and tipped the contents into his palm. There were three gold coins, one of them showing a head covered with laurel leaves, a length of silver chain and several small coins and metal fragments. Not over-generous, but just and fair, for the paying off of a mercenary. Much the same as he would have got from Red Thorstein.

'Fair pay?' she said.

'Fair pay,' he agreed, tipping the coins back into their pouch and storing it into his belt.

'So then, now a gift,' said Lady Aud, 'a gift such as a fighting man should receive, who has deserved well of his lord.' And she brought from under her great cloak a long bundle wrapped in oily fleece. She turned back the folds and set in his hands a sword, the iron hilt wreathed and braided with silver wires, the pommel formed from a great lump of yellow amber; and when he drew it from the scuffed and age-worn horsehide sheath the blade sang against the metal lip in the way the very finest of smith's work would do. A blade with ancient magic in its forging.

Bjarni looked at it with the eyes of instant love. Then he felt a pang of disloyalty, and his gaze shifted to the serviceable blade already hanging at his belt. 'I have a good sword of my own,' he said. 'One sword is enough for a man with only his own way to make.'

'Yet once a man has made his land-take and so is looking to the time ahead, he can be doing with two good blades,' said the Lady Aud. 'One for his own hand, and one for giving to his son when the time comes.'

Bjarni sheathed his new sword. The belt-thongs were somewhat worn and would need renewing, he thought, before he could hang it at his belt. He stood nursing it across his forearm and looking at her, gravely at first, then with a sudden delight. 'My thanks, Lady, and the thanks of my maybe someday son.'

Later that morning, with the voyage safely blessed by Brother Ninian, with the women and the last of the gear finally on board and the oars already swung out, Bjarni stood with those who had shared the forest winter but were not sharing the Iceland faring, and watched them head out from the shallows, *Seal Maiden* in the lead and *Fionoula* following behind, and wished for the moment that he had made his choice the other way; and a small pang of loss knotted in his belly.

Then a hand came down on his shoulder, and for the one instant he thought that it was Erp. But he had just taken his leave of Erp on the tide-line; when he looked round it was only one of the shipwrights.

'Come away, lad, we've a keg of ale to drink to fair seas and following winds for the old lady. Reckon Iceland doesn't know yet what's coming down on them.' The man grinned.

Bjarni turned to the broached ale-keg, with a feeling of stumbling forward over a new threshold: and when he looked out to sea again, *Seal Maiden* and *Fionoula* had almost disappeared into the morning murk that hung above the swinging waters of the Pentland Firth.

17

Storm at Sea

Only a few days after the Lady Aud sailed for Iceland,
a band from the main settlement started out by way
of the Great Glen to fetch up the first women and
bairns and breeding beasts. And with them, carrying
his few possessions and his old sword slung behind
his shoulders, went Bjarni Sigurdson.

Presently there would be a steady coming and going
along the way between the Islands and the new Caithness settlements; galleys on the long chain of lochs,
and portage-ways and drove-roads of a sort through
the forests and across the moors in between. But for
now the way was hard and hazardous, and slow to
travel. Three of the band were dead in one way or
another, and early spring was drawing on towards
summer when the air began to take on the soft familiar
tang of the West Coast, and they came down at last
to the blue waters of the Firth of Lorne.

They managed to gather up a few skin-clad coracles
from the fisher-villages down-coast, and so came at
last into the home-harbour of Mull. The first thing
Bjarni in the foremost coracle saw as they came
bobbing past Calf Island into sheltered water was the

fat familiar shape of *Sea Cow*, beached above the tide-line.

The second thing was a wild and joyful baying and a familiar black shape ploughing out through the shallows to meet the coracle. Then he was out over the side with the rest, to haul the light craft up the beach; and Hugin was plunging and circling round him like a black seal. Bjarni abandoned the coracle – it would not take more than the three of them anyway to handle her – and gave himself up to being greeted and half drowned by his dog.

Among the high-tide kelp he squatted down, his eyes shut and his arms round the wriggling and ecstatic body, while Hugin lunged against him, licking his face from ear to ear. And when the great hound's joy had somewhat abated and he opened his eyes again he saw *Sea Cow*'s master standing straddle-legged grinning down at him. He scrambled to his feet.

'Heriolf! Here's a fine meeting! Why did the sea news not tell me I'd be seeing you before the day was out?'

'But I knew I would be seeing you,' said the merchant, 'for has not this black devil of yours been sitting on the ship-strand since first light, staring out to sea?'

The other coracles had been dragged ashore by now, and a crowd was gathering, women for the most part, calling for word of sons and husbands, for there had been little enough news since the first ill tidings of their Lord's death. Bjarni took his share with the rest, giving what answers he could to the eager and anxious questions. But the affairs of the Caithness settlements were no longer any concern of his; in a little he collected his sea-kist and, once again slinging his worldly goods over his shoulder, headed with

Heriolf for the ale-house at the far end of the ship-strand.

And later, when the rest of the returned ship-carles had scattered to their own homes or were eating in the Chieftain's Hall – men still ate there, passing the harp among them, where Egil, Thorstein's former warband captain, now sat in the High Seat – and news of their return was already running to the farthest headlands of Mull, Bjarni sat taking ease with *Sea Cow*'s crew around the ale-house drift-wood fire, with Hugin sleeping at his feet. Some of the faces in the firelight were strange to him, but most were familiar enough, and there was a certain warm contentment in him because in the new life that he knew he had walked into, the old life could still reach out to him friendliwise. They passed the ale-jack from hand to hand, and exchanged the news of the past three years. So Bjarni heard of *Sea Cow*'s long voyage south and east into the Mid-Land Sea for dark-skinned slaves for the Dublin market, and told in his turn of Onund Treefoot's visit to Jarl Sigurd of Orkney and how he gained the right to water ship from his springs, and of the deaths of the two Chiefs before the Caithness settlements came into being, and of the Lady Aud's departure on her Iceland faring. But a good part of these later stories they had heard already, and so were more interested in his own part in them.

'And what reward did the Lady Aud give you for the slaying of her son's slayer?' one of the men asked, leaning forward into the firelight.

'Na, na, I was but first blade in that hunting,' Bjarni told him quickly. He still remembered the young Pict's face too clearly for comfort. 'When I told her that I was for taking back my sword-service, she gave me much what the Chief would have given me in paying-off geld.' He hesitated, looking down at the sword in its horsehide sheath at his side. 'Then she gave me another sword. So I am a two-sword man now.' He half drew it, rejoicing as always at the song-note of the blade on the metal sheath-lip and the way the light slid and rippled on the pattern-forged blade.

'Sa, sa . . . One for you and one for the son to come after you. A man of property, you are,' said Heriolf in kindly mockery, and leaned forward for a closer look. 'That is a good blade. And where will you carry it, I am wondering? Will you try Dublin once again?' His small dark eyes narrowed in laughter. 'A fine beard you have now.'

Bjarni shook his head. 'My five years are up and my debt is cleared. I am to Rafnglas again, I and my black devil. You would not be heading that way?'

He did not really expect it, but Heriolf, looking into the fire, said slowly, 'Well now, I was thinking of a run south through the Islands before the old lass heads for the far seaways again. Like enough there's buying and selling to do in Rafnglas . . .'

Bjarni slapped the pouch at his belt. 'I can pay my passage, this time.'

Heriolf took a swig at the ale-jack and passed it over. 'Nay now! There's twice you have come with me as bodyguard, and as the Fates who mark the future on men's foreheads seem to have decreed a third time, let you not spoil the pattern.'

Sea Cow sailed two mornings later. Normally Heriolf would have spent longer over his trading, for the Mull settlements were rich in skins and a fine market for luxury goods, bronze and amber and the goods of foreign lands, but now the whole island was restless, poised for flighting like the wild geese in the spring, and restless yet, too full of the change that was upon them to have much mind to spare for the splendours of bronze and amber, the unusual beauties from Eastern markets or thick snow-bears' pelts.

'When Egil has had time to settle into the High Seat, the market will come back,' Bjarni said.

But Heriolf was less sure. 'Maybe, in a while, a longish while. If Egil is strong enough to hold the settlement together meanwhile, and hold the raiders off . . .'

So they ran *Sea Cow* down into the bay and out past Calf Island and headed south.

They took the in-shore route, in good weather. They ran the keel ashore on the white ship-strand of Islay and put in a day's trading, and then put into the south-west end of Argyll, to trade for fine wildcats' skins from the forests inland. Then to Arran, and then the Islands fell back, and they were out into open water with the empty sea space of the Solway Firth to the east, and the dim blue-drawn line of Ireland edging the world to the west. And away and away south-eastward, unseen for a long while as yet, but suddenly Bjarni seemed to smell it as a horse smells its own stable, the long mainland coastline and the Lakeland settlements. He had sailed these seaways before, in five summers' sea-faring, but this time was different, this time he was for his own landing-beach, and the settlement that was home for him, so far as any place was home. And the shallow side-valley far up Eskdale, where he would make his land-take and build his bothy that would one day be a house, with a woman spinning beside the fire and the son he had his second sword put by for.

It was a good prospect, and yet it lacked the fierce joy to it that he had expected when he came at last back to his own landing-beach.

Rafnglas was the most northerly of all the Lakeland settlements. Soon now, well before dark . . .

It was then that the storm reached out to them. First, no more than a dark cat's paw eddying after them, dying away once more into a flat calm, and then a great buffeting wind from the north-west that leapt upon them as they lost the shelter of the land, out of the emptiness beyond the Solway Firth beneath the ragged scurry of wind-cloud flying low.

The sea began to get up almost while they looked at it.

After five sea-faring summers among the Islands, Bjarni had come to know well enough the weather signs of clouds and flying birds sounding strange and the indefinable smell of coming tempest, but this was one of those rare storms that come up without any warning, taking even the most experienced of seamen unawares, as though the storm gods had opened a hand and loosed the winds on an instant's whim, chancing, for the moment, to have nothing else to do.

'Put the dog below and tie him up,' Heriolf said. 'We're in for some ugly weather.'

Bjarni twisted a hand in Hugin's collar and hauled him down under the loose deck planking, and tied him up to a spar with a bit of free rope, not too far in in case the bales began to shift, the dog barking and protesting. The movement of the ship was growing uneasy even as he did so, and when he came back on the deck he found that even in the few moments that he had been away, the world had changed. It had grown darker and wilder, the sea had turned a bad colour, the waves torn into ragged white along their crests. They were shortening sail, the wind whining in the rigging above the sails as they flapped like huge ungainly wings, and the spindrift dashed across the heaving deck.

'We'll not make Rafnglas this tide,' someone shouted.

Presently the light began to go, though it was not yet time for sunset. And the shape of Heriolf, standing poised and braced at the steering oar, began to fade into the general murk, and only his voice came to them out of the dark, shouting orders. Presently they furled the sails and she was running before the wind under bare spars.

Far into the night they fought the sea, Heriolf feeling for the sides and crests of waves which with a less skilled ship chief must have swamped them. Whole hills of water came at them with great valleys between. Now and then *Sea Cow* checked and staggered on the climb, but always she reached the crest, hung there an instant as the wind that had been shut out in the troughs caught her, then slipped down on the far side.

On they drove, before the great following seas, their trust in the unseen man at the steering oar. Once, when the moon rode free of the clouds, far off to the west something briefly showed that must have been the southern tip of Man, and then all was lost once more in the trough of the next wave and the next, and the next . . .

There was no time, no distance, no possible knowledge of distance or direction, nothing to do but keep the bailing going, crouch with their hunched backs to the lashing spray, eyes searching the turmoil ahead for any sight of land, trust to the man at the steering oar to keep them from being broached by the next following wave – and always the mad stampede of whitecaps racing alongside – crouch ready for whatever might happen next, pray to the White Christ and to Thor, that he had been able to keep them far enough out to clear the thrusting coast of Wales to ride the storm out on the open sea.

Presently there began to be a new note in the

turmoil all about them, a deeper booming menace that could only mean one thing, waves pounding on an open shore. Bjarni, crouching in his place in the stern, was aware of Heriolf's figure beside him leaning his full weight against the steering oar, struggling for a further westing in their course. A tension was added even to the tension of that night, and then almost in the same instant, as it seemed, two things happened. Hugin came scrambling out from the hold with the chewed end of his rope hanging from his collar – it was as if he knew, Bjarni said later, telling the story of that night – and came skidding and sprawling to crouch at Bjarni's feet; and the moon, sliding suddenly free into a ragged lake of clear sky, showed from the next wave-top the white fury of great rollers pounding onto a rocky shore, a great headland thrusting to catch them like the jaw of a trap.

'Out oars,' Heriolf shouted above the wind. 'If we can keep her off the rocks, there's sheltered water westward of the Ness!'

And almost before the order could be obeyed, a great cross sea came charging down upon them, sweeping before it all that was not tied down or clinging to something. For a horrific moment Bjarni saw the dark shape of Hugin trying desperately to swim against the great sluice in mid-air, and then the wave was past, leaving *Sea Cow* waterlogged and staggering behind it. And of Hugin, no sign. 'Bail!' the shout went up, and men staggered into desperate action. But Bjarni saw only the black head of Hugin, like a seal's on the wild moon-bright water. He was up on the side. 'Leave the dog, you fool!' Heriolf shouted behind him. He leapt clear.

Spray-drenched as he was already, he scarcely felt the shock of the cold, only the immense power of the great swinging seas. He tried to call, 'Hugin! Hugin!'

but his mouth filled with sea water. Hugin was trying desperately to follow the ship. And Bjarni headed the same way. He reached the thrashing dog and got a hand twisted in the chewed rope. 'Come!' he shouted, and dragged the dog round, striking out to where he had seen the waves on the distant shore. Maybe there was an ugly death waiting for them both on such a coast in such a sea, but maybe not, and they had no other chance. The ship could do nothing for them.

Swimming one-armed with his hand on Hugin's collar now, he struck out for the white menace of the shore. But the current within the storm took them and swung them eastward away from the great headland and towards a lower shore. And when, it seemed a life-time later, Bjarni was suddenly aware of land almost under his feet, and a great wave swept him and the black dog shoreward, it was onto smooth sand.

18

Angharad

The next wave all but dragged him out again, but before the third came creaming in, he had got somehow to his feet and staggered up clear of the high-water mark, dragging Hugin after him. The tide had only just turned, the amber sea-wrack was behind him, and the sand dry and soft under his feet. Dimly he was aware of great dunes rising to meet them. Then he had collapsed onto his face and was being direly sick. Hugin was lying all along his length against him, limp and cold and motionless as a swath of seaweed. He thought the dog was drowned, and then as the world began to swim and darken, and what felt like half the sea came rushing salt and cold up out of his belly, he thought he was. Lying on his face with one arm over the dog's sodden body, he simply let go and the darkness took him.

The next time he knew anything, he was lying on his back and Hugin was standing on him, licking his face from ear to ear. The gale had died down a little, and it was raining, but in the shelter of the dunes there was some shelter, and he lay looking up at the tall hillocks crested with marram grass that was half torn from the sand. He could not tell what time of day it was, for the sun was hidden behind moving cloud. But something in the light told him that it was well past noon, and with no knowing how far they were from food and shelter, it was time that he and Hugin stopped lying here above the tide, and set out to find it.

He felt quite strong as long as he was lying down, but when he sat up, every muscle in his body hurt, and the dunes swam around him, and just for a moment the fragile yellow flowers of a half-uprooted horned poppy in the dune slope seemed the most important thing in the world.

He shook his head to clear it and struggled to his feet. The world was still swimming, but he could walk, and Hugin was shaking himself so that sand and sea water flew in all directions. And so he turned inland, unaware of what they were doing, only that he was heading away from the waves behind them.

Beyond the dunes was rough grass islanded with gorse, and then higher ground, a rolling country of low hills. Ahead, to the west, half seen and then lost again in the driving rain – outside the shelter of the dunes the wind was still blowing hard in long weary gusts – rose the great shapes of mountain country, bloomed with darkness and still streaked with the white of last winter's snow. But Bjarni, his head down against the rain, his feet seeming not really to belong to him, and the black dog trailing miserably at his heels, was scarcely aware of these things.

How long he stumbled on through a land that had no sign of any human settlement, he did not know. He knew presently that he was in wooded country but that half the trees were down, so that he stumbled on a fallen branch and fell, hitting his head on something, and staggered up again with blood running into his eyes. But it all seemed oddly dreamlike and he did not even curse. In a little he came out on the far side of the trees – it was only a thin belt of woodland – and wiping the blood out of his eyes with the back of his hand, saw a shallow valley opening before him, and at the head of it, a small huddle of roofs that spoke of shelter.

It was still raining before the squally gusts, but away to the westward on the shoulder of the mountains the sky was breaking up and a long beam of sodden daffodil light showed through. Stumbling on down the hillside, he headed for the promise of warmth and something to drink. He did not want food, but the longing for the smooth sweetness of milk was in his salt-parched throat. Yet as he drew near, the place began to look more and more derelict. No sign of sheep or cattle in the home pasture. No sign of anything living; but from the roof of the house-place, a pale plume of smoke trailed sideways on the gusts. Not quite deserted, then, and with a fire on the hearth. He stumbled on towards it.

As he reached the gate-gap in the thorn hedge that surrounded the steading garth, a figure appeared round the corner of the house-place, and crossed the garth towards a tumbledown byre; a boy with a bundle of hay on one shoulder and a pail in the other hand, and a stocking cap low on his head against the rain.

He checked at sight of Bjarni in the gateway and stood looking at him, wary as a wild animal. Probably few strangers came that way. Then as Bjarni came slowly on through the gap towards him, he said something that had the sound of a question in it.

But the tongue was not Bjarni's. He shook his head, his gaze fixed almost painfully on the pail. 'Drink,' he said.

And that was clear enough. The boy held out the pail and echoed, 'Drink.'

Bjarni took the pail and drank. It was water, not milk, but clean and sweet, and he drank deeply, then handed it back. The boy set it down, and the hay beside it, in the door of the byre; said something to the shadows within, from which came the stamp of an impatient hoof and the familiar smell of horse. Then he turned back to Bjarni, and looked him up and down with a little frown between his brows. All at once he seemed to make up his mind, and his frown disappeared, and he half turned, pointing to the house-place door. 'Come.'

Bjarni lurched after him through the doorway. Inside was warmth and firelit darkness, and the peat smoke that hazed the shadows caught at his throat. He choked and lurched off balance, and could not right himself again, and the boy steadied him in a headlong fall into buzzing and spinning darkness.

When the darkness gave him up again, he was lying by the fire, and somebody was kneeling over him with a bowl of something. Squinting upwards he saw that it was the boy. Then the boy's arm was under his shoulder, raising him, and the bowl was against his mouth, and the boy was saying with a kind of concerned roughness, 'Drink, then sleep and grow strong; do not you dare to die under my roof. I have enough on my hands without that.'

Bjarni understood about half of what he said, but he understood the first command, and gulped down the stuff that was being tipped into his mouth. It was a kind of warm and watery oaten gruel with honeycomb in it, and somewhere behind the sweetness a bitter taste of herbs. Close by, Hugin was slurping his way through a bowl of what looked like the same gruel with household scraps in it. They finished in almost the same moment, and the great dog lifted a mealy muzzle from his empty bowl, and whimpered on a puzzled note, deep in his throat.

The boy's hand went out to touch his head behind the ears. 'All's well,' said the tone of his voice.

Bjarni mumbled urgently, 'Careful, he's not one for strangers.' Hugin lifted his head under the hand, and thumped his tail behind him.

'All animals are for me,' said the boy. 'It's one of the reasons . . .' He broke off. 'Now sleep,' he said again, with an odd authority in his tone. The warmth of the gruel and the taste of herbs seemed to be rushing in a kind of pleasant fog into Bjarni's head, and he slept.

When he woke again it was daylight; he was as weak as a half-drowned puppy but there was a feeling of morning within him, and his head seemed to be working again, which it had certainly not been doing last night. He became aware almost in the same instant of two things. The first, that he was naked, lying under the warmth of an old weather-worn cloak, with the rags of his breeks and tunic still steaming gently beside the slurried remains of last night's fire. The boy must have stripped him while he slept and set his clothes to dry. But his sword – he dragged back the cloak in a sudden panic to find his sword, and there it was, laid beside him under the cloak, the hilt almost in his hand – his left hand. His fingers closed on the grip, and he relaxed with a sigh of relief. But as he did so, he became aware of the second thing: that he was being watched.

Hugin was sitting beside him, watching his face, with small hopeful thumps of his tail behind him, but there was someone, something, other than Hugin, whose presence he had sensed. He looked round and saw that in the far corner of the house-place, where he had thought last night were only crowding shadows, an old man was lying on a pile of heather, straight and still under a rug pulled to his chin as someone lying on his funeral pyre, but with his head sharply turned, and his eyes, bright and desperately full of life, fixed upon him.

Bjarni let out a kind of croak but there was no response. And a few moments later the boy appeared in the doorway with the morning light behind him. 'That is Gwyn, he was my cattleman,' he said. 'He is very sick and cannot speak, but he knows what is going on.' He spoke slowly and carefully, mostly in the Norse tongue, though with an outlandish accent that made the words hard to understand.

He came across to the fire and picked up the bowl that had been keeping warm on the smoked peats, then came and squatted down beside him. And watching, Bjarni made the discovery that he was not watching a boy at all, but a girl clad in breeks and sark instead of a woman's kirtle, and with her hair – since the storm had passed she had laid aside her stocking cap – knotted close behind her head as men knot up a horse's tail to be out of the way.

'You are a girl!' he told her.

'Yes, I know,' she returned gravely, but he had the feeling some part of her was laughing at him.

'Why breeks?'

'Easier it is to do a man's work in a man's clothes,' said the girl.

'You alone here?' He frowned up at her.

'Except for Gwyn. Eat now.' She slipped an arm under his shoulders. There was a horn spoon in the bowl, and she began spooning the stuff into him. He ate abundantly; the stuff was thicker than last night's gruel and seemed to have something else, an egg maybe, stirred into it.

In a little, seeming to decide that if he was strong enough to ask questions he was strong enough to answer them, she began to ask the odd question in her turn. 'Who are you? What fortune brings you to my door?'

'Bjarni Sigurdson. I am from the sea.'

'Ship?' she asked.

He realised that it was not such a daft question as it sounded; not when you thought how he had landed on her threshold out of the worst summer storm in years; and him left-handed and with a great black dog at his heels.

'Ship.' He nodded.

'Shipwreck?'

He had not thought of Heriolf or *Sea Cow*, or wondered as to their fate, until that moment. 'I think – yes,' he said and pushed the bowl away, suddenly not wanting any more to eat.

'There are many wrecks on Dragon's Head, though few at this time of year,' said the girl. 'But sometimes a ship escapes and finds shelter in the great bay facing towards Anglesey.'

He only understood about half of what she said, but he heard in her tone the comfort she was trying to give him, and felt a little warmth in the sudden cold desolation within him.

She set the bowl aside, and he was grateful to her for not being one of those women who cluck like a hen and try to force food into a man when he has not the stomach or heart for it.

He humped himself together under the cloak, and said, 'I get up – my clothes . . . '

She pressed him back. 'The rags that the sea has left you will not cover your nakedness. Lie quiet now.

Sleep and grow strong, and in the evening if I judge you ready we'll find you clothes to dress you in, and you shall get up and sit beside the fire and eat meat, and clean your sword before the salt water can do it harm.'

'Now?' he croaked.

'Not now,' said the girl. 'I have not the time to find you clothes. Lie still, and this evening will come.'

And suddenly she was gone, leaving him to wonder whether she was always like that with a man when she had him at her mercy.

Most of the day he dozed, drifting in and out of sleep and wakefulness, vaguely aware of the girl coming and going about her own affairs, and seeing to her outdoor tasks, tending to and feeding the old man in the corner; but gradually the sleep-time grew less and the waking times more.

And then it was evening, and he was restless with impatience, and the girl had taken a pair of home-spun breeks and a tunic of good rowan-red wool out of a carved kist against the far wall. 'These were my brother's,' she said, and dropped them beside him, and turned away, about the evening meal.

He put the breeks and tunic on – they were much about the right size – and buckled on his own belt with the pouch containing his three gold pieces. When the evening meal was over he sat, comfortingly full of eel stew and beginning to feel more like a living man again, with his sword across his thigh, burnishing the blade before the cold sea salt could rust into the ripple-patterned blade. Hugin lay outstretched beside him gnawing a pig bone, and on the far side of the fire the girl sat spinning. It looked odd to see her spinning there, in her breeks and sark.

Sometimes they talked to each other, managing

none so ill, with her slight knowledge of Norse. With traders and settlements along the coast, most people had a few words of it. The British tongue, though a different branch of the one that Bjarni had gained in the three years he and Erp had talked friendliwise together, helped too, eked out with gestures. Sometimes they sat silent, a silence made up of small sounds: the flutter of the flames on the hearth, the purr of the spindle and the dog gnawing his bone, the faint rasp and hiss of Bjarni burnishing the sword across his thigh.

He had only one sword again – it had been good to have two, his own to hold his land-take, and one for his son; he remembered Aud saying that as she gave it to him. It made a good feeling inside, as though the land-take and the son were already part of him. But now his old sword, his son's sword, was lying somewhere among the rocks off Dragon's Head, among the wreckage of *Sea Cow* and the bodies of men who had been his friends, and he felt rootless again, a man without any place of his own in life, and only his one sword for sale again.

For the sake of something else to think about, he looked up at the girl on the far side of the fire, watching her through the faint fronds of peat smoke. The light of the fading day shining in through the doorway showed her clearly. Beautiful, she would have been, he thought, if she had not always had the look of a harp too tightly strung, the hair pulled up behind her small head so black that when the light touched the blackness it was almost blue. Her eyes were dark under brows like slim black feathers, her skin silky where it rose out of the worn neck of her sark and had not browned in the sun and wind like the rest of her face. On the creaminess of it a red mark showed, like . . . like . . . as though somebody had laid their wine-stained fingers on it close together. He had not noticed the mark before, because he had not sat really looking at her before.

She looked up and saw where he was looking and, dropping the spindle, made a quick movement as though to pull up the neck of her sark, then with a gesture that was oddly disdainful, picked up the spindle again. Proud, that one, Bjarni thought, a woman wearing the clothes of a man, but who carried herself like a queen.

'Tha's known my name since morning,' he said. 'But tha's not told me yours. Fair's fair.'

She answered him gravely, for the exchange of names was a grave matter, after all. 'I am called Angharad, and my father was Iowan, son of Nectan, of the line of Erin.' She spoke like a queen, too. Then she grinned like the veriest urchin, but somewhat wryly. 'The Lordly Ones do not give their names to mortal kind, so now at least you know that I do not come from the Hollow Hills, despite the faery mark on my neck.'

19

Witch Mark

That night Bjarni slept by the fire again; but the next
morning he woke in the normal way of things, and
got up, in the clothes he had slept in, when he heard
Angharad moving behind the curtain that shut off the
far corner of the room. He wondered whether he and
Hugin should be on their travels again before the day
was through, and if so, which way they should go.
East and northward, probably, heading for Rafnglas
on their own feet, but somehow he seemed to have
lost his roots there again. Or maybe across to Anglesey, where he had heard that Anarand the King of
Gwynedd had many Danish and Norwegian soldiers
for his wars on the kingdoms further south . . . Meanwhile, he did odd jobs for Angharad, cutting wood,
turning the old dun horse which seemed, apart from
five ducks, to be the only livestock about the place,
into the home pasture to graze and mucking out the
stable behind him. She gave him his share of the
morning meal, and afterwards, when she had gone
about some business of her own, he took up his sword,
which until now he had left lying under the old cloak,
between his bed place and the wall. He was just going

to belt it on, when suddenly he bethought him that he did not own the clothes he stood up in. He did not doubt that Angharad would give them to him. He had the price of them several times over in his pouch, but surely they were part of her hospitality. And he had the feeling that to offer to pay for hospitality would be as unforgivable among her people as it would be among his.

While he stood considering, he heard a small grunting sound, and looking round, saw that it came from the old man in the corner. Gwyn clearly wanted something, and Angharad was not here. He crossed over to the still, bundled shape. 'What is it, old father?' he asked, forgetting for the moment that Gwyn had no power of speech. Then following the direction of the old, terribly bright eyes, he saw the pannikin of water on a stool close by. He squatted down and picked it up. 'This?'

The old man gave a faint nod.

Bjarni slipped an arm under Gwyn's head, and lifted it, and held the cup to his blue lips. A horrible sour smell came up from the old man. He drank after a fashion, some of the water going down his chin. 'We'll do better another time,' Bjarni told him, without really thinking what he said, and laid him back again on the plaited straw pillow. Pity, almost the first time Bjarni had felt such a thing, rose in his throat.

There was a faint movement behind him and he looked round to see Angharad in the doorway.

'I think he's fouled himself,' he said. 'Shall I help you?'

When it was done, and the old man made clean and seemly again, and the soiled rushes taken out to the midden behind the house-place, Angharad said, 'Let you stay another night at least. The salt water is scarce dried out of you yet. And you are not in any state to be out on the moors heading for – wherever you are heading for, you and the dog.'

But Bjarni had the feeling that it was only partly for his sake that she bade him stay, and partly for her own; that to have a hale man with a sword about the steading was a respite from something, some kind of fear maybe.

So he stayed the night, sleeping on piled bracken in the byre, with his sword beside him and Hugin and the old horse for company; and the next night also. And by day he helped her with the work of the steading. The hay was ready for the first cut, in the meadow that ran down to the stream, and they gathered it between them and laid it out in silvery swaths to dry. And he helped her tend the old man. 'He was my cattleman,' she said, that first day, but there was no sign of any cattle about the place, nothing living except the old horse and the five ducks that followed Angharad wherever she went. But the whole place gave signs of having dwindled from something much more than it was now; the fine Hall and the surrounding byres and barns, half in ruins, showed signs of being the steading of a big and busy farm, with the in-take lands spread far up and down the valley. And one girl in breeks who carried herself like a queen, working just enough of it to feed herself and one sick old man, and a horse? Surely there was a story here . . .

On the fourth morning the wind was blowing from the west, not hard, but enough to silver the young green barley in the one small crop-field all one way. And on the wind Bjarni, coming back from turning out the horse, caught very faintly the sound of a distant bell. It was the first sign he had had since the storm that there was anyone outside the valley.

'Do you hear the bell?' he asked Angharad, who was collecting duck eggs.

'Yes,' she said. 'It's the chapel, you can hear it when the wind is in this direction, calling the folk of the valleys to worship God.' She reached into the hollow of the peat-stack for another egg.

'Best you had be on your way then,' Bjarni said.

'I cannot leave Gwyn.'

'I will stay with Gwyn,' said Bjarni.

She put the last egg gently into the bowl. 'You are not Christian?'

'I am a prime-signed Christian,' Bjarni told her. 'But I will stay with Gwyn.'

She said, speaking steadily, 'I think I am not welcome where that bell calls; nor among the folk it calls to.'

That evening as they sat together over the evening meal, she asked him, 'Where will you go, after you go from here?'

'Wherever the wind sends me,' Bjarni said. 'It was in my mind to go back to my own settlement at Rafnglas, where the Lakeland rivers come to the sea. That was before the storm came and blew us off course. Now I am not so sure.' By that time he and Angharad were beginning to be able to talk to each other quite well in the bastard Norse and British tongue that they seemed to be weaving between them, but he did not feel he could tell her about his second sword in it, not in any way that would make sense. 'It's five years that I have been away; and I am not sure that I belong there any more.'

'Five years with the sea-faring merchant kind. That might make it hard to strike sword?'

Bjarni shook his head, tossing a half-gnawed knuckle bone to Hugin. 'Not the merchant kind, though *Sea Cow* was a merchant ship and the ship-master was my friend. When the Chieftain bade me out of my settlement – an ill thing that I had done – he gave me a sword, not this one, which I carried for pay among the ship companions of Onund Treefoot, he that had his nest on Barra in the Outer Isles, and then with Red Thorstein of Mull. I was with him when he died in Caithness last autumn, and now my sword is my own again. I was hearing that King Anarand has Danes and Northmen among his war-bands on Anglesey.'

The girl looked at him in silence a long moment through the peat-reek; then she said, 'Maybe, one day. Meanwhile, let you bide here with me.'

He returned her look, startled for the moment, and then demanded, 'What as? You don't need a cattleman.'

'As my hired sword,' said Angharad. 'No, no cattleman . . .'

Just for the moment he thought it was a jest, and then he saw that she was in slightly desperate earnest; and again he had the feeling that she was afraid of something.

He held out his hand to her – palm up – above the fire. Hers came to meet it and they shook hands as men do on a bargain.

So Bjarni Sigurdson, who had hired his sword to Onund Treefoot and Thorstein Olafson, was hired sword now to the lady of a derelict farm. And for the moment surprisingly content that it should be so. He went on working with her about the house and farm much as he had in the past three days, work that might have been done by a thrall, or the lord of the household come to that.

He hunted and fished for her so that there was food

for them both. It was a life nearer to the life he had
grown up with than anything he had known in the
past five years. Yet not quite like it – and he always
wore his sword.

At times, Angharad would disappear into the
woods or up onto the high moors with a big wicker
creel, and the growing things she came back with she
hung up to dry above the fire, or pounded in with
goose grease from a great jar in her store-shed, or
infused in water from the stream, timing the process
with incantations in a strange stately-sounding tongue
that was neither British nor Norse. So it was not many
days before Bjarni realised that young though she was
– maybe no older than himself – she was herb-wise
as an old village crone; but maybe something a little
more, a little other . . .

'Why do you do all this, and nobody comes for
your salves?' he asked one day, finding her tying dried
herbs into bundles.

'People do come – sometimes,' she told him. 'When
they come, what they need is ready for them.'

And sure enough, one day when it would have
been past sheep-shearing time if there had been any
sheep, a man came over the edge of the valley holding
his right arm in his left, with an ugly gash on his
wrist that had sickened with neglect and was oozing
yellow pus.

Angharad cleaned it for him and salved and bound
it with clean rags. And she dosed him with something
dark and pungent-smelling, and gave him more of
everything in a bundle. 'Come back in three days,'
she said.

But watching him go away over the rim of the
valley, she said, 'He'll not come back, not unless he
gets so sick that all my leechcraft is undone.'

'Why so?' Bjarni said.

'Because he's afraid. Did you not smell how afraid he was?'

'But he came, this time he came . . .'

'Because he was more afraid for his arm.'

'But what is he afraid of?'

'What they are all afraid of – me,' said Angharad.

They were leaning side by side on the empty pigsty wall in the late sunshine, and he looked round at her quickly, not quite sure if he had heard her aright.

She returned his look for a moment, then turned her gaze down the quiet valley. 'When my father knew that he was dying he sent me to the nunnery over beyond . . . thinking, I suppose, to find safety for me there.' Her hand moved up to the wine-coloured mark on her neck, as though it was linked somehow with what she was saying. 'I was not made for the cloisters, but there was an aged sister there – Sister Annis – who was their infirmarer, very wise in leechcraft. I was set to help her because I had some knowledge of herb-lore myself, and from her I learned all that she had to teach of healing; some that the mother superior maybe did not know about, that came from part of an old book that was saved when the Emperor Theodosius burned the great library at Alexandria. Such knowledge is forbidden to us because it came from the ancient world, before the birth of Christ. But Sister Annis did not believe that any knowledge that might heal men's suffering could be ill, and she passed on to me what she still remembered. So my father died, and when my brother was killed three winters ago at the boar hunting – I was close to taking my final vows, but I had not yet taken them – I left my nunnery and came home to handle the farm. At first the people of the valley were glad of my coming, for they had no wise-woman. But there have been bad harvests, and last year many of the cattle dropped their calves too soon. And when they brought their ills to me for healing, they were frightened of Sister Annis's spells in the Latin tongue, though I told them that they were but Paternosters and words of healing power.'

She had been talking in a level, hurried tone, as though having started to tell these things that maybe she had never told before, she could not stop. But now her quick rush of words fell away.

'Could you not use the spells that they are used to?' Bjarni said.

She shook her head. 'The spells and the salves and the draughts are part of each other. I could not change one without the other. This is the leechcraft that I have learned and I will not betray it. Beside, I cannot turn away the bad harvests. Nor can I charm this away.' And again she touched the strange mark on her neck.

The man did not come back; but a few days later, a girl of maybe ten summers came to the door, clutching a bunch of wilting wild flowers, tormentil, and bedstraw and crushed silken poppies, and holding out her left hand with a large wart on the forefinger and two more at the base of the thumb. Most of those who came to Angharad for healing brought payment of some sort: a pot of pig-fat, a few eggs, a handful of wool combed and ready for the spindle; though if they did not, it seemed to make no difference to Angharad. She took the flowers, and put them in a crock of water which she set beside Gwyn's bed. Then, returning to the child in the doorway, took her hand. 'Oh, you have knocked the big one, it is bleeding,' she said, and took out from the breast of her sark something – Bjarni had never seen what it was – that she wore always on a silken cord round her neck and, kneeling, rubbed the wart with it. The child stood quiet to have it done, but Bjarni saw that she was shivering, and that the other hand behind her back was making the sign of the horns against the evil eye.

Angharad rubbed each of the warts in turn. Then she dropped the thing back inside her sark. She cupped the girl's face for an instant, looking deep into her eyes. 'The Sea Beast will have taken them all away before the old moon dies,' she said.

The child remained still for a moment, then twisted away and turned and ran.

'She was making the sign of the horns behind her back, all the while,' Bjarni said.

'I know. But none the less, the warts will go.'

20

Harvest Weather

Most of the summer had gone when one day Bjarni
returned from fishing the tail of the upstream pool
with two fine spotted char in his hand. There was a
small mean wind blowing and a fitful scudding of
rain, and he looked somewhat anxiously to the
weather, for the barley was near to harvest. There was
a feeble wailing coming from the house-place, as of a
sick lamb trying to bleat without enough breath to
bleat with. And another sound, a low rhythmic murmuring that he knew well enough by now was the
sound of Angharad at her leechcraft, and timing
something with one of her strange Latin spells.

He checked at the doorway, for often Angharad did
not like a watcher at such times. But she did not seem
to notice him, and nor did the woman who sat beside
the fire, bent all together over the child in her lap,
almost as though she would gather it back into her
own body. There was a thick pungent smell, and
something was bubbling gently on the fire, while a
pot of some kind of dark greasy stuff stood near by.

'Paternoster . . .' murmured Angharad, watching

the pot and moving it a shade to one side when the bubbling grew too swift and again, 'Paternoster . . .'

The woman was rocking a little, as though already in grief.

Angharad finished the Paternoster, and drew the pot aside. 'Don't do that,' she said. 'If you do as I tell you, the child need not die.'

She fished a soggy mass of leaves from the pot as soon as it was cool enough to put her hand in. 'Now put back your cloak from him and hold him steady.' She spread the hot leaves on the baby's small panting chest, and it broke its wailing to sneeze at the fumes. She bound all in place with clean rags, then drew the edges of the soft fawn-skin in which it had been wrapped close about it. She poured something into a little flask stoppered with wood, and gave it to the woman. They were on the threshold by this time: and Bjarni had drawn aside to let the woman pass.

'Give him the draught as often as you can,' Angharad said. 'That is to bring the fever down. Keep him warm and still. And tomorrow I will come. Don't bring him out again, not in this wind. I will come.'

And the woman nodded wordlessly and, gathering her cloak close about the thing she carried, turned and walked away.

'Would it not have been better to have kept her and the child here overnight?' Bjarni asked, entering and dropping the fish that he had caught.

'Much, but nothing would make her keep it here after sundown. This way she will save its immortal soul, even if the body dies.'

And the note of forlorn bitterness in her tone made him suddenly angry, so that he wanted to hit somebody.

*

'Don't go,' he said the next morning when she gathered her things together and flung on her cloak.

'I must,' she told him. 'If I don't, the child may die.'

'Then I'll come with you.'

'No! Bide close to the house lest Gwyn has need of you. He grows weaker these days.'

He stood in the clearing to see her away, wondering why he should obey this chit of a girl in breeks as though she was the Lady Aud. And as she disappeared down the track, he heard behind him in the corner of the house-place the difficult grunting sound that meant that Gwyn wanted something. Hunching his shoulders, he turned and went to find out what it was.

The old man had had his morning stirabout, so the most likely things were that he wanted a drink, that the rushes of his bedding had got into a lump somewhere, or of course that he had fouled himself again; but it seemed that it was none of these things. His feverish gaze fixed itself on Bjarni's face, then went straining to the doorway and back again. He went on grunting; he seemed to be trying to speak. The need was so desperate that, though it was not speech, it was more like speech than Bjarni had ever heard from him before. 'Go.'

'Rest easy, old father,' he said. 'I'm going. I'll leave Hugin with you.' And to the great dog who stood beside him with gently waving tail, 'Sit and stay.'

He heard a protesting whimper behind him as he left, and turned in the doorway. The dog was half up again, tail and eyes beseeching. 'On guard,' he said, and the dog collapsed with a protesting sigh.

He went on through the steading gate and down past the barley-plot, then towards the rim of the valley. He had never actually been into the village before, but his hunting had brought him above it more than once, and he knew the way well enough. In a short while, coming down a hill shoulder above alder woods, he saw Angharad only a short way away, and checked his long loping pace. He had no wish to catch up with her yet. So long as he could keep her clear in view . . .

He overtook her on the edge of the village's intake land. Frowning, she looked round quickly at the sound of his footfall on the turf behind her. 'I bade you not to come, but bide with Gwyn,' she said.

'Gwyn bade me to come with you,' he told her flatly. 'I left Hugin with him.' Suddenly he grinned. 'Where should your hired sword be but behind you when you walk abroad?'

The small fierce moment passed, and they went together down the drift-way, Bjarni walking a couple of paces behind in the proper place for a hired blade.

The village when they reached it was much the same close scatter of turf and furze thatched bothies and a few larger house-places that he had known elsewhere, save that it was not huddled below any chieftain's hall, which gave it an incomplete look in Bjarni's eyes, though he knew well enough that among the Welsh the lesser folk gathered in hamlets while the chiefs and greater kindred had their garths and steadings scattered solitary over the countryside – such steadings as Angharad's must have been in its great days that were past.

The drift-way became the village street wandering down through the turf-roofed houses and their byres and barns. The place had seemed busy enough when they came down towards it. Men were at work in the wood-wright's yard and the smithy, someone was driving a pig up the stony street, women with their cloaks huddled about them against the thin rain were moving between house and byre and gathered bucket

in hand around the spring head, children and dogs
were busy about their own affairs. But at their coming
the place grew quiet, children were called indoors,
and men and women melted away, or drew well back
from their passing. Only the dogs came with tails
wagging friendliwise, and the smith – a man of power
working with cold iron and bending it to his will had
no need to fear witchcraft or any other unchancy thing
– worked on unheeding of their passing by. Yet Bjarni
had the feeling that eyes were watching them, even
where no one seemed to be.

At the next bothy, where an old cat lay dozing
on the midden, Angharad turned and ducked in
through the doorway, Bjarni following, blinking
through the peat smoke. Yesterday's woman sat
beside the fire, the sick child in her lap. She looked
up as Angharad entered, seeming for the moment to
shrink back a little, then let her caught breath go,
and moved to show the child. The two women spoke
together, low-voiced, both looking at the babe. There
was water in a crock set ready by the fire.

'The fever is lower,' Angharad said, her hand
exploring the little creature's head. She poured some
water into the small bowl she had brought in her
bundle, and while it was heating, undid the binding
rags and lifted off the leaves, dry and crackling now,
and wrapped the deer-skin close again.

Then she brought out more of the same leaves and
dropped them into the water. The hissing and pungent
steam arose, and she began again the same low murmuring that Bjarni had heard before. 'Paternoster . . .'

To Bjarni, leaning his shoulder against the doorway,
with his ears twitching for any sound from the street
outside, it all seemed to last a very long time. But at
last the fresh poultice was bandaged on, another vial
of something changed hands, and all the other things

that must be done, and Angharad gathered her bundle together and rose to go.

The woman's hand reached out desperately to cling to her. 'Will he live?'

'I think so,' Angharad told her. 'His fever is down and his breathing easier. If he grows worse again, send Anyl for me, and I will come.'

Gently she drew back out of the woman's hold, and came out past Bjarni into the street and turned uphill once more.

On the way down it had seemed that Angharad had had no thought in her mind but the sick child, but now, with the thing that she had come to do safely accomplished, she seemed to have awareness for other things. Where the drift-way led through the first of the crop-land, she paused, her gaze running out over the barley paling, with its scatter of scarlet poppies. The rain had stopped, and a faint waft of sunshine ran before the wind.

'By Our Lady's Grace, the weather is kind; there will be a better harvest this year,' she said, and turned to the steep track once more.

A man was coming down the drift-way towards them, a dog at his heels and a bundled fleece on his shoulder. He stopped as they drew near each other, then turned abruptly and disappeared behind a haw-thorn windbreak. Angharad looked after him a moment, without checking her pace. 'That was one of our farm hands until he drifted away last year.'

'One of them? There were others?'

'You can't work a farm the size of Gwyn Coed – the size Gwyn Coed used to be – without hands. There were two more, and a bond-woman about the house.'

'And they all – drifted away?'

'I think maybe they were afraid to find the Horned One some stormy night sitting beside my hearth.' She spoke lightly, but there was a faint bitter ache in her voice that made him look at her quickly. By now they were walking side by side. She did not return his look, but walked on with her head up and her gaze lifted to the high valleys that ran toward the foothills of the snows. 'No, it is in my mind that far back behind all things is Rhywallan, my kinsman.'

'A poor sort of kinsman, I would be thinking.'

'There's only one thing he loves,' Angharad said simply, 'and that is land, land . . . He wants mine. He has offered me gold for it.'

'Has he not land of his own?'

'Plenty,' Angharad said, her eyes still on the valleys. 'Up that way towards the broad in-take lands. Chieftain and Lord of three valleys he is, and corn-land on Anglesey that the King gives him for services as his falconer. Still he would have mine to add to his own, and he has the King's ear.'

They dropped over the rim of Gwyn Coed and descended through the thickets of oak and hawthorn and wild apple, and the hill flank rose behind them, shutting out the high valleys. And below them the burn came curling down through the in-take land.

'Would you take gold for Gwyn Coed?'

'I had sooner die.'

'It's in my mind,' Bjarni said, suddenly stopping on the bank, 'that you should let him have Gwyn Coed, you should wish him joy of it, and come away with me. I will take you back to my own settlement.' He heard his own words, not quite believing that he was actually speaking them.

'No,' said Angharad.

'There's danger here. And you know it. Afraid you are. Come away.'

'Of course I am afraid. Why else did I cling to you when you came out of the sea with your great man-killing sword at your side? I'll not leave the land that was my father's and my father's father's father's before him.'

Bjarni shook his head, baffled. 'My kind can build their home and hearth and strike root wherever the keel comes to shore.'

'But I am not of your kind. And there is one thing you are forgetting in all this – I cannot leave Gwyn.'

And from that, he knew that there would be no shifting her.

When they got back to the steading, all was as they had left it, the old man lying with his bright gaze turned towards the door, the great black hound sitting beside him, who leapt up and came with swinging tail to thrust his lowered head between Bjarni's knees in greeting. And for a moment Bjarni wondered whether the whole thing was only a fancy in Angharad's mind, brewed up by being too long alone, and in some way passed on to him. But then he remembered the emptying village street, men's hands making the sign against ill luck as she passed . . . and he felt for the sword-thongs at his belt.

21

Harvest Wrath

The weather held, and in three days' time the barley in the crop-plot was ready for harvesting. 'Do you know how to handle a sickle?' Angharad asked him a little nervously and Bjarni, unaccountably annoyed at the suggestion that he knew the handling of nothing but a sword, said harshly, 'Why not? The raiding season ends with the start of the harvest.'

But at the harvesting they made a team that worked together easily enough, Bjarni going ahead with the sickle, and Angharad following after to bind up the sheaves. In a way it was different from any harvesting that he had known before, for always the harvest had been a matter of wide fields, and the whole settlement gathering to each other's aid. But this little harvesting, just himself and Angharad, and Hugin hunting field mice among the stooks, had an odd goodness about it that he knew suddenly he would not forget.

They got the harvest in, sheaves piled high on the farm sled drawn by the horse, Swallow, and stored in the barn ready for threshing. The last sheaf, the maiden, they brought in and bound high on the crossbeam of the house-place for next year's harvest. And that night Angharad made a feast; the best that she could contrive with soaked barley and meat, honey cakes and heather ale from her carefully hoarded store in a long-necked red pottery jar with a hunting scene embossed round its sides. But the thing that made it into a feast instead of the evening meal that on other nights, with the day's work done, they had shared wearily together, was that Angharad, sitting on the women's side of the fire, had changed her breeks and sark for a kirtle of saffron-coloured stuff, and washed her hair and brushed it out until it shone, and made herself a crown of flowers from the harvest field, moon-daisies and cornflowers and the like.

'I have never seen you in woman's garb before,' Bjarni said, sitting on the men's side and gazing at her through the peat smoke.

'What good is a golden gown for mucking out the stables in?' said Angharad simply. But she said it with a smile, rising to take more honey cake mushed in ale to the old man in the corner. Gwyn had been growing noticeably weaker over the past few days, spending more and more of his time in sleep, seeming less and less aware of what went on about him; but the harvest feast was for him also. Bjarni watched her kneeling beside the old man, spooning the pap into him, talking softly.

He watched her come back to the fire. He had the oddest feeling that it was not only the first time he had ever seen Angharad in a gown, but the first time he had ever seen her at all. It was not only the gown; it was that for that one evening Angharad seemed to have relaxed something in herself, and laid it aside like a weapon. The string of a harp that was always too tense was slackened off to its true pitch, so that

the tune she made was good and sweet... A good
harvest after two bad ones would maybe make the
villagers not so sure now she was a witch, or that it
was her coming that had made the bad harvests.

Bjarni was not used to thinking that kind of thought.
It took him by surprise, and the surprise of it made
him choke into his ale-jar; and Angharad shifted
round the fire and thumped him on the back, which
turned the strange moment back to normal again.

The neck of her saffron gown fell open a good deal
lower than the sark she usually wore: and as she
leaned towards him the thing that she wore on a
silken cord around her neck swung out through the
opening, and he saw that it was a ring; a heavy golden
ring, much battered and set with some dark green
stone. She made as though to catch it up and thrust
it back inside her gown, then seemed to change her
mind and left it hanging in full view, from which he
judged that he might speak about it if he wished.
'That's what you rubbed the bairn's warts with.'

'A gold ring is the best thing for charming warts
with, except a black cat's tail, and I have not a black
cat.' On a sudden impulse she slipped the cord over
her head and held it out to him.

He hesitated a minute before taking it. 'Is it magic?'

'Only to the child whose wart it charms away. I use
it because it is precious to me. It was my father's and
his father's before him, right back to the ancient times
– from the time of the Redcrest soldiers who built the
great fort to guard the Anglesey strait.'

Bjarni sat turning the ring between his fingers,
catching and losing the firelight in the green stone.
There was something engraved on it, a fish of some
kind... he bent closer and saw that it was not a fish
but a dolphin. 'Seamen say that when dolphins follow
a ship, the voyage will be lucky.'

He handed the ring back to her, and she slipped the cord over her head and stored it once more in the breast of her gown. 'It is too big for my hand,' she said. 'But now there is no man to wear it . . .'

There was a lovely quietness of heart about her this evening, and sitting by the peat fire, beneath the corn maiden on the tie-beam, with Hugin chasing dream hares in his sleep close by, they talked together as they had never quite done before, telling things in exchange for other things, much as children may do when putting out tendrils of friendship to each other. So Bjarni found himself telling her about his boyhood in Norway before he came west-over-seas to join his brother in the Rafnglas settlement; things that he had scarce thought of in more than five years, and had not known that he remembered or cared about at all. And in return Angharad told him of the time when the half-derelict farm was alive and busy, when her father and brother still lived, and before the shadow came. And then Rhywallan's name came into it. Bjarni sat forward with a jerk.

'Oh yes, he was part of those days,' Angharad said. 'He was fostered here for a while, at my father's hearth. He and my brother were close companions. He was greedy even then – land greedy, greedy for what he wanted; and because his father was the King's Chief Falconer he had the right to the champion's portion in all things.'

'Is the King's Falconer so great a thing to be?' Bjarni asked. 'To work the king's hunting birds?'

She laughed. 'The King's Falconer does not work the King's falcons, he has underlings who do the work – the King's Candle-bearer only walks before the great candle on feast days, the King's Woodman does not himself carry in the wood and peats for the fire in the great hall. Only the King's Harper, and the King's Chaplain, and the King's Champion must be always with him, to carry out their own duties. For the rest it is a title of power and honour, not a task to be performed. When Rhywallan became the King's Falconer in his turn, he thought still more that all things he wished for were his by right. And he wished for me – I was twelve years old by then and of marriageable age, though ten years younger than him. He went to my father, but my father would not give me against my will. It made for bad blood between the households. And my father was already a sick man. I think it was for that reason that when he felt the hand of death upon him, he sent me to the nunnery, to have me well out of the way of whatever might come after.'

'Did you wish it so?' Bjarni asked. He could not see Angharad shut away in a house of holy women.

'It pleased me more than to be married to Rhywallan,' Angharad said simply.

Outside, the wind was rising, setting the smoke of the peat fire sideways, filling the far end of the house-place with blue haze. The old man coughed, and Angharad rose and went to give him a drink, then returned to sit by the fire again. The talk drifted to other things, and she began telling about her time in the nunnery, about Sister Annis who had taught her leechcraft, about Sister Garniflaith who was greedy and stole the honey cakes that the Holy Mother liked to keep for guests, and then tried to blame it on Mousis the nunnery cat . . .

Presently Hugin raised his head and listened, muzzle lifted, grumbling softly in his throat. Bjarni glanced across at Angharad, and she was listening also, though as yet there was nothing to hear under the long slow gusts of wind. Bjarni put his hand on the dog's neck, and felt the hair lift a little under his palm. A few moments more and they all heard it, in a trough of quiet between gust and gust; the flying beat of horses' hooves coming up the valley.

'Now who would be riding this way like the Wild Hunt at this hour of night?' Bjarni said, and got up, his hand going to his sword hilt.

'I can only think of one.' Angharad was on her feet also and turning to the doorway. 'And we were talking of him a while back . . .'

Outside it was almost as light as day, with a great harvest moon casting sharp-edged shadows, and silver-fringed cloudlets scuttling across the sky. And almost as they reached the foreporch doorway, a man on a horse yelling like the fiends in Hell leapt the thornwork gate, two hounds as white as moonlight leaping ahead of him, and a moment later brought the horse to a rearing and plunging halt almost on the threshold.

'Rhywallan!' Angharad said, but Bjarni had known that before she spoke. 'And what brings you here at this hour of night?'

'It is a fine white night for the hunting,' said the man on the horse. There was enough torchlight through the house-place doorway to show that the snorting and fidgeting animal was red – a bright bay – and the man's mantle was red also: in sunlight horse and rider would burn like flame, but now in the moonlight they were as dark as something out of the Hollow Hills, until Angharad stepped forward with one of the torches which she had taken from the wall sconce. 'And finding myself this way, I thought to ride up valley and ask after your harvest.'

'The harvest has been good,' Angharad said on a note of quiet triumph. 'A good harvest after two lean ones. Maybe the shadow will pass.' Bjarni caught and understood the note of challenge.

Harvest Wrath

'I see for myself the thing the countryside talks of – the fair stranger with a black dog at his heel, who came to you up from the sea on the night of the great storm.' His gaze flicked over Bjarni with a curious mingling of looks: part curious, part jeering, part – and this was the dangerous part – on the edge of fear. Bjarni gave him back look for look, not answering, aware of Hugin pressed against his leg.

Angharad answered easily enough, the goodness of the harvest still within her. 'So, now you see for yourself: this is Bjarni Sigurdson, a seaman washed up from the wreck that night, he and his dog together. And a good storm it was for me too, left with no hands but my own to work the farm since Gwyn was struck down.'

The man laughed. 'That's the kind of tale that you would tell – or that maybe he would tell you – of course.'

'It is the truth,' Angharad said.

'So. It's the truth.' Rhywallan's voice was mocking. 'But to return to the harvest – it is for that that you have put on your best gown and tied up your hair with the flowers of the corn?' Bjarni saw the man's eyes moving over her with a kind of smirking delight, and knew that for Rhywallan too, the sight of her in woman's gear was doing strange things. And yet all the time, the fingers of his bridle hand, half lost in the folds of his cloak, were making the sign of the horns.

'Of course – down the valley the village will be doing much the same this night.'

'And bidding any guest come in for a cup of harvest ale?'

'I will bring you ale if you wish it, but I cannot bid you enter. Gwyn is at the end of life, and I will not have him disturbed.'

'So.' His face changed suddenly. 'Forget the ale. Best

not, I'm thinking, to eat or drink of this house. And as to the village harvest, forget that too. The deer broke into the crop-lands two nights since. There will be empty grain stores in the village this winter.'

Angharad caught her breath, and Bjarni felt her tighten – all the strings of her harp tighten. 'The corn was in good heart when we passed that way three days since.'

'Aye, you were seen to stand and look at it, and him with you. It was the next night the deer broke in.'

'It was none of my doing,' Angharad said, speaking in a clear careful voice, like a woman standing trial before the moot, the village court.

'No? But there are those in the village who fear otherwise, and fear is a dangerous animal when it breaks free. My advice to you is to get you back to your nunnery. I will give you gold for a second dowry if you have forfeited the first by this reckless return to the world.'

Angharad said in the same clear level voice, 'I would not sell the land to you for my dowry into Heaven, though Hell yawned at my feet!'

Rhywallan showed no sign of being flicked on the raw by her tone, but his fidgeting horse flung up its head, snorting as though from a savage jerk on the bit, shivering and trampling.

Hugin, who had been rumbling softly in his throat all the while, let out a deep warning growl. Rhywallan made a curious sound high up behind his nose, and in the same instant the two hounds, who had been standing stiff-legged and with lifted manes, launched themselves upon Hugin.

Hugin was no fighter, but it was not in him to turn tail. He sprang joyfully to meet the double menace, and next instant a snarling and whirling dogfight was going on almost on the house-place threshold.

Rhywallan reined his frightened horse a little aside, and sat looking on with interest, but the fight could not last long, two against one, and the one not a killer by instinct. Angharad cried, 'Call your dogs off!'

Bjarni plunged into the ugly tangle of struggling bodies rolling over each other and savage tearing jaws. Hugin was down, and one of the pale hounds had him by the throat. Bjarni's hands were on the hairy neck, trying to strangle him off, but even as he struggled to force the clenched jaws apart, the other hound crashed into them, taking his legs from under him, and he felt the slash of teeth in his shoulder. Hugin was still struggling but the strength was going from him. With no time to think, Bjarni's hand went to the dirk in his belt, almost as it seemed of its own accord ripping it from the sheath, driving it into the attacker's throat. He felt the warm blood spurting over his hand as the hound collapsed with a grunt. His hand was on Hugin's collar as the black dog staggered to his feet, choking and whistling for breath with the second dog already upon him. But in that same instant, fire came over his shoulder spitting and sparking – Angharad's torch, and Angharad beside him driving it into the snarling face; and Rhywallan's remaining hound giving back, swinging his head from side to side and whining like a kicked puppy.

Everything seemed to go quiet with extraordinary suddenness, as the fight fell apart. Only one dog was trying still to growl, without as yet enough breath to growl with, and one whining and pawing at his scorched muzzle. And the third lying twitching while the blood fountained red from his throat. Then the twitching stopped.

'You have killed my best hound,' Rhywallan said in a grating voice.

'Who was for killing mine, he and his brother – sicked on him by you,' Bjarni said. For an instant it came into his mind that Rhywallan might demand Hugin in place of his dead hound, and he wondered how best to deal with it if he did.

But Rhywallan seemed to read the thought, and his full lips curled in mockery. 'Do you think I would take the like of that into my hunting pack?'

Then Angharad's voice, cool and sweet and edged like a sword, came between them. 'Rhywallan, my kinsman, you have seen what you came to see, and said what you came to say; now let you be on your way while the harvest moon is still high to light you back to your dunghill.'

The man turned a little in his saddle to look down at her as she stood with the torch held high. 'Surely I have seen what I came to see – what all the valleys are talking of: you with your left-handed, devil-handed Sea-Demon and your black familiar. What spell did you cast to set the faery finger upon me all those years ago before ever you went to the Holy Sisters?' He had been speaking quietly, almost musically, but suddenly, horribly, his voice rose almost to a shriek. 'Aye, I have seen you with the harvest flowers in your hair while the down-valley harvest fields lie wrecked and trampled. Best you remember that, you with the witch mark on your long white neck!'

22

Witch Hunt

Rhywallan was wrenching his horse's head round as he shrieked his last words, jabbing in the spurs as the poor beast plunged away, the single hound streaking in its wake.

A few moments more and they were out over the thornwork hedge, leaving a trampled and forsaken place behind them, and a wild thudding of hooves down the drift-way, like a rider of the Wild Hunt, then out over the open turf lifting out of the valley, growing faint, dying away. When there was no sound left but the wind under the moon, Bjarni fetched a long breath, and leant to pull aside Hugin, who had padded over, still grumbling deep in his torn throat, to nose at the body of the dead hound which lay before the threshold. 'I'll get rid of the dog,' he said.

Angharad shook her head. 'The dog can wait until I have tended your hurts and Hugin's. Back into the house, both of you.'

And turning back as she bade him, Bjarni was aware for the first time of the pain in his fang-gashed shoulder and blood spreading through the torn stuff of his sark, aware too of the reddened blade in his hand.

When Angharad had him stripped to the belt and squatting by the hearth where the light fell strongest, she pushed up the sleeves of her gown, and set water to heat among the peats, while she brought clean rags and salves from the kist in her sleeping place, and bathed and searched the gashes, dripping in some fierce spirit and spreading on a dark, evil-smelling salve that burned like fire.

Looking from her frowning intent face to the ruthless work of her hands, Bjarni told her, not complaining but purely as a matter of fact, 'You are hurting me – more, I think, than you are given to hurting the folk who come to you for tending. Is that because of your kinsman's coming?'

'If you mean because I am angry or afraid, no!' Angharad said, reaching for a strip of clean rag. 'There are ills on a dog's teeth that must be knuckle-kneaded out before they may breed poison in the wound they make.' She began to bandage his shoulder and upper arm.

Bjarni watched her. She had not denied that she was angry or afraid, and he knew she was, with good cause, all tied in with the sense of danger that he had known here all summer long; and having for its centre, the eye of the storm, the young man on the red horse who had left the dead hound on the threshold. 'I am sorry I had to kill the dog,' he said, 'I have made you an enemy – or added to the venom of the one you had already.'

Angharad knotted the bandage. 'Tomorrow we will let the air get to it, but for tonight best keep the salves close.'

'If I carry sword for you, I would fain know the ill that I may have to fight with it. Your kinsman wanted you years ago, and he wants you still – I saw that in his eyes when he looked at you. Yet he bade you go back to the Holy Sisters, and I do not think that I understand.'

'It's quite simple,' Angharad said. 'He is greedy, as I told you before, land-greedy. He wanted me even without the land, then when my brother died and I came home to run the farm, he thought he might have both of us, and when he found that he could have neither, the want began to fester inside of him – oh, long before you and Hugin came out of the storm. He wants both still, but if he can drive me back behind the walls of my nunnery, he might at least have the land.' She laughed a little wildly, her hand going to her throat. 'But he will not take me by force, lest this on my neck really is a witch mark, after all.'

She turned to the black dog, who had lain by the fire pawing at his torn muzzle. 'And you now, my black darling.'

And while Bjarni held the dog against his knee, she bathed and salved his hurts, which were many, for beside his muzzle and fang-slashed throat he had a long shallow gash on his flank, and one ear flying like a war flag from the thick of battle.

When it was done, Bjarni went to get rid of the dead hound in the garbage pit behind the house-place, and cleaned his dirk by stabbing it again and again into the peat-stack. The broken-down thornwork would have to wait till morning.

But the events of the night were not yet over. When he came in again through the foreporch, the house place was full of rasping breathing not like anything that he had heard there before. And Angharad was kneeling beside Gwyn in his shadowy corner, the torch again in hand, the fingers of her other hand resting, somehow as though she were listening through them, against the old man's neck.

She looked up as Bjarni crossed to stand beside her, thrusting Hugin's enquiring muzzle back with his heel.

'He knew what was going on around him earlier this evening,' she said. 'I am thinking that he is beyond that now.'

The old man's face had darkened. He lay staring straight upwards, but not as though he saw the rafters overhead; his mouth sagged open, and from it came those terrible snoring breaths. 'Is there nothing that you can do?' Bjarni asked.

She shook her head. 'Nothing save be with him, so that if he knows anything, he knows that he is not alone.'

Old Gwyn died soon after dawn, with the green plover calling over the head of the valley.

Angharad carried out for him the ancient tasks of womenkind for their dead, keening for him the while, according to the custom of her people, as she made the old man ready for burial. And all the while, Bjarni, not quite knowing why, stood in the doorway, his sword across his thighs, staring down at the valley as though on guard.

When all was finished and the old man made decent and dignified, he asked, 'Will I fetch a priest – if you tell me where to find him . . .'

She shook her head almost fiercely. 'He would not come to this house. Nor will I hand Gwyn's body over to the folk down-valley, who like enough would deny him Christian burial as my servant.'

'What then?' Bjarni asked.

'When the light goes, we will take him up to High Cross and bury him there.' She sounded as though the thing were clear in her mind and had been settled long since. 'It is a place he loved in his herding days, and surely the cross will make it hallowed ground.'

So when the light began to fade, Bjarni harnessed Swallow to the farm sled, and brought it round to the house-place door, and they laid the old man's body on it wrapped in the blanket under which he had lain so many months. And with the first dark they set out up the valley, Angharad going ahead to lead the horse, Bjarni bringing up the rear with a spade on his shoulder, Hugin loping at his heel, to make sure the sled's rigid burden was not jerked off over the uneven ground.

At the head of the valley where the rough pasture was islanded with heather and furze, the ancient Celtic cross had stood through the lifetimes of many men, forming a boundary mark for the farm, and close before it Angharad brought Swallow to a halt. From up here the light of the day still lingered in a bar of dim gold far out beyond Anglesey. But the moon was coming and going through the drift-light for them to see what they had to do. Bjarni unslung the spade from his shoulder and began to dig.

It was hard going at first through the tough surface net of old heather roots, but lower down the earth was softer. The sound of steady digging and earth cast aside was almost lost in the soughing of the wind across the heather, save for a sharp ringing note from time to time when the blade caught a stone. Presently he had opened up a large pit too deep to be dug from the surface, and was standing in it, flinging the spadefuls of earth over his shoulder.

The smell of the earth was in his nostrils, and the sound of the earth heavy behind him as it fell. Hugin would have joined in, and had to be thrust off.

'That's deep enough,' said Angharad.

Bjarni straightened up and judged the depth of the

grave in which he stood, then nodded. 'Aye, it will keep off the wolves.'

He climbed out and between them they lifted Gwyn's body from the sled, and slid him, as gently as might be, down into his grave. At the last moment Angharad, who had been hunting among the heather while Bjarni dug, bent down and laid a loose handful of harebells on the man's blanket-covered breast. Then with spade and hands they shovelled back the earth, pressing it well down, and adding the heather last of all. The old man's body was so thin that the ground scarcely rose higher than it had done before he was laid in it. By daylight there would be signs, for any who came looking. But who would come? No one would know that the old man was dead, and no one but the two of them would ever care.

It was very quiet now, only the wind, and somewhere far off in the woods below an owl calling, and the faintly raised place before the High Cross the quietest thing of all.

And against the quiet Angharad was speaking words in the strange stately tongue that he had heard her use for timing her potions.

She went to the old horse and got him and the sled turned, and they set off down the valley. Where the valley looked westward round a shoulder of the moor, the sky was lighter than it should be, and the wrong colour, a reddish glow behind the dark shoulder of the moors. Bjarni saw it the instant before Angharad, and checked, putting out a hand to check her also.

'What – ' she began, and then, 'Oh no! Oh, Holy Mother, no!'

'Wait here with Swallow,' Bjarni said, and started forward again up the gentle slope towards that angry stain that was growing stronger in the sky.

For answer, she flung Swallow's bridle over the branch of a tattered hawthorn tree, and in a few steps she was beside him again. He did not argue; he had learned now that there was little use in arguing with Angharad; and anyhow this was not the moment to be wasting time in argument, so they went on together. 'Down!' he whispered as the slope levelled just before the skyline, and they covered the last axe-throw of distance on their bellies. On the lip of the ridge they lay still, looking down, Bjarni with his hand on Hugin's collar, half strangling the great hound into silence. Below them, across in the pasture, the steading lay clear, horribly clear in leaping flamelight. Byre and barn were blazing, and even as they watched, fire sprang up from the house-place roof, bending over before the wind. Figures too, dark and flamelit and running with bits pulled from the blazing buildings to spread the fire, and amongst them, on the edge of the firelight, urging them on as it seemed, a figure in a great crimson cloak on a red horse; and on the wind, the sound of voices, crazed voices, shouting, screaming, 'Burn her! Burn the witch!'

Bjarni drew a deep whistling breath through his nose, and for a moment his free hand went itching for his sword hilt, his whole instinct to go leaping down across the home pasture and fling himself into what was going on there, and kill and kill and kill, beginning with the rider of the red horse. That way, he would account for a good few of them before they pulled him down.

But once dead, what use would he be to Angharad? He fought the rage down in him, and his free hand, going out, found the girl's arm and gripped it. 'Come away,' he said.

She started at his touch, as though she had not known that he was there at all, but then, without another word said, allowed him to draw her back from the ridge.

Safely out of sight of the steading, he got up and, catching her hand, pulled her after him. She came unresisting, but not as though she were afraid or escaping or even aware of what she left behind her.

And when they got back to the hawthorn tree she stood beside it unmoving while he searched about for the spade and drove it deep among the roots of the heather, and unharnessed Swallow from the sled.

'Can you walk?' he asked. 'Better, maybe, not to risk tiring Swallow until we have need.'

She did not answer, but fell into step beside him as he turned eastward, leading the old horse and with Hugin padding at their heels.

A while before dawn they struck what remained of a paved road, knowing it by the ditches on either side and the feel of a metalled surface under the heather. Maybe it was one of the roads that the Redcrests had made. Bjarni had heard of such things. No good to ask Angharad walking beside him as she had done all night, like a creature bound by some dark spell out of the Hollow Hills.

Anyhow, the road seemed to run more or less in the right direction. Just on the edge of dawn it brought them to the ford of a narrow stream coming down from the high moor between banks tangled and arched over with hazel and rowan. And turning aside from the road they came some way downstream to a backwater that broadened into a small sky-reflecting pool.

A good place to pause for a while, out of sight of the road – if anyone had used it this past hundred years. He brought his little party to a halt, and the moment she was no longer moving forward, Angharad folded at the knees and sat down. Bjarni left her where she was, sitting between the roots of a rowan tree, her arms around her updrawn knees, and staring straight before her, and took Swallow over to the pool, watering him and, knee-hobbling him with his rein, turning him loose to graze. By the look of it there might be fish for tickling in the tail of the pool. But first Bjarni went back to see if there was anything more he could do about Angharad. He was getting sorely worried, wondering how long it was going to be before she stopped being like a shadow and started to look out of her eyes again.

Maybe it would be better for her to go on like this for a while ... But when he got back to the place where he had left her, Angharad was sitting up and looking about her like somebody just wakened from a deep sleep. The first light of a low sunrise was slanting under the rowan branches into her face. 'So it was not a dream,' she said when she saw him.

Bjarni shook his head, suddenly very weary, and folded up beside her. 'No, it was not a dream.'

'I must go back.'

'You can't go back,' he said heavily.

'I must. I can't leave the farm to Rhywallan's taking.'

'I am not thinking that you have much choice,' Bjarni told her flatly. 'You couldn't even marry your kinsman now.'

'I never could – or would,' Angharad said in a small hard voice. 'But I must go back. Gwyn Coed was my father's and his father's father's.'

And he realised a little desperately that he had not even dented her resolve. Anxiety made his voice a little rough. 'Land is but land, and somewhere, always, there is another land-take to be made, with fire carried round it. With Gwyn gone to his rest, there is nothing left to fall living into your kinsman's hand.'

'Except the ducks,' said Angharad on a sound between a laugh and a whimper.

'Grief is on me that we could not save the ducks. We have saved Swallow.' To his own surprise he put out his left hand, a little clumsily, and set it over hers. 'I will take you back to your nunnery if you'd have it that way. If you're not for the Holy Sisters, then there's not much you can do but come back to Rafnglas with me.'

Until that moment he had not thought what he was going to do with Angharad, where he was going to take her, only that he had to get her away from the burning farm; and he heard his own voice saying the words as though they were not quite his own, and he was as surprised as it seemed that she was. She pulled her hand from under his and looked at him with her brows up. 'And what makes you think that I would marry with a blue-eyed barbarian?'

Anger and hurt took Bjarni by the throat. 'Who spoke of marriage? You have not even a dowry!'

For a moment they looked at each other, on the verge of a scene that might have put bitterness between them for all time. Then Angharad said, with a hand going to the marred side of her neck in a familiar gesture, 'Nor any beauty to take its place.'

And the moment tipped over into something else, and Bjarni swallowed his own hurt and anger to take hers from her. 'Tha's bonny enough for me, though,' he mumbled awkwardly. And suddenly he was realising something that he had not realised before; that while he came of a people who could uproot easily, whose home was as much the sea as the land, she was of another kind. And save for the nunnery years she had known no home, no familiar place, but the valley and the farmstead that now lay in black ruin behind her. She was flung out into a strange world that held nothing familiar, a cold place; he could feel the cold in her. He was the only thing she knew in it; and though they had worked together through the summer, and come close in many ways, he was still a stranger to her in others.

He searched around in his weary mind for the right thing to do, the right thing to say. He was not practised in love talk, but suddenly his arms were round her and his face buried in the side of her neck, speaking softly where the red flare was.

'I have done something that I never did before. Last night I ran from a fight for your sake. Because I would not see you killed.'

And this time she did not draw away. Instead she put her arm round his neck, and he felt the beginning flicker of warmth, of life in her. 'I *have* a dowry to bring,' she said with a kind of weary laughter. 'I have a horse and a ring that cures warts.'

'And that's a fine dowry after all,' Bjarni said as they slipped down into the growing warmth of the streamside grass.

23

The Return

It was late in the autumn when Bjarni brought them
all down to Eskdale and turned seaward down the
long winding drift-way that linked the older and
lower steadings of Rafn's settlement. The journey
behind them had not been so long, as journeys go,
but they had made slow travelling across high moors
and through forest land so dense that even when they
had the firmness of a Redcrests' road underfoot, it
was as though no mortal had ever passed that way
before them. They had travelled slowly, trapping
game and tickling trout for food as they went, sometimes stopping for a whole day to rest Swallow; once,
in vile weather, claiming shelter from a solitary holy
man, though of what faith even he did not seem quite
sure. Once a shuffling brown bear came out of the
forest too near to the camp fire, setting Hugin raving,
which they had to drive away with a flaming branch.
More than once driven eastward by mountains or
unfordable rivers, they had seemed to lose the sea –
the only thing that Bjarni really knew about his way
back to Rafnglas was that he must keep in touch with

the sea always on the left – and he almost doubted whether he was going to get back at all.

Yet here they were at last, towards evening on a day with drifting skies, with the wind booming through the woods, the burn that they followed swimming yellow with fallen birch leaves, coming down into Eskdale.

Most of the way they had walked, leading Swallow, occasionally riding and then never more than one of them at a time. But at the first boundary-stone of the in-take, he mounted the old horse and took Angharad up before him, being minded to ride home as a man should do who had been away five years making his fortune. He had the feeling Angharad understood this and was laughing at him, but when he looked down at her, her face was perfectly grave.

Grave still, she pulled off the old stocking cap and let her hair fall free, shaking it out over her shoulders. She too had an entrance to make.

And so they rode down into Rafnglas.

At that time of day there were not many to see them pass, for the men were still away in the in-take fields about their daytime work, and the women within doors making ready the evening meal. But once or twice an old woman spinning in a doorway, a child playing in the dust, a man with a bundle of faggots on his back, the smith with a plough-share on his anvil in the mouth of the wayside forge, looked up to see them go by; a tattered and journey-stained young man riding on an old horse, with a woman dressed like a man mounted before him in the curve of his bridle arm, and a huge black hound slightly lame in one paw loping beside them. The settlement had grown in five years, and there were faces that were strange to him. Others that he knew had grown; but none of them knew him. For a while he had somewhat the feel of a ghost returning to the place where he had lived long ago. He did not attempt to make himself known even to them; there would be time for all that later.

The rowan tree with the double trunk still stood beside the foreporch of his brother's house-place, and below its branches, Gram was working grease into a new ox hide. He looked up when Bjarni reined to a halt beside him and for a moment they looked at each other. 'You don't know me?' Bjarni said.

And saw the other's eyes light slowly as the knowledge came. 'The beard makes a difference,' he said.

Gram got up, rubbing his greasy hands on the seat of his breeks. Suddenly as Bjarni dropped from Swallow's back, he let out a shout. 'Bjarni! After all this while!'

They had their arms around each other, beating each other about the back and shoulders. 'Five years! It's been five years, and we thought you were drowned!'

'I thought so too, one time,' Bjarni said. 'But here I am, back again. It's good to see you, big brother.'

But he was taller now than Gram.

Angharad also had dropped to the ground, and stood holding Swallow's bridle and looking on. Bjarni reached back for her and drew her forward. 'I bring home with me Angharad, my woman.' He felt her stiffen slightly and remembered that she was not his woman as yet, not in the eyes of other men and women; well, that could be set right in the next few days. His hands tightened over hers.

Then a thrall had taken charge of Swallow and they were crowding into the house-place, the familiar house-place grown strange after five years, and Ingibjorg grown strange after five years too, her face startled now as she looked up from her cooking pot, grown heavier with a downward droop to the mouth. Bairns too, one still in a cradle, one sitting almost in the fire playing with a little wooden horse, making it gallop on the warm hearthstone. Dogs too. He looked among them for Astrid, but she was not there. Well, it was five years and more; very old, she would have been.

Gram was saying, 'Ingibjorg! See what the tide has washed up on shore.'

'I see,' Ingibjorg said through the steam of the crock she was still stirring. 'The gods' greeting to you, Bjarni, my husband's brother. And this that the tide has washed ashore with you?'

Angharad spoke up for herself, carefully in the Norse tongue, 'I am his woman, and Angharad is my name.'

'Angharad, that is surely no name of our Norse tongue.'

'No,' said Angharad. 'I am of an older race than the Northmen.'

'She does not speak our tongue freely as yet,' Bjarni said.

'So, a woman of the British, then?'

'Aye, from Wales. The Danes burned her house over her head.' He was going to have to lie about Angharad's story anyway, so he might as well make the lie a good one and well fleshed out.

The two women looked each other up and down, taking stock, much as Hugin and the two hounds who had risen from the hearth were doing, hackles a little raised.

'Ingibjorg – go you and bring drink for our homecomers.' And when she had risen and gone into an inner chamber, Gram drew stools to the fire, and they sat looking at each other with suddenly five years of silence between them.

'We never thought to see you again,' Gram said after a few moments. 'Heriolf thought that you had drowned.'

Bjarni leaned forward eagerly. 'Heriolf? He has been here?'

'Aye, back in early summer. He told how *Sea Cow* had come near to shipwreck on Orme's Head in the great storm. He told how you were on board heading back to Rafnglas even then, and a black hound with you – this one?'

'Aye, this one.'

'And how the dog went overboard, almost among the breakers, and you after him. And nothing that he or his crew could do about it, save try to keep *Sea Cow* off the rocks . . .'

'But they got clear?' Bjarni said, with a great gladness in him.

'They continued to beat round the point, and at last found shelter to make good their storm damage in Conway Bay. But you they gave up as lost – yet they left your sword and sea-kist here for you if ever, against all odds, you should come back to claim them.'

Bjarni looked around him as though expecting to see it propped in a corner. 'My sword? I might have known it would be safe with Heriolf. But I grieved for him dead as he did for me. You have it here?'

'Na, na, he left blade and kist together with the Chieftain.'

Ingibjorg had returned with a leather jack of buttermilk that she gave first to Bjarni and then to Angharad, saying as custom demanded, 'Drink and be welcome.'

She had brought dried meat and oatmeal back with her too, and made to add it to the bubbling contents of the pot, but checked a moment before doing so.

'You will share the evening meal with us? It will be ready in a while and a while.'

'They will share more than the evening meal with us,' Gram said, and to Bjarni, 'This was your hearth before you went on your wayfaring; it is yours again, and your woman's. Our roof is yours, little brother, until we can build on a further bothy; and add to our land-take – and so, we shall do well enough.'

But Bjarni saw the anxious look in his eyes, saw Ingibjorg's mouth tighten. And he was glad that he had made other plans. 'Nay, big brother, the offer is a kind one; but I am minded to make my own land-take and build my own hearth for my woman and me, somewhere further up the dale.' And he saw relief begin to take the place of anxiety in his brother's eyes. Gram had never been any good at covering what he was feeling; and a faintly sour thought woke in Bjarni. 'We will come back to share the evening meal with you, and gladly. For the rest – I shall find a sleeping place up at the Hearth Hall. If you will give Angharad shelter while she makes her bride-cake and a gown to be wedded in, there is no more that I ask.'

And ignoring their somewhat thin protests, he got up. 'For now I must find Rafn. I have a sword to claim back, and a message for him that he will fain hear.'

He turned to Angharad. The older child had already climbed into her lap, and as she made to move it, he said, 'Na na, leave the bairn be.' He lifted a wing of her hair and leant to place a kiss under it on her neck, as though sealing her for his own in sight of family.

He laid his free hand kindly on Gram's shoulder in passing. 'Keep the good stew hot for me.' He whistled quite needlessly to Hugin, who had already sprung up and come to his heel, and together they went out into the thickening last of daylight.

*

He ran Rafn the Chief to earth on the boat-strand, overseeing repairs to the figurehead of his ship which it seemed had suffered damage in one or other of the past summer storms.

In the shoreward part of the way, one or two among the faces that Bjarni remembered had remembered him; greetings there had been, and word of his coming had run on ahead of him; so that when he came down to the boat-strand, the big grey-gold man sitting on balks of timber in the mouth of the boat-shed turned from the work of the shipwrights without surprise.

'Bjarni Sigurdson!' he said, and then, 'Aye, Bjarni Sigurdson and not his weed-dripping ghost. We had scarce thought to see you in these parts again.'

'I was in my brother's house-stead as I came by,' Bjarni said. 'He told me that Heriolf Merchantman was here in the summer, and thought me drowned, as I thought him and all *Sea Cow*'s crew.'

'Aye, but before that, five years before, on the day you sailed with *Sea Cow* for Dublin, I think that you had little thought ever to return.'

'Not until my fortune was made, at all events,' Bjarni said. 'But many things may change in five years, and I have a woman to build a hearth for, when she has baked her bride-cake.'

The Chief nodded, his eyes thoughtful and a hint of a smile at the young man's face. 'So, and what better reason to make for the home keel-strand? And the fortune?'

'At least I have come back richer than I went.' Bjarni grinned. 'For I have this dog that followed me from the black alleyways of Dublin town, and a fine horse, and three gold pieces. And there is my sword and sea-kist that you hold for me.'

'And a fine tale to tell in the Hearth Hall after supper, I am thinking.'

'That too. I am pledged to eat with my brother and his woman – our two women – this night, but after, I will come back to tell it, and to claim my sea-kist and my sword that Heriolf left for me.'

'You carry a better sword now than the one I gave you,' Rafn said, his eyes on the beautiful weapon that Bjarni was nursing across his knees.

'Aye,' Bjarni agreed. 'And I earned it. But the giver bade me set aside the other for my eldest son.'

Laughter sounded deep in Rafn's throat. 'Sa, sa – and a sorry thing it would be to rob the eldest son.'

So far they had spoken lightly enough, in the hearing of men at work on the galley and now packing up work for the night; and not one word had been spoken as to the reason for Bjarni's leaving in the first place; and linked with that the message he had carried so long was with him still.

'Rafn Cedricson,' he said, very quietly with the half-laughter all gone, 'I have a thing to tell, a message that I have carried three years for you.'

Rafn got up, and they strolled together around the side of the boat-shed among the blown dune-sand laced with marram grass.

'What message?' Rafn asked, checking in the shed's lee. 'Who from?'

'Three years since on Iona, I was prime-signed for the White Christ, and the holy man who stood sponsor for me, he gave me the message.' Bjarni was looking out over the saltings and winding waterways into the pale brightness of the silver-gilt sunset, but he felt the man beside him grow suddenly tense. 'I had told him of the ill thing I had done, to the east out of the settlement. I told him all; and when he was told, he said, "When your outcast years are accomplished, and you go back, tell Rafn your Chief that Gisli his foster-brother forgives him the oath-breaking ..." That is all.'

'It is enough,' said Rafn the Chief.

And when Bjarni looked round at him he also was looking to sea, and there was something in his face that might have been only the sunset, but Bjarni thought was something more. 'It is enough,' he said again. He brought his gaze back out of the sea distance. 'Aye, it is enough.'

They had begun to wander back towards where the high gables of the Hall upreared themselves above the close gathering of lesser roofs. Beside the mill they stopped again, the soft wet rush of the mill wheel in their ears. 'It is good that you have returned,' the Chief said, not a man to whom the softer ways of speech came easily. 'Away with you now to the woman you left beside your brother's hearth. Later come to claim your sea-kist and your sword for your someday son, and to tell us the tale of these five years – a fine tale, I make no doubt – the Sword Song of Bjarni Sigurdson.' His great paw was on Bjarni's shoulder, spinning him round. 'The settlement has grown since you left it, but there is good land still for the in-taking, further up the dale.'